SUMMER SECRETS AT DUCK POND COTTAGE

DELLA GALTON

Boldwood

First published in Great Britain in 2025 by Boldwood Books Ltd.

Copyright © Della Galton, 2025

Cover Design by Alice Moore Design

Cover Images: Dreamstime and Shutterstock

The moral right of Della Galton to be identified as the author of this work has been asserted in accordance with the Copyright, Designs and Patents Act 1988.

Every effort has been made to obtain the necessary permissions with reference to copyright material, both illustrative and quoted. We apologise for any omissions in this respect and will be pleased to make the appropriate acknowledgements in any future edition.

A CIP catalogue record for this book is available from the British Library.

Paperback ISBN 978-1-83518-543-8

Large Print ISBN 978-1-83518-542-1

Hardback ISBN 978-1-83518-541-4

Ebook ISBN 978-1-83518-544-5

Kindle ISBN 978-1-83518-545-2

Audio CD ISBN 978-1-83518-536-0

MP3 CD ISBN 978-1-83518-537-7

Digital audio download ISBN 978-1-83518-540-7

This book is printed on certified sustainable paper. Boldwood Books is dedicated to putting sustainability at the heart of our business. For more information please visit https://www.boldwoodbooks.com/about-us/sustainability/

Boldwood Books Ltd, 23 Bowerdean Street, London, SW6 3TN

www.boldwoodbooks.com

For Adam Millward, with my love.

1

Where was the best place to make one of the most important phone calls of your life? Finn McTaggart shielded his eyes against the flaming June sunshine as he scanned the smallholding, which was comprised of a scattering of stone outbuildings encircled by fields in the middle of the Wiltshire countryside. The mobile signal was notoriously bad at Duck Pond Rescue. The animal sanctuary was both his home and his place of work, but it was better outside than indoors, and the higher up you were, the stronger it got.

The landline in reception was the obvious place but Finn had already discounted it because of the risk of interruptions. Reception was also currently the home of Mr Spock, a very talkative parrot who was prone to yelling out swear words or mimicking fire alarms if the mood took him. Finn definitely couldn't risk Mr Spock yelling obscenities in the background.

He frowned. He'd have to use his mobile. Holding it up in front of him so he could see when one bar changed to two, he strolled around the yard. Past the feed store, the haybarn and the horses' paddock on his left. Past the cattery and the kennel block on his right, then on past the small pink caravan opposite the wooden pub-style picnic table where volunteers often paused for a cuppa and a chat. The field nearest the road where the ex-battery hens roamed sloped upwards. That was a possibility.

Ideally, he'd have got into his car and driven up to the village. There was plenty of signal up there, but Jade Foster, who was both his fiancée and the founder and owner of Duck Pond Rescue, was out on an urgent rescue mission. He'd promised to stay on site until she got back.

This call couldn't wait any longer though. He'd have to make the best of it. Sighing, he climbed over the five-bar gate into the hen field. The sun felt hot on his face and his fingers were slippery on the cool metal bars, but he knew it wasn't just heat. It was excitement, anticipation and plain old terror that were making his hands sweat and his heart beat out of his chest.

He'd felt like this on and off for the last few days, which had been a whirlwind since Eleanor Smythe, owner of Artline, a top London agency, had contacted him. 'I'd like to talk to you about an art exhibition that's happening in Salisbury,' had been her opening line, and Finn had been so stunned at this out-of-the-blue phone call that all he'd been able to stammer in reply was, 'Is this a wind-up?'

'It is not a wind-up, Mr McTaggart. I've seen some of your work. I'm interested in seeing more. I don't have time to discuss this now. I'll call you on Monday.'

'Um, great, thanks... I've—' But she'd already disconnected. Yesterday had been Monday. Despite the fact he'd carried his phone everywhere with the volume turned up full, she hadn't called. There had been no messages, no missed calls.

Then this morning, he'd had a voicemail, saying she'd tried to call but hadn't been able to reach him and maybe he'd do her the courtesy of returning the call within the hour if that wasn't too much trouble. There had been a distinct tone of 'This is your last chance, my patience is running out' on the voicemail, which had come in just after Jade had left.

Finn had hoped against hope that she'd be back within the hour, but she wasn't here yet. And this felt like his last chance.

He walked swiftly up the slight slope of the hen field towards the coops at the top end. The signal changed to two bars on his phone and then flickered. Two bars would have to do. If the worst came to the worst, he could arrange to call Ms Smythe at a more convenient time. He sat on the flat roof part of the coop with his feet swinging about a foot from the ground.

It was a great spot to concentrate too. Nothing but the fresh summer breeze rustling through the trees, the distant sound of a tractor and the soft clucking of a few curious hens. It was beautiful up here – an oasis of peace.

He took a deep breath, plugged in his wired headset, which was better at blocking out external noise than his wireless earbuds, and dialled the number. It rang and rang. Finn had just started to wonder if he was too late when a brusque voice answered.

'Eleanor Smythe.'

'It's Finn. Er, Finn McTaggart. I'm just returning your call.'

'Ah, yes. Finn.' Her voice changed from brusque to honeyed sweetness. 'I was just thinking about you. I'm glad we've finally connected. I'd like to arrange a meet, but if we could just exchange a few details. Is now a good time?'

'It's a great time. Thank you.' His heart thudded against his ribcage. She'd been thinking about him. The *top* agent in London had been thinking about him. It was unbelievable. It was a dream come true – no, it was beyond his wildest dreams. If someone had told him a year ago that he'd be talking to Eleanor

Smythe about his work, he'd never have believed them. He hadn't even really thought he could paint back then. His art had been a hobby for so long that he still suffered from imposter syndrome when anyone told him he was good.

'We'll start with some background information if we may.'

'Of course. What would you like to know?'

Finn became aware that a brown hen had fluttered up onto the roof to join him. She put her head on one side and studied him with round beady eyes. A couple of her mates were heading towards him too, running purposefully across the grass. Humans meant food to Jade's flock of ex-battery hens. They were all so tame they ran to greet her when they saw her, knowing she was the bearer of tasty treats. They weren't usually quite so tame around him.

'First of all,' Eleanor Smythe was saying, 'maybe you could tell me if...'

Finn felt a violent tug at his ears and everything went silent. 'What the...?' He was so shocked that he swore loudly, not sure for a moment what had happened.

It took a few seconds to compute. The brown hen who'd been sitting beside him was now racing across the field, her wings flapping for extra speed, with his headset dangling from her beak. His mobile, still attached, was bouncing across the long grass in her wake. Finn leaped off the hen house and set off in hot pursuit. But the hen had the advantage of wings and she wasn't stopping. Several other hens had joined in the chase. They were clearly of the opinion their mate had something worth stealing.

Spaghetti, Finn realised in horror. Jade gave them spaghetti as a treat and they loved it. The hen must have mistaken his white headset for a piece of dangling pale spaghetti, her very favourite food, and there was no way on earth she was giving up her prize.

* * *

Jade was driving along opposite the perimeter fence of Duck Pond Rescue when she saw something really odd going on in her top field. What on earth? A man – Finn, she realised, as she slowed the car for a proper look – was chasing a flock of hens across the grass.

There was one out in front and it looked like Finn was gaining on her. There were a lot behind him too. As she watched the curious race unfold, she saw Finn launch himself into the air and rugby tackle the hen. Oh, my goodness. Jade couldn't believe her eyes. Was this what went on when she was out? What on earth was he doing?

Making a split-second decision, she pulled over to the grass verge, bumped one wheel onto it, leapt out of her car and slammed the door behind her. She ran across the road, and then along the perimeter of her field, which was stock fenced, until she reached the gate. A few seconds later she was over it and charging across the field. From what she could see, Finn had caught the hen but he hadn't got up; he was sitting down in the field, fiddling with something, but he had his back to her so she couldn't see what.

Before she reached him, he let out a yell. A mixture of rage and frustration by the sound of it as he bent over something in his lap. At least he'd let go of the hen, Jade saw with relief. The rest of the flock had begun to scatter away across the field, some shaking out their feathers in that way they did when they'd just had a dust bath, or an encounter with a human they didn't much like.

Jade was panting by the time she got close enough to shout. It was a hot day and maybe she wasn't as fit as she thought. Finn didn't seem to hear her. He was now busy talking into his phone, which was pressed to his ear, so she shouted again. 'Finn...!' and finally he turned. His expression of surprise and shock would have been comical if she'd had the faintest idea of the context.

'Jade.' He looked at her sheepishly as he lowered his phone and brushed bits of dried grass from his cut-off jeans. 'I didn't know you were back.'

'Clearly.' She caught her breath and looked him up and down. 'So. Er... are you going to tell me what's going on?'

'Sure.' His grey eyes were guarded.

'Is that hen all right?'

'The *hen* is absolutely fine.'

Jade nodded. Finn was her soulmate. She loved the bones of this man and although they hadn't known each other long – they'd met fourteen months ago when he'd started working for her – she would have trusted him with her life. She also trusted him with the lives of her animals. Every last one of the four-legged and feathered creatures that she'd given a home to were just as important – or in some cases more important – than the humans in her life.

No doubt Finn had a good explanation for what she'd just witnessed. Although she couldn't for the life of her think what it might be.

She let out a breath. 'Shall we head back to the house and you can get cleaned up?'

'Get cleaned up?'

'Yeah.' She suppressed a smile. 'You've got something that looks very much like chicken poop in your ear.'

2

Less than twenty minutes later, Finn and Jade were sitting in Duck Pond Rescue's reception, a converted stone outbuilding containing a desk, a landline, coffee-making facilities, a visitor's chair and a dog basket. The dog basket belonged to Mickey, one of the first dogs Jade had ever rehomed.

She'd once told Finn she'd kept him because she didn't think anyone else would want him. He was supposed to be a cockerpoo but Finn thought he looked more like a shaggy brown rug on legs. He certainly wasn't going to win any beauty contests and he was an adept thief, but Jade adored him. She was a massive pushover when it came to the underdog. And underdog was a description that could have been invented for Mickey.

Currently, an oval brass bird cage took up one corner of reception. It was five foot high and three foot wide, and decked out with various perches, although Mr Spock didn't spend much time in it because Jade said it was too small. The bird cage door was tied back with a reusable cable tie and only closed at nighttime. Apparently, Mr Spock's previous owner had given the parrot free rein in his spacious house, but when he'd had to downsize to a flat which didn't allow pets, that was no longer possible and he hadn't felt able to keep him.

While Finn had got cleaned up, Jade had made a pot of coffee and now they both had a mug on the desk in front of them. Finn explained what had happened as they drank it and Jade listened without interrupting. In fact, there'd been no interruptions at all, Finn thought, which was pretty ironic. Mickey was asleep and even Mr Spock, who was perched up on the top of his cage, hadn't let out so much as a peep. Typical. He'd have been better off making the call here in the first place.

'So did you phone Eleanor Smythe back?' Jade asked.

'Yeah. I was doing that when you arrived. It went straight to voicemail so I left a message explaining what had happened. I hope I haven't blown it. I was swearing like a trooper when that bloody hen nicked my headset. The most important agent in London must now think I'm totally bonkers.'

'You *are* totally bonkers.' She smiled at him.

He did not smile back.

'Sorry. Too soon?' Her face sobered and she leaned forward and caught his hand. 'I'm sure you haven't blown it. Artists are supposed to be eccentric, aren't they?'

'Eccentric, maybe. Rude – not so much. I was calling that hen all the names under the sun while my phone was bouncing around the field.'

'I bet.' Jade had her hand over her mouth but he could still see the laughter in her eyes.

'It's not flaming funny.'

'Sorry. No. I know how much this means to you.' She looked so contrite that Finn relented.

'It is a bit funny, I suppose. Hopefully you're right and she'll decide that my bonkersness – if that's a word – is an asset.'

'She will. Anyone who's got the slightest sense of humour would think it was funny. Did you get your headset back?'

'Yep. Still firmly attached to the phone. I doubt the chook would've run so far with it if half the flock hadn't been chasing her. She'd have stopped somewhere, realised it wasn't spaghetti and spat it out.'

'I'm sure you're right. That rugby tackle was spectacular, by the way. Did you hurt yourself?'

'It was mostly my pride. Enough of me. How did the rescue mission go? What were you rescuing, anyway? You never did say.'

'It was a snake in an outdoor swimming pool.'

'Jade!' Finn looked at her in alarm. 'I'd have gone with you if I'd known. It might have been dangerous.'

'It wasn't dangerous. It turned out to be a toy. A rubber snake to be precise. It *was* pretty lifelike.'

'For pity's sake! Didn't they think to check before they called you out?'

'Apparently, they did. The pool cleaner poked it with a broom and it wriggled. But I imagine it's quite hard to differentiate between a wriggle and a normal movement when you're prodding something floating in the middle of a swimming pool.'

'*You* managed it OK.'

Jade clicked her tongue. 'I'm an expert. Ben used to have a rubber snake when he was younger. It was part of a set of zoo animals Sarah bought him one Christmas. I think she regretted it the minute she did it because the snake was his favourite. He thought it was hilarious to leave it in odd places to scare the living daylights out of her.'

'I bet he did.' Finn felt a warmth steal through him at the mention of Ben, his seven-year-old son. Until recently, he hadn't even known of Ben's existence. It still felt odd that Jade, who'd known Ben since birth because his mother Sarah was her oldest and best friend, knew more about the details of his childhood than Finn did.

Not that Jade had known Finn was Ben's missing father. Sarah had kept the identity of Ben's father a secret for the first few years of his life, which hadn't been difficult because Finn had lived up in Nottingham where he'd been born and where his father, Ray, still lived.

It hadn't become an issue until Finn had moved back to Arleston and by some quirk of fate Jade had employed him and later the two of them had become more than friends. There had been a short time when Jade had known the truth because she'd guessed it, but Sarah had insisted she keep it secret. That secret had eventually blown up in all their faces and had temporarily ended Jade and Finn's relationship.

Fortunately, love had won through. Finn had forgiven Jade for her part in the deception and he'd forgiven Sarah too. She'd been young when they'd conceived Ben after a one-night stand at a party. When she'd realised she was pregnant, she'd been terrified that Finn, who she'd never set eyes on before and had never seen again afterwards, would somehow jeopardise her keeping him.

It was all water under the bridge now. Since Finn had discovered he had a son, he'd been making up for lost time. He saw Ben as often as he possibly could.

'Penny for them.' Jade's voice interrupted his thoughts and he was jolted back into the present.

'I was just thinking about Ben. I've got him this weekend. Did I say?'

'You did.' Her eyes warmed. 'Are you going anywhere special? Or will you guys be under my feet all weekend?'

'I've promised him a picnic at Stonehenge on Saturday.

That's if I can drag him away from the animals. I need to take some photos for a painting I'm planning and he said he wants to come. Do you fancy joining us?'

'On my busiest day of the week – hmmm, that might be tricky. No. I think you two should go and have some father–son bonding time. As you say, he spends enough time here. He thinks it's hilarious that Mr Spock says rude words. Why, oh why did I take on a parrot that swears?'

'Because you're you. The kindest, loveliest person I've ever met.' Finn gathered their empty mugs. 'I can't believe it's so quiet round here. Have you unplugged the phone?'

Jade shook her head. 'No. Why don't you go up to town and try ringing that agent again? You'll be able to get a good signal up there so at least you can explain properly what happened. I've got some free-range egg deliveries that need dropping off at the pubs too, if you don't mind?' She winced. 'Although I do get that hen-related tasks might be a bit of a sore point at the moment.'

They both laughed as he nodded and went out into the yard, and he thought how weird it was. The most important phone call of his life had been sabotaged by a flaming hen, but already it didn't seem the disaster it had felt earlier.

It was while Finn was at the Red Lion, doing his first egg delivery, that he heard the news that the farmer next door to Duck Pond Rescue was thinking of retiring.

Mike, the landlord of the traditional old English pub with its thick cob walls, ancient beams and big old inglenook fireplace, knew everything that was happening in the village, and he leaned forward across the long wooden bar to tell Finn, his face conspiratorial.

'If you guys are looking to expand, it's a good opportunity.

Does Jade need any more space for her ever-growing menagerie? It's worth an ask, isn't it?'

'I guess it is.' Finn wondered about Mike's angle. He rarely did anything without an angle. He found out in the next breath.

'There's talk he might sell up for development. There's space for at least fifty houses on that site. We definitely don't want another new housing estate on our doorstep. Once they get planning permission for that, there's no knowing where they'll build.'

'Won't that be good for you? Lots of new customers.'

'I wouldn't mind but they don't put the infrastructure in. It's hard enough to get a doctor's appointment round here as it is.'

Finn nodded thoughtfully. There'd been a lot of building in Arleston lately. Two new housing estates had appeared on the other side of the village. A few people had protested but it hadn't made any difference.

Mike paid Finn for the eggs and put several empty egg boxes on the bar. 'And I've long since given up trying to get a dentist.'

He had a point. Not that Finn wanted to get into a long discussion about the state of the country, which was one of Mike's favourite subjects.

'You won't want a lot of building on your doorstep either,' Mike added. 'All those diggers and dust and noise scaring the animals.'

'I'll definitely mention it to Jade,' Finn promised.

As he got back in his car, his mobile buzzed in his pocket. He snatched it out and saw Eleanor Smythe's number flash up.

He answered immediately. 'I'm so sorry about earlier,' he said in his most professional voice. 'I'm afraid I had an unfortunate interruption.'

'I see.' There was a long pause. 'I did wonder...?'

Deciding honesty was the best and simplest policy, Finn

explained what had happened and, to his surprise, Eleanor burst out laughing.

'I must admit I was shocked at your outburst, but as we've never met, I'd assumed it wasn't aimed at me. So let's get down to business. How about you come into my Salisbury office for a proper meeting? I'm there in a couple of weeks. Would the third of July suit you?'

'Yes, that's perfect. Thank you.' Finn felt a huge surge of relief. So he hadn't put her off. She still wanted to meet him. There was a God.

* * *

At Duck Pond Rescue, Jade had just rescued a hapless mouse from Diesel, a big black cat she'd kept because, like Mickey, he'd been one of her first rehomes. Diesel, who had free rein at the smallholding, was a skilled hunter. He had endless patience and would wait for hours for a fieldmouse to venture into open ground where he could outrun it.

Fortunately, this one had been alive when Jade had intervened. Many of them weren't. Diesel often deposited the bits he hadn't eaten in reception.

Dawn Layton, who'd once been a volunteer but who Jade now paid for thirty hours a week, grinned as she scooped up a protesting Diesel in her arms.

'I'll lock him in the cattery while you liberate the mouse,' she suggested, her eyes narrowing speculatively. 'Otherwise he'll have it back here in five minutes, minus its head.'

'Thanks,' Jade said gratefully as Dawn disappeared down the yard, her blonde bob swinging around her shoulders.

Dawn, who was sensible, middle aged and kind, was one of the few people Jade trusted totally with her animals. Dawn had owned dozens of animals across the years, was a shrewd judge of character, and was as passionate about animal welfare as Jade was. She helped out with home checks, was always happy to keep an eye on things if Jade had to go out and did a lot more hours than Jade paid her to do.

Jade felt warmed as she nipped across the unmade road with an interested Mickey at her heels to the duck pond opposite the house that had given both the lane and the cottage its name. It was people like Dawn that helped to make the rescue a success. She released the mouse near the weeping willow into the green tangle of undergrowth that edged the pond and watched it scurry away to safety.

She hoped Finn had managed to get in touch with the agent. He might have made light of it in the end but she knew how important it was to him.

She WhatsApped him.

> How did it go?

Finn may not have much confidence about his work, but he was very talented and he'd dreamed of a chance like this all his life. It was a mark of his strength of character, Jade mused, that he hadn't been crosser about the hen mugging.

Finn messaged her back almost immediately with a thumbs up emoji and the words:

> All good. Tell you later.

Jade breathed a sigh of relief.

Their romance had got off to a tricky start, partly because of the secret of Ben, but they both had trust issues because of their backgrounds too. Finn's mother had left when he was six years old, never to be seen again. His father had brought him up singlehandedly. Ray had been brilliant, Finn had told Jade, but taking on the role of both Mum and Dad was an impossible job.

Jade knew this only too well. Her own father had left when she was tiny and she'd been brought up by a succession of nannies while her mother, Elizabeth, focused on her hotel empire. Their relationship had always been fractured. Elizabeth hadn't been maternal and Jade had always felt she mattered less than the hotels which had been her mother's pride and joy. When Elizabeth had died from a stroke three years ago, leaving everything to her only daughter, Jade had sold the hotels and ploughed the money into buying the smallholding that had become Duck Pond Rescue.

She felt guilty that she hadn't followed in her hotelier mother's footsteps, but she'd always preferred animals to people. She'd once trained to be a vet in Bristol, but had come back home when her mother had first been taken ill and had never completed her studies.

Having a relationship hadn't been part of her plans and it had taken Jade a while to trust Finn, just as it had for him to trust her, but now they were together it felt wonderful. Knowing someone had your back was amazing. It was one of the reasons Jade hadn't gone in all guns blazing when she'd seen Finn in hot pursuit of a hen. She'd known there would be a good explanation.

It was a great feeling knowing there was another human on the planet who you could trust with your life. Finn had asked her to marry him the previous year and she'd said yes. They'd bought an engagement ring, a tiny beautiful diamond that Jade wore proudly, but they hadn't yet set a date. Just knowing they would marry one day was enough. They hadn't promised each other anything as big as forever. They'd just promised they would never again keep secrets from each other.

3
———

'So all's well that ends well,' Jade said to Finn when he came back from the village bubbling with excitement about the conversation he'd just had with Eleanor Smythe.

Bubbling with excitement was an exaggeration because Finn was one of the most incredibly self-contained people Jade had ever met. Nothing ever seemed to ruffle him for long but his angular face was flushed and his grey eyes were lit up.

They were standing in reception and Finn had just told Jade the esteemed agent had been quite amused to hear he'd been mugged by a hen.

'That's brilliant. What else did she say?'

'She thinks my work could be suitable for an art exhibition in Salisbury in September. She can arrange for that to happen, and basically she'd like to represent me. We've arranged a meeting in a couple of weeks. She has an office in Salisbury as well as London, but in the meantime she's getting her PA to send me a draft contract so I can look through. I can't believe it, Jade. I really can't. It's...' He paused for the right word and ran a hand through his fair hair. 'Validation... if that makes sense.'

'It makes perfect sense, honey. It's brilliant. How did she know about your work anyway? Did she see it somewhere?'

'She did. Do you remember the art dealer I met via Mike in the Red Lion last year? We got on well and I had high hopes it might go somewhere but it didn't in the end.'

'Yes, I remember.' She also remembered how disappointed he'd been, but in typical Finn fashion he hadn't dwelt on it.

'Well, it turns out the guy knew Eleanor Smythe. He showed her some photos he'd taken of my work and she was interested enough to get in touch.' He blew out a controlled sigh. 'The price tags she was talking for my work were mind boggling. She'd take her cut, of course. But I'm trying not to get too excited in case nothing comes of it.'

'It sounds like it already has if she's sending you a contract.' Jade kissed him. 'You totally deserve this. Congratulations.'

Behind them, Mr Spock burst into song. 'Congratulations and celebrations...' They were treated to the parrot's rendition of Cliff Richard's old song, followed by a long cackle of laughter.

'Mr Spock's on a roll. How on earth does he know all the words?'

'According to Phoebe Dashwood, his previous owner had weird musical taste. You remember Phoebe, the vet at Puddle-duck Farm?' she added when Finn looked puzzled. 'Phoebe rehomed Mr Spock originally. She had his cage in her practice, but his swearing was putting off her clients. It's tricky having a parrot swearing like a trooper in a professional workplace.'

'It's tricky here.'

'No, it isn't. Most people who come in here think it's hilarious.' Jade chuckled and Mr Spock let out another cackle of laughter. 'Parrots are amazing mimics. They only need one word or a familiar sound to trigger them. It's astounding, isn't it?'

In his basket, Mickey yawned, got up and stalked out of the office.

'He doesn't look very impressed,' Finn remarked.

'He's not. He can't get a decent nap in here any more. If he could talk he'd be telling us the sooner we rehome that parrot the better.'

The landline on the desk began to ring and a couple of teenagers who'd been helping with dog walking came into reception. Jade reached for the phone. 'Let's catch up properly later, honey.'

* * *

They caught up in bed in the end. Running an animal sanctuary was a 24/7 commitment and even though Jade adored her work, she was well aware it didn't leave much time for anything else. They usually took it in turns to cook – neither of them was big on cooking and as Jade was vegetarian and Finn wasn't, it meant either making two meals or one that could be adapted. Stir fries or omelettes were handy because they were easy to add meat to or leave it out. Pasta and pizza worked well too, and sometimes they went to the Red Lion or got a takeaway. Tonight had been Jade's turn to cook but she'd been tired when she'd got in and Finn had been going through the contract Eleanor had emailed, so they'd ended up having microwave porridge instead of a proper meal.

'I'm sorry about dinner,' Jade murmured, snuggling up to Finn in bed.

'I wasn't that hungry.' He kissed her hair. 'Or I'd have made something. Anyway, I like porridge.'

'Me too. Hey, maybe when you're a famous artist earning a fortune we could employ a chef. And a cleaner.'

'Yeah. That sounds good. Although I wouldn't be holding your breath. Most artists make a fortune when they're dead.'

'It's lucky Mum's stocks and shares are doing so well then, isn't it?'

'*Your* stocks and shares,' Finn corrected, his gaze holding hers, and Jade mumbled an agreement.

It was weird how she still thought of her inheritance as her mother's money.

'It's still difficult to believe she's gone, Finn. I used to feel really sad that Mum and I had so little in common, but I'm glad I inherited her skill at investing money. Especially as the dividends help to support this place.'

He glanced at her face. 'I thought we were pretty much self-sustaining with the adoptions and sponsorship you get from local businesses.'

'We are, but I don't like to rely on those. The economy's been quite bad lately, hasn't it, and that has a knock-on effect on us. Charitable donations are the first things people stop when money is tight. Also, more people give up their animals when they're broke. We're bursting at the seams.'

'And on that note, you've just reminded me of something Mike said earlier. Apparently, the farmer next door is retiring and Mike's worried he's going to sell up to developers. He mooted the idea you might like to buy a bit more land and expand this place.'

'Did he now?' Jade sat up in bed. 'Doesn't Farmer John have any family to take over? Farmers usually pass on the baton to their offspring.'

'Mike didn't seem to think so. There's not a Mrs Farmer John anyway.'

'No, that's true. How interesting.' Jade's mind buzzed with possibilities. 'I must admit I hadn't considered expanding. But maybe we should. It's a good opportunity and I shouldn't need too much of the capital. Perhaps I should go and see Farmer John.'

'I wish I hadn't mentioned it now.'

'Why? It's a great idea.'

'Yeah, it might be, but is there any chance we can talk about it tomorrow?'

'Sorry. Are you tired?'

'I'm not tired.' He sat up, then leant across and cupped her face in his hands. 'I'm just thinking that bed's not the place for heavy discussions about finance. I can think of "far more interesting things" we could be talking about... or... ahem... doing.'

She kissed him back and for a long while there was no more talking.

* * *

Over the next couple of days, the idea of expanding the sanctuary grew in Jade's mind.

When she'd first bought the smallholding, she'd thought there would be plenty of space to set up an animal rescue. Five acres had seemed like a lot, but in the beginning she'd only really considered having cats and dogs. They'd ended up with horses as well – but they only had enough room for two or three and they had two already.

The other two-acre field was used for dog walking and Finn had fenced part of that off for the ex-battery hens. The dog kennels, the cattery, the hospital block, which was a converted pigsty, the storage areas and the reception took up the rest of the space. When she'd told Finn they were bursting at the seams, she hadn't been exaggerating.

And her investments were doing well. It wouldn't hurt to

find out how much Farmer John wanted for a couple of fields. There was one big one – she judged it to be about five acres – that abutted the hen field. That would be perfect.

Also, if she bought that, there would be enough space between Duck Pond Cottage and any housing development for it not to be a problem even if the farmer did sell the rest to a developer.

By Friday night, she'd made up her mind. 'I think I might go and see Farmer John,' she said to Finn as they cleared up after supper.

He'd cooked tonight – spaghetti, which he'd joked he'd never be able to eat again without thinking of hen muggings, and a roasted red pepper garlicky sauce, which was amazing. He was definitely a better cook than she was.

'You're serious about getting more land, then?'

'I think it's worth finding out what his intentions are. We don't know for sure he's even selling up. He might have a niece or nephew tucked away somewhere who wants to take up farming. But if he hasn't, it's a great opportunity.' She paused for breath. 'Is Sarah dropping Ben off here tomorrow or are you collecting him?'

'She's bringing him here about ten.'

'Brilliant, so I'll get to see him. It's ages since I saw Sarah too. Did you tell them about the hen mugging?'

'No, I thought we could do that when we're all together. Maybe over pizza tomorrow night. I bet he'd like to hear the snake story too.'

They smiled at each other. Finn opened his mouth, as if he was about to say something else, and then hesitated.

'What?' she asked him, tuning in, but then her phone buzzed and she saw a WhatsApp from Sarah. The part of it she could read said:

Can't wait to see you tomorrow. I've got news.

Sidetracked, she opened the message and by the time she looked up again, Finn had finished drying up and had put down the tea towel.

'Sorry. That was Sarah. Were you going to tell me something just now?'

'It'll keep.'

'Are you sure?'

He yawned. 'I'm sure.'

* * *

Finn wondered later if he should have told Jade what was on his mind. But he was still so undecided himself.

A couple of days ago he'd had a curious WhatsApp message from his father.

Getting a WhatsApp message at all was curious because until recently, Ray had been a complete technophobe and although he owned a mobile, he mostly didn't charge it.

But just over a year ago, Ray had started a relationship with a lovely sixty-something lady called Dorinda, who lived three doors up from him.

Dorinda, or Dorrie as she preferred to be called, had given Ray a whole new lease of life. She was lively, upbeat and massively social – she actually called Ray 'Pumpkin', something he didn't seem to mind at all – and bit by bit she'd drawn the ultra-reserved Ray out of his shell. Recently she'd encouraged him to buy a smartphone to replace his old Nokia.

To Finn's surprise, Ray had loved the smartphone and had taken to it like an old pro. He mostly used it to look at the BBC news and he'd started sending Finn links to news stories he thought might be of interest to his son.

They were often animal or art based, but the most recent one had been a news item about estranged family members being reunited and the joy that could bring. At first Finn had thought his dad might be referring to the fact he'd only recently met his grandson, Ben. But Ray and Ben had never been estranged – they just hadn't known about each other's existence.

At the foot of the news item had been a link to a tracing agency. Finn had wondered if his father was hinting, in that not-too-subtle way he had, that he wouldn't mind if Finn wanted to contact his own mother. This didn't seem very likely in view of the fact that for most of Finn's life his father had clammed up if he'd raised the subject of his mother. 'Least said, soonest mended' was a phrase Ray was very fond of. Living for the day was more important than digging about in the past.

On the other hand, Dorrie had worked wonders at changing Ray's outlook in other ways. Maybe it had been her influence. Whatever the reason Ray had sent the piece, it had stirred something up in Finn. For the first time in his adult life, he had wondered if he should try to track down his mother. He suspected this was because he now knew what it was like to have a son. And having met Ben, he couldn't imagine a life without him. He certainly couldn't imagine having a child and then abandoning it. Ben had been five and a half when he'd first met him. Very similar to the age Finn had been when Bridie had abandoned him and Ray. All he knew about his mother was her name and the fact that she'd gone back home to Northern Ireland soon after she'd left his father.

He wanted to discuss all this stuff with Jade, but he needed to find the right time.

Jade's relationship with her own mother had been difficult.

And she'd never known her father. She'd once told Finn she wasn't interested in tracking him down either. One rejection had been enough. She wouldn't risk facing a second.

The whole subject of parents was a minefield. And the truth was that Finn might not be able to find his mother even if he did look for her. So he'd decided to put out a few feelers first. It wouldn't hurt to type her name into a search engine and see what came up. If there was no trace of her – or if there was and she didn't want to see him – then there was no sense in telling Jade and rocking the boat.

4

'Auntie Jade, I'm here. I'm here. Where are you?'

Jade heard Ben long before she saw him. She was in the stone-built feed store, partway through the Saturday breakfast routine, topping up a container with chicken feed, when she heard his high distinctive voice out in the yard.

She put down the scoop and went to the door to look out. Sarah was keen. Hadn't Finn said she was coming at ten? It was barely nine.

Ben was by reception. He'd clearly already been in to see his dad, who was standing just behind him in the doorway. Jade felt gratified that Ben was just as keen to see her as he'd always been. She'd adored the little boy since he'd been born and she'd been ever so slightly worried that once he had both a mum and a dad in his life, not to mention Callum, Sarah's partner, he might not be so eager to see her. But her fears had been unfounded.

She wasn't conceited enough to think she was the main attraction. Ben was besotted with animals. He'd live at Duck Pond Rescue if he could.

'I'm in here, love.' She stepped out into the sunlight, which was bright after the cool shade of the stone feed store, and shielded her eyes.

'Auntie Jade.' Ben flew across the yard to give her a hug and she bent down to lift him, which was a lot harder than it used to be.

Ben tugged away from her. 'Mr Spock is very naughty.'

'Is he, love? Why's that then?'

'He says bad words.' Ben widened his grey eyes and tried to look serious but then ruined it by bursting into peals of laughter.

'That's very naughty. But he's a parrot and parrots don't know any better, whereas little boys do, of course.'

'I'm not allowed to say words like—'

Jade put her hand over her mouth and shook her head quickly before he could elaborate further. 'Do you want to come and feed the hens with me and collect the eggs? Where's your mum?'

'She's talking to Dad.'

'Come on then. Let's go and see if we've got any hungry hens.' She handed him the canvas bag with its individual egg pockets which helped to avoid breakages and they set off.

A few minutes later they were in the hen field and Ben was running ahead of her up to the coops. Jade wished she had his energy as he flew across the patchwork grass, heedless of what he might be treading in. Luckily he'd got his scruffy old clothes on. Sarah would have brought a bag with his going-out stuff in. There were already several hens hurtling towards Jade and a few had diverted towards Ben – recognising him as another soft touch.

It usually took Ben about five minutes to get totally filthy when he arrived at Duck Pond Rescue. It was worse in the winter when the place was all mud and manure, but even in the summer there were plenty of ways to get mucky.

By the time Jade reached the coops, Ben had already unlatched the back of the first one and had liberated several eggs, which he put carefully into the bag.

'They're not too poopy, Auntie Jade.'

'That's good to hear.'

'This one's really warm. I think she only just lied it.'

'Laid it,' Jade corrected gently. 'That's brilliant.' She filled up the feeders from the container and hooked them back into the coops one by one. She'd always adored Ben but she'd never let herself think about having kids of her own. You needed a relationship for that and until she'd met Finn, a relationship had been the last thing she'd wanted. Sarah had once accused her of hiding from the world in the Wiltshire countryside so she didn't have to meet anyone.

Jade had vehemently denied this at the time, but deep down she knew her best friend had been right. She had been hiding. But she wasn't any more and since she'd fallen in love with Finn, Jade had started to feel differently about having children too. She must be feeling broody, she realised with a little start, letting her gaze rest on Ben's fair head and serious profile as he hunkered down and re-latched the coop where he'd got the eggs.

It was a more sedate walk back to reception with Ben taking the job of carrying the eggs very seriously.

Sarah and Finn were in the yard when they got back. She was congratulating him about his new agent and the prospect of an art exhibition. 'You're definitely going to be famous,' she murmured, and winked at Jade.

Sarah looked tanned. Her honey-blonde hair was swept up

in a ponytail and her summer-blue eyes were sparkly and happy.

'I wondered where you two had got to.' She bent and wiped a smudge of dirt from her son's face with her fingers. 'Oh, Ben, you're filthy already. How do you do it?' But the warmth in her voice belied her words as Ben shrugged her off.

'It's OK, Mum. I'm wearing scruffs.'

'That's very true,' Jade said as Sarah rolled her eyes, and the two women hugged.

'Finn made a pot of coffee but I think some volunteers just finished it.'

'I'll do some more. Let's sit in reception for a bit. I think Ben and his dad have plans to make. And the eggs need to be cleaned up at the house.'

Finn got the hint. 'We'll do that while you ladies catch up,' he said, and he and Ben disappeared in the direction of the cottage.

'So...?' Jade said, ushering Sarah into reception as soon as Finn and Ben were out of earshot. 'What's this exciting news?'

'I don't remember saying it was exciting.' Sarah's freckled face flushed and her eyes brightened even more. 'It is though. You're right.' She held out her hand and the engagement ring she'd taken off last Christmas, when she and Callum had split up temporarily, sparkled as it caught the morning sunlight.

'The wedding's back on,' Jade said, without even a question mark in her voice. 'Oh, that's brilliant. Give me a hug.'

She breathed in the wild musk scent Sarah always wore, and as they drew apart she said, 'I thought you'd decided you didn't need a bit of paper.'

'Yes, I know we said that but we've changed our minds. We're totally happy with each other. We want to shout it to the world and I fancy being Mrs Callum Wilson.'

'Well, congratulations,' Jade said, instantly regretting it as Mr Spock launched into song, and even the laid-back Mickey, who'd been sitting peacefully in his basket, put his ears back with a look of pained disbelief and wandered off into the yard to escape the noise.

'That parrot's unbelievable – where did he come from? He was swearing like a trooper earlier.'

'I know. Ben told me. I probably shouldn't keep Mr Spock in reception. It's not the best impression if I'm trying to have a serious conversation with someone, but I could hardly say no when Phoebe Dashwood asked me. She's always helped me out. Maybe we should see if we can get Ben to teach him some more appropriate words.'

Sarah laughed out loud. 'Good luck with that. He loves Mr Spock just as he is. Anyway, I didn't just want to tell you the wedding's back on, I want to run something by you.'

'Go on.'

'What do you think about us having a double wedding? Me and Callum, and you and Finn.'

Jade was so taken aback she spluttered on her coffee.

'I didn't expect it to be that much of a shock. You guys are still getting married, aren't you?' She glanced meaningfully at Jade's ring. 'It'd be brilliant fun to have a double wedding. Great for Ben too – having his mum and dad being centre stage on such a big day. Not that I wouldn't have invited you and Finn to our wedding obvs. But this way we'll all be getting married together.' She broke off. 'Tell me you think it's a good idea.'

'Um… I don't know. I mean, yes, it probably is. But when were you thinking? Finn and I haven't made any plans at all yet. We haven't even set a date.'

'Exactly. So you won't even need to change anything. And we

can probably get a super good deal if we have a double wedding. Think about it – only one church booking, only one reception. Only one set of posh gear.'

'What does Callum think?'

'He's more than happy to go along with whatever I want,' Sarah said with a hint of satisfaction in her voice.

Of course he was. The big flame-haired Scotsman loved the bones of her. Jade was pretty sure that if Sarah had asked him to get married on a moving train or in the depths of the ocean dressed in full scuba gear, Callum would have said yes without hesitation.

Jade's head was spinning a bit. 'I'm fine with it in principle. I mean, obviously Finn would have to agree but...' She broke off as Finn came back in the door.

'What would I have to agree?' he said, looking between both of them.

'Where's Ben?' Sarah checked over his shoulder. 'I haven't mentioned it to Ben yet,' she said in a quick aside to Jade. 'I know he's going to love the idea but I wanted to check it out with you two first.'

'He's just gone off with Dawn to the kennels,' Finn reassured them, coming fully into the room. 'So come on. Out with it. What are you two plotting?'

To Jade's surprise, Finn, who'd always been quite private and not a big socialite, wasn't entirely against the idea.

'I can see where you're coming from as regards Ben,' he told Sarah. 'Although I think we'd need to have a really good chat about it all. Make sure we're all on the same page as far as the type of day we want goes. Won't you and Callum want something closer to his family? Kilts and Scottish castles and the like?'

'We definitely don't want Scottish castles. Although I'm not averse to men in kilts. Callum looks good in a kilt.'

Finn put up his hands. 'No way.'

Sarah laughed out loud. 'I'm joking. My God, your face. Don't worry. No kilts. Callum's parents are surprisingly lowkey. We were never looking for a massive do when we planned it before, if you remember. We were going to get married locally and go to the Red Lion for pie and chips.'

'That's true,' Jade said as the landline leapt into action.

She spoke to a woman wanting to check their opening hours, but she'd barely disconnected when Sarah gave an ear-splitting scream.

'What on earth…?' Jade stared at her in alarm.

Sarah was pointing with a shaking finger at the door. 'Diesel's got something in his mouth. I think it's a mouse.'

She leapt up onto her chair as the big black cat nonchalantly dropped a wriggling mouse on the floor, which then scurried towards Sarah's chair.

'Catch it,' Sarah yelled at Finn. 'For God's sake. I'm terrified of them.'

'No shit, Sherlock!' Finn leapt into action and caught the mouse. 'What shall I do with it?'

'I don't care, just get rid.'

A few minutes later when the mouse had been unceremoniously dumped over at the duck pond, and Diesel had been shut in the feed room so he couldn't recatch it, Jade glanced at Sarah.

'Why don't we all get together for a drink soon? We can talk it all through and decide. Finn and I need to have a good chat about it too.' She stole him a glance. He might just be going along with the idea because he thought she wanted to do it. Neither of them was in a rush to walk up the aisle.

'Are you free Friday after next?' Sarah asked, nervously

checking the floor, presumably in case the mouse had been stupid enough to run straight back in again. 'Come round for supper. Ben's got a stopover with his mate Darren so that would be a good time. I don't want to get his hopes up if it's not going to happen.'

They agreed supper would be a good start, and when Sarah had finally left, Finn and Jade exchanged glances.

'Do you really not mind, Finn? Sarah did rather spring that on us.'

'I wouldn't mind getting married in a shed as long as I was marrying you.'

'I think that's the most romantic thing you've ever said to me.'

'I try.' He flashed her a wry smile. 'Talking it through with them doesn't commit us to anything. And as we're not even doing that for a fortnight, there's plenty of time for us to talk through the pros and cons first. But right now, I'm going to track down my son and see if he's still up for Stonehenge and a picnic.'

Finn breathed a sigh of relief as he walked up the yard. The truth was the wedding talk was a welcome distraction. He hadn't slept well and he knew it was because he felt guilty. Last night he'd had a conversation with his father that had led to him doing something he knew he might live to regret. He'd set the ball rolling in the search for his mother.

He'd acted on impulse and he hadn't told Jade because so far every time he'd tried, fate had intervened. Maybe nothing would come of the Facebook message he'd sent. Maybe it was best to put it right out of his mind. He still wasn't sure. But hopefully he'd be able to clear his head and get some perspective if he was away from the sanctuary for the day.

Being with Ben at Stonehenge, the beautiful and ancient

world-famous heritage site, which was a mere fifteen-minute drive from Duck Pond Rescue, was the perfect place to get some perspective.

An hour later, Finn and Ben were walking under the bluest of cerulean skies towards the ancient, great grey standing stones. No matter how many times Finn visited the huge circle of stones, they never failed to strike a sense of awe into his soul. And somehow it was calming walking around the neolithic site, which had stood for what was believed to be more than 5,000 years.

It was two days after the summer solstice, when people came from all around the world to see the moment when the sun rose behind the heel stone in the north-east part of the horizon and shone into the heart of Stonehenge. It was a custom that must have gone on for centuries, and there was still evidence of the 15,000-strong current-day crowd that had gathered to welcome the daybreak this 21 June.

A litter picker in a fluorescent yellow jacket with a black bin liner called out a cheery good morning and Finn and Ben stopped to chat.

'Need any help?' Finn asked.

'Thanks, but we're on it,' the man told them. 'It's actually not too bad. The event's pretty organised these days, and most people are responsible.'

'Can we come to the summer solstice one year, Dad?' Ben begged.

'I don't see why not.'

'Can we dress up as penguins?'

'Um...'

The litter picker laughed. 'I think it's pagans, not penguins, although I suppose you could dress up as a penguin. I'm sure no one would mind.'

Ben looked disappointed. 'What's a pagan, Dad?'

'I think it means someone who doesn't hold conventional religious beliefs?' Finn looked at the litter picker for support.

'That sounds about right. I think there are quite a few druids too.'

'What's a druid, Dad?'

'I think they're a kind of ancient priest. They wear white cloaks.'

The litter picker nodded in agreement and Finn glanced at Ben's animated face. Luckily they had a whole year for Ben to forget he wanted to dress up as a pagan or a druid or indeed a penguin. Finn had no more desire to wear fancy dress than he had to put on a kilt. 'Let's go and take some pictures of the stones and we can think about it,' he said diplomatically.

'OK, Dad.' Ben ran ahead of him and Finn tried to concentrate on why they were here as he took pictures from various angles on his phone. He sometimes brought his easel out to the landscapes he was painting, but it was good to have photos too so he could work from home. He wouldn't just do one painting of Stonehenge. There would be several.

He rubbed his eyes, still feeling tired, as his mind flicked back to the conversation he'd had with his father last night.

They'd been on their usual weekly catch-up when Finn had asked about the estranged family news item.

'Dorrie thought I should send it,' Ray had said gruffly, and Finn had heard the reluctance in his voice. 'She's got this idea you might want to trace your mother. I told her it was a waste of time. If your mother had wanted to stay in touch she'd have left me some means of contacting her.'

'I know that, Dad.' Finn had felt like he was traversing a field of unexploded mines. 'And it's no reflection on you, but I am curious about her.'

'Well, the only thing I can tell you, lad, is her name. As you know, her family lived in Belfast. I doubt she's got the same surname but for what it's worth, it was Neale back then. Bridie Neale – and there must be a thousand of them in Northern Ireland. It will be like looking for a needle in a haystack.'

'It's better than nothing.'

'There was a sister called Caitlin. Same story. She probably won't have the same surname either.'

'Thanks, Dad.' Finn had changed the subject at that point, knowing it was unsettling his father. The only other thing he knew about his mother was that she was eleven years younger than Ray. Which would make her around fifty-five now.

It wasn't much to go on, but it was a start.

Jade had still been out on a home visit when he'd finished speaking to his father, so Finn had gone onto an old Facebook account he'd set up years ago and typed in Bridie Neale. He'd quickly drawn a blank. None of them were in the right age bracket, at least as far as he could tell from their profile pictures. One or two didn't have profile pictures. He'd considered sending an innocuous message to these, leaving his phone number, but what if they were bots or scammers? He didn't fancy giving his phone number to a scammer.

When he'd typed in Caitlin Neale he'd had more luck. There were three Caitlin Neales and one of them lived in Belfast. She was the right age and it was the right area. Finn looked at her profile photo and decided she had kind eyes. It might not be her, but he knew he'd kick himself if he didn't try. So he'd typed out a bland message saying he was trying to track down a friend in the area and thought she might be able to help. He'd read it through to check he wasn't giving too much away and pressed send.

As soon as he'd done it, he'd had second thoughts. He really should have discussed it with Jade first. They talked about everything and this was a biggie. Bigger than him getting an agent. Possibly even bigger than them planning a wedding. On the other hand, if Caitlin didn't answer there was no harm done. That would be the end of it.

He'd consoled himself with the fact he could tell Jade when she got in.

But she hadn't got in until gone ten and Finn hadn't wanted to start the conversation then. So in the end he had said nothing. It had seemed logical at the time. It wasn't a conversation they could have in a hurry. But his subconscious mind clearly had other ideas. Guilt had invaded his dreams.

He hadn't told her this morning either. There was never any time in the mornings for more than the briefest of conversations. Not that Caitlin had answered his message. So maybe he was putting himself through all this stress for nothing.

'Daaaaad?' Ben's voice interrupted his thoughts, and judging by the thread of impatience, Finn realised it wasn't the first time he'd spoken.

'Sorry. I was miles away.'

'I know.' Ben rolled his eyes. 'You've been staring at the

stones for ages. Have we got enough photos yet? I'm getting hungry.'

'We'd better go back to the car and fetch that picnic then, hadn't we, son?'

'Yay! Did you get cheese and onion crisps?'

'I did, son.'

Ben beamed in delight and Finn swallowed his emotion. He felt an ache in his heart every time he said the word 'son'. The more time he spent with Ben, the less able he was to understand how Bridie could have vanished so completely and utterly from his life.

He knew that half of him was hoping to find his mother alive and well and half of him was hoping he wouldn't. Because if she was alive and well and had simply not bothered to contact him for all of these years, he didn't think there was an explanation on earth that could convince him it had been worth all the heartbreak.

With a spike of insight, Finn realised suddenly that this was the real reason he hadn't told Jade what he was doing. If there was no trace of Bridie then he could just rebury the past. But once he told Jade, then it all became real. So maybe on balance it really was better to wait until he knew what he was dealing with.

He and Ben laid out their picnic on the perfect spot Ben had found, not far from the car, in sight of the stones. Finn had got scotch eggs to go with the crisps and shop-bought sandwiches to save making them, and a handful of Ben's favourite chocolate bars. A feast that neither Sarah nor Jade would have approved of on health grounds, but it didn't hurt once in a while.

Treats were OK as long as they weren't too often. Maybe that applied to old secrets too. Finn breathed a sigh of relief that he'd made a decision. Stonehenge had worked its magic. He wouldn't tell Jade for now. There was no sense in both of them stressing about a message that might never be answered.

He looked at Ben, who'd got sidetracked from the food and was watching a beetle crawl across the worn-down grass. Finn couldn't imagine a life without his son. It made the possibility of finding Bridie even more poignant, and yet even more painful if it came to nothing. Yes – the decision he'd made was the right one for now.

He had no more insight into what the future held than the ancient people who'd positioned these stones must have done, he thought as he glanced over at the heel stone silhouetted starkly against the deep blue June sky.

The only certainty was that, like those ancient people, Finn hoped there would be another sunrise. Another blank canvas on which to paint a picture. Another day to unravel whatever the fates had in store.

6

Once Jade had got used to the idea of having a double wedding and she'd realised Finn wasn't averse to it either, she was excited.

'To be honest, I'd envisaged us having a really quiet do with just your dad and Dorrie and Ben. And Sarah and Callum, of course,' she told him when they chatted about it over the next few days. 'But it would be fun to tie the knot together.'

'It could be – as long as Sarah hasn't got anything too crazy planned. I think Ben would love it. She's right about that.'

'So, are we going to say yes then?'

'Subject to us all agreeing on the type of day it is, I don't see why not.'

Jade grinned. She didn't imagine Sarah would want too quiet a day. Quiet and sensible weren't adjectives she'd ever have used to describe her best friend, but there was wriggle room. The two of them had always complemented each other well because they were such complete opposites.

Sarah wasn't keen on exercise or getting her hands dirty, unlike Jade who had always been more comfortable pottering outside beneath a big sky. Sarah was a genius on a computer.

She wrote the software for marketing databases that sold to multinational companies, which was where she'd met Callum, who sold the databases. Jade was never sure which one of them made the most money, but they were both high flyers.

Jade was serious and tended to play by the rules, whereas Sarah had always been a natural rebel, whose instinct was to do exactly the opposite of what she was told.

Sarah hated authority and Jade thought it was a necessary evil which occasionally had to be tolerated. Although deep down Jade had an anti-authority streak too. If she hadn't she probably would have followed her mother into the hotel business, which was what had been expected of her, instead of rebelling and insisting on following her own path.

Fortunately, they loved each other dearly, and the only thing they'd ever really fallen out about had been the issue of Ben's father. Jade had always thought Sarah should try to track down the stranger she'd met at a drunken Christmas party and Sarah had always flatly refused.

Thankfully that had been resolved when Finn had come back to Arleston two years ago and both women had finally realised who he was.

Things had ended happily when it came to that dangerous secret.

Keeping secrets from Finn was not something Jade ever planned to do again.

What with all the excitement of Sarah's proposition, Jade forgot all about her mission to ask Farmer John about his retirement and selling up plans.

Finn had been busy too – he was spending all his spare time painting, which was apparently the only advice his new agent had given him. He took his easel into the surrounding countryside at every opportunity. As well as Stonehenge, he painted other famous local landmarks like the Westbury White Horse, a fifty-five-metre-high white horse carved out of chalk on a hillside. There were seven chalk horses dotted around Wiltshire but Westbury was the biggest and most distinctive.

Occasionally Finn just painted ordinary scenes with no recognisable landmarks. One of Jade's favourites was an old wooden stile by a footpath that led across a field of golden barley. Scarlet poppies dotted the field of gold while the dusty brown path meandered into the distance before disappearing over an unseen horizon into a bright blue sky. There was something about the picture that made Jade's throat ache.

'If you can't sell that one, maybe we can put it in the lounge,' she said when she told him how much she loved it.

'We can put it in the lounge now. It's my favourite. It reminds me that there's always hope, if you just keep on the right path.'

'That's very spiritual,' she said, looking at him in surprise. Finn rarely came out with profound sayings like that.

'Is it? That must be Eleanor's influence. She said I should think about titles for my work, based on what I was trying to capture when I was inspired to paint them. I've called that picture *Hope*.'

Hope went up in their lounge on the biggest wall. Every time Jade looked at it she thought about what he'd said. Hope was one of those things everyone needed.

A couple of days after this conversation, Jade bumped into Farmer John as she was walking some dogs in her field. It was a mid-week morning and he was in the field alongside them doing something to the wheel of a tractor but when he straightened up, he saw her and strolled across to the fence that divided their land.

'Jade. It's good to see you. It's been ages.'

'Yes, I know. It seems mad when we're next-door neighbours. How are you?'

'I'm good, Jade, thanks. Hello, boys.' He put a hand through the fence to greet the two waggy-tailed terriers, now dancing on their hind legs on the ends of their leads. 'There's a fine couple of ratters if ever I've seen them.' He met her gaze again. 'I'm counting down the days to retirement. Never thought I'd be saying that but the day has finally come.'

'You're not old enough to retire, are you?'

He laughed. 'Oh, I'd say seventy-six is old enough even for a die-hard old farmer like me, wouldn't you?'

She was genuinely dumbfounded. 'You can't possibly be.'

'I've been lucky with my health, there's no doubting that. But yep, I'm afraid I am and farming's a young man's game. I've slowed down lately. The bits that haven't already fallen off are getting decidedly creaky.'

It was the perfect opening. 'So, do you have a young niece or nephew to take over the reins?' She was fairly sure he didn't have children.

He shook his head and his eyes shadowed. 'Sadly, I don't, no, so this place is on the market. I'll miss it, that's for sure, but there's no point in having all this land if you're not going to farm it.' He gave her a direct look. 'I'm not going to lie to you, Jade. I've had a couple of developers sniffing around already. I'd rather sell it to a farmer, or another landowner like yourself, of course I would, but the reality is I'll sell to the highest bidder.'

'Would you consider splitting it up and selling off some of it to me?' The words were out of her mouth before she could change her mind. Until that moment she hadn't even fully made a decision about expanding. But now, in that split second, she was certain.

The old farmer put his head on one side. 'I'd consider a

reasonable offer – yes. Of course I would. What did you have in mind?'

She told him and he nodded thoughtfully.

* * *

Finn, who was out collecting Calor gas refills, which they used for the stoves that heated the outside animal enclosures and also for the caravan cooker where volunteers could heat up soup, had just had a call from an unknown number. He hadn't answered it because his hands were full, and it was probably a sales call anyway. But his phone had just pinged to indicate they'd left a message.

He put the gas cylinders in the back of his Toyota and then sat in the driver's seat and listened to the message.

An unfamiliar Irish accent filled his ears.

'My name's Caitlin Neale. Am I talking to the voicemail of Finn McTaggart? If I'm not talking to him, I apologise, and please put this message out of your mind. But if I am talking to the right number I'd be grateful if you could give me a ring back, Finn, at your convenience. I think you've been trying to contact me.'

Finn sat bolt upright in the car as shock straightened his spine. It had been over a week since he'd sent the Belfast Caitlin Neale a message, and he'd already decided she couldn't be the right one or she'd have got back to him.

For a few moments he wondered what to do. His instinct was to phone her back instantly right now while he had a decent signal and she was obviously available – her message had been left less than five minutes ago – but what would he say?

He didn't want to scare her off by going in too heavy and

telling her he was her long-lost nephew. Especially as he was a nephew she might not know she had.

On one long-ago drunken evening, when Ray was half cut on Christmas whisky, he'd told Finn that Bridie's family had never approved of him.

'They thought I was too old for her and the wrong religion. She never told them about you. She didn't dare.'

With hindsight, Finn had realised this was probably why she'd never come back. She'd literally blocked out this part of her life, him included, and while he'd been devastated at the time, once he'd reached adulthood and had been able to re-examine the past with fresh eyes, he'd understood how she might have been able to do it. If not one single person in her own birth family knew she'd ever had a child then maybe she'd managed to block out the fact too.

Or maybe she'd missed him every day since and longed to see him again. Finn had swung between these two extremes for much of his life. The not knowing was tough but it was better than finding out she hadn't missed him at all and had gone on to have another six replacement children, all of whom she loved far more than her firstborn.

Now he was on the brink of finding out, he felt as though he'd opened a Pandora's Box. Even though, right now, it was still firmly locked. Like his mobile, which felt slippery in his hands. He glanced at it. He should go back to Duck Pond Cottage, tell Jade everything, and see how she felt about it all.

They had a rule. No secrets between them. Especially not a whopping great big one like this.

The sun through the windscreen felt hot on his face. He did up his seatbelt, glad he had a plan. But then his mobile burst into action again and Finn looked at the incoming call and saw the same number that had left the voicemail flashing on his screen.

He answered it. 'Finn McTaggart.'

'Hello there, Finn. I was wondering if I'd phoned the right number, so I was. Would it be you who sent me the Facebook message?' She sounded even more Irish than she had on her message.

'It was me.' His voice came out croaky, which wasn't surprising as his tongue was so dry it felt like a bit of old leather in his mouth. 'Thank you for calling me. I was just going to phone you back.'

'Now I've saved you the bother. How can I help?'

Finn gathered his courage and launched into his prepared generic spiel. 'I'm trying to track down Bridie Neale. She knows my father. They were friends back in the early nineties when she was living in England. We think she moved back to Belfast some time towards the end of 1998.'

There was an intake of breath. 'OK, I'm with you.' Caitlin sounded more surprised than anything else. 'Now let me see. That is going back a bit. Would you bear with me?'

'Sure.' He heard her shout something to someone else in her vicinity. 'Sean – can you remember when our Bridie went over to England to live?'

The answer was too muffled for Finn to hear the reply and there was some more back and forth conversation which he couldn't catch either. She must have either moved away from the phone or muffled it somehow.

He held his breath. There was sweat pouring off his face now and running down the back of his neck. Stress. It wasn't that hot. But he opened the driver's door to let some air in while he waited for Caitlin to come back to the phone.

It seemed to take forever, but then she was back and talking again.

'Sean, my better half, he's agreeing with you – Bridie went to live in England in the early nineties. We're saying the summer of 1990 would be about right. So that would fit in with what you think. Am I right?'

Finn could feel himself quivering with impatience. He'd managed to work that bit out already – although he realised he'd never asked his father where they'd first met. Or how long Bridie had been in Nottingham – or even what she was doing there. He felt so ill prepared for this conversation. 'But she came back again to Ireland,' he went on hesitantly. 'Would you have any address for her? Somewhere we can contact her?'

'I'm afraid we don't know that, son. That's as much a mystery to us as it seems to be to you. Bridie never came back to Ireland. She stayed in England, so she did.' Caitlin sounded suddenly sad. 'It's years since we've heard from her. The last known location we had was the south of England. Hampshire. Or it could be Wiltshire. We're not entirely sure. I am sorry.'

'Hampshire or Wiltshire?' Finn felt shock ricochet through him for the second time that morning. It didn't make sense. Why would Bridie have left him and his father and stayed in England? He'd always thought – because that was what his father had told him – that she'd run back home to Belfast.

He gathered his wits and forced himself to speak casually. 'Do you have any idea of a town or a city?'

There was another long pause and more muttered discussion. Then Caitlin finally came back to the phone again.

'We think maybe a place called Southampton. Would that be in Hampshire or Wiltshire?'

'It's in Hampshire. Do you by any chance have a contact number for her?' He held his breath.

'I'm so sorry, I don't. I wish I did. I miss her, but...'

'It's OK. Don't worry.' He hoped his despair didn't show in his voice, even though his heart was sinking. 'You've been really helpful.'

'No problem. Good luck, son. And if you do get hold of her, tell her Caitlin sends her love and would love to hear from her. She won't be Bridie Neale though. We're pretty sure she got married.'

Finn heard the ache of regret in her voice and he wished he could tell her who he was. Caitlin was his auntie – one he'd never known he had – and she'd sounded as though she'd missed Bridie too. Why had his mother decided to cut off so completely from her whole family?

7

For a long time after he'd disconnected, Finn stayed where he was in his car, with the driver's door cranked open, trying to process what he'd just discovered. He felt hot and cold and shivery, all at the same time.

For his entire childhood he'd envisaged his mother being far away in a different country, which explained why she'd never come back to see him. It had helped knowing she was far away – a princess in a foreign land. When he was small, he'd thought of her as a princess.

She'd been beautiful enough to be one. He remembered sweet-smelling golden hair, spidery eyelashes and a gentle voice.

He'd been just six years old when she'd left and at about the same time he'd read a fairy tale at school in which a beautiful princess got a piece of glass in her eye and it made her see the world differently. For a long time, he'd wondered if that was what had happened to his mother. She had got some glass in her eye which had made her think she no longer loved him. She was a bit like a beautiful princess, but no one seemed to want to tell him. No one seemed to want to talk about his mother at all.

When he was older, he'd stopped thinking of her as a princess. That fairy tale image had slowly died, along with the hope that had ebbed away as each year passed and she never returned. She'd never sent a birthday card. She'd never called. It was as though she had vanished without trace.

Imagining her across the seas had helped him to cope. She couldn't come back because she was too far away. Sometimes he imagined that some dreadful accident had befallen her, just after she'd left him and Ray. She'd died and that was the reason for the years of silence. In this scenario, Finn had imagined her lying on a hospital bed and in her dying breath thinking of him, the child she'd abandoned, and regretting that she'd left him.

In every scenario Finn had conjured up for his mother's departure, there had always been an element of huge difficulty – the feeling that Bridie hadn't come back because she couldn't. Not because she didn't want to. He had never played the blame game.

Perhaps because his father hadn't either. His father had only ever said, 'She was too young, Finn, for a family, and she knew I'd always take care of you. She did what she thought was best for you.'

Finding out Bridie hadn't gone back to Ireland at all was a crushing blow. Knowing she must have been living a stone's throw – less than an hour if it was Southampton – from where his paternal grandparents lived but had still never once asked after his wellbeing felt like a huge betrayal.

Bridie had known Benjamin and Evie McTaggart and she'd known their Arleston address. She could easily have asked them how he was. She could easily have sent him a card or a letter.

He was struck by another possibility. Maybe she *had* done this. Both of his grandparents had died within a few months of each other before he'd moved to Arleston, so Finn couldn't check with them. But surely if Bridie had contacted them, they would have said something. Unless they hadn't wanted to rock the boat and upset their son. That was a possibility too.

Maybe they even had something hidden away – some evidence, a card or a letter they'd kept.

He shook his head, caught between shock and denial. Ray had inherited their cottage when they'd died, and Finn had overseen the clearing out of its contents. If there had been anything to find he would have found it. He'd sorted through countless files and pieces of paper and he'd not seen anything. But then he hadn't been looking. What if he'd missed a letter from his mother? A birthday or Christmas card. There'd been plenty of old cards. He hadn't read them all.

He tortured himself with the thought that it was too late. Whatever might have been in his grandparents' cottage was long gone. His head hurt with the churning of what ifs and if onlys.

It was another text that finally pinged him out of the past and into the present. He glanced at his phone and read the notification from Jade.

> Are you on your way back? I've got some
> exciting news.

Finn realised he'd been sitting in his car for over half an hour. This was crazy. He should get back. Find out what Jade's news was and tell her what he'd just discovered.

He gripped the steering wheel. At least he no longer felt hot. He felt weirdly numb and calm. He manoeuvred the Toyota out of the car park, the clinking of the Calor gas cylinders in the back bringing him firmly back to reality. No wonder Jade had texted him. A twenty-minute trip had turned into one that had taken over an hour.

'Was there a queue in the Calor gas shop?' Jade greeted him

cheerily. 'Or did you get sidetracked looking at the tools section? I love that shop. I always spot something I need, although I didn't know I needed it until I saw it.'

'I had a couple of phone calls and I didn't want to talk while I was driving.'

'Anything important?'

He shook his head. She looked so happy. Finn didn't want to burst her bubble with a bombshell from the past. Besides, this wasn't the right time anyway. He couldn't tell her here on this bright blue summer day. He had to get his head around it all first. It was going to have to stay secret a bit longer.

He busied himself changing the cylinders on the pink caravan.

'So what's this exciting news?' he asked as he worked.

'I saw Farmer John earlier and it's true about him selling up. Mike was right about him considering selling to developers. But I've negotiated a deal. He's going to sell me the field adjacent to the dog field.'

'Wow.' He finished with the cylinders and met her eyes. 'Tell me more.'

When she told him Farmer John was happy to sell her the five-acre field that directly abutted her land and the price they'd agreed, Finn looked at her in admiration. It was crazy cheap.

'How did you get him to agree to that?'

'I'm a very good negotiator. My mother may have missed out on any maternal genes, but she knew how to screw down a deal and she taught me everything she knew.'

She gave a little bow, and as she straightened, he stepped forward and hugged her. 'You're amazing, do you know that? Has he got a buyer for the rest?'

'There are a couple of developers interested. I think he's going to let them fight it out.'

'But he's definitely agreed to sell you the field.'

'Yes. We shook hands on it and he won't renege. He's always been a gentleman. Come on, I'll show you. I've got plans, and they involve you and some nifty fencing.'

'Good. I feel like I haven't done much to earn my keep lately.'

'That's only because you've done most of it already. This place has had a complete makeover, thanks to you.'

Jade gestured towards the kennel block as they passed. Finn had given the kennels a new roof, and the cattery had been completely refurbished. All of the old stone outbuildings had been given the Finn touch, which meant they'd been updated and weatherproofed and would last for a good long while, and he'd done it all with minimal outlay. Finn had been brought up with the motto make do and mend. Ray had never had much money to spare and everything had been recycled in their house. It was a way of life that settled itself into your bones.

Even the pink caravan had been given a paint job and replacement window seals so it no longer leaked when it rained. Jade had insisted it was still pink as she'd said she could never get used to calling it a blue caravan or a cream caravan so Finn had humoured her, although he'd negotiated her down to a slightly less disgusting pink than the faded cerise it had originally been.

A few moments later they were standing in the hen field, looking out at what would become Jade's new land.

'There's a natural tree line that runs down towards the road,' Jade pointed out. 'It's the land between here and there that I'm buying. Farmer John said we may as well include the bit the trees are on. They'll only be felled if we don't. He's getting some plans drawn up that will show all the boundaries properly. He's got a solicitor already so I just need to instruct ours.'

He loved the fact she said 'ours', not 'mine'. That was so

typical of Jade. This whole setup was hers. He'd had nothing to do with buying any of it, yet she still referred to it as 'ours' and she consulted him on every decision.

Finn felt guilty about that sometimes. He had some savings, which included an inheritance from his grandparents, although these had dwindled of late because he insisted on paying his share of the bills and he also paid Sarah maintenance for Ben. He'd never really envisaged he'd make any proper money from his art, but that had happened too lately, and with luck – and Eleanor Smythe's help – he hoped it would continue.

If it didn't, he'd need another job. When he'd first moved in, he'd been working for Jade, and she'd paid him a small wage, with accommodation thrown in. But things were different now they were a couple. He was desperate to be more of a provider than he was.

'Is the outer boundary on the road?' he asked Jade now.

She nodded and he felt a hint of unease. From what he could see, that didn't leave much access for the developers and he'd have thought access would have been a big consideration.

'What?' Jade asked, picking up on his hesitation.

'I was thinking that a developer might need more access to the road. They'd need an exit that wasn't on a bend, I'd have said.'

'I wondered that too, but Farmer John seemed happy enough about the boundary we agreed. And he's pretty shrewd. So I don't think it will be an issue. We've shaken on it anyway, so he can't pull out.'

'Great,' Finn said, glancing back at her face once more. He wasn't so sure. But once again, it didn't seem fair to burst the bubble of happiness that surrounded her. He'd just have to hope she was right.

8

The day before Finn and Jade went to dinner with Sarah and Callum to chat about all things wedding, Finn had his meeting with Eleanor Smythe in Salisbury.

Jade knew he was a lot more nervous than he was letting on. He'd put on his smartest clothes, which meant a shirt and trousers, and now he was standing in reception while she fielded calls.

'Do you think I should wear a tie?' He had a maroon one rolled up in his hand.

'If you want to – would you feel comfortable?'

He put it on, tying it expertly, and Jade remembered he'd once had another life where presumably a shirt and tie was the norm. He'd been an electrical engineer in a switch-making company. Since he'd come to work for her, he'd lived in faded cut-offs and tee shirts in summer and jeans and striped rugby shirts in winter – they rarely went anywhere you had to dress up.

'You scrub up well, darling.'

'Thank you.'

'But I don't think you need the tie.'

'No, me neither.' He took it off. 'I feel less nervous without it.'

'You'll be great.' She stood up to hug him. 'She'll be lucky to have you – that Eleanor.'

His grey eyes warmed. 'Thank you. Have a good day. I shouldn't be too long. Is there anything you need doing in Salisbury?'

'Not unless you fancy doing a home check. I've got a couple interested in rehoming a small dog.'

'I could do that. What does it entail?'

Surprised, she glanced at him. Finn didn't usually get involved with anything directly animal related.

'It's just common sense, really. They sounded like nice people when they rang, but it's easy to pretend on the phone. One of the reasons I do a home check is to make sure they are who they say they are and that they're not bonkers. Then I ask them a few pertinent questions. Have they considered what they'll do when they want to go abroad on holiday? Are they aware of the costs and commitments of owning a dog? These two said they've had dogs before so they should be. I also make sure they've got a fully fenced garden, which literally means walking around the perimeter and checking there's no gaps. We did a home check once before if you remember – we went out to see Reg Arnold, our dog food supplier.'

'I do remember. That one worked out well, didn't it?'

'It did. He's still got Candy. He takes her around in his van when it's not too hot and she always looks happy.'

Jade handed Finn a leaflet. 'I usually give prospective rehomers one of these. All the ins and outs of dog ownership are on here. There's also the contract we get them to sign – so you can leave that for them to look through as well. Don't get it mixed up with your art contract.' She chuckled.

'I'll do my best. It will be a nice diversion from art. Are they expecting me?'

'They said a Wednesday or Friday afternoon was good and I said I'd ring before I went. I'll text you the address and phone number. Thanks, honey.'

He blew her a kiss from the door. 'Happy to help.'

Jade watched him out of the reception window as he strolled across to his car. He'd been quieter than usual for the last few days. She knew how much this meeting meant to him. Having Eleanor Smythe as an agent could really launch his career, but until that contact was signed, nothing was in the bag. Hopefully he'd be back to his usual upbeat self after today.

Once or twice, she'd wondered if anything else was bothering him. But Finn had assured her it was just the stress of the impending interview and Jade was pretty sure he'd have said if there was anything else.

Maybe he was having second thoughts about the double wedding. She decided she'd quiz him on that later too. They could make sure they were on the same page before they saw Sarah and Callum.

* * *

The meeting with Eleanor Smythe wasn't quite what Finn had expected. He'd known what she looked like, because he'd seen photographs online, but she was older, smaller, and more casual than he'd anticipated. She was wearing jeans and some kind of flower print top that looked expensive.

She had asked him to take some canvases with him. She'd specified which ones she wanted to see from the photographs he'd sent her, but to Finn's surprise that didn't seem to be as important to her as the interview itself.

So far, she'd barely glanced at the two canvases he'd lugged up in the lift to the top floor, which was where her office was. She gestured him to a seat opposite a large wooden desk in a room strewn with other artists' work. The walls were dotted with it too, and Finn recognised a couple of famous names, which made him feel even more nervous. He hadn't realised she represented so many well-known artists.

For about half an hour she cross-questioned him about his plans. Was he serious about his career? *Yes.* Did he have another full-time job? *Not exactly.* Did he have a family and were they supportive? *Yes. Very much so.* How much time did he have to paint? *Time wasn't an issue.*

Throughout her quick-fire questions, Eleanor nodded and occasionally paused to think, but made no notes despite the details she was eliciting from him. He wondered if she had a photographic memory.

But then at the end of the interrogation, she leaned across the desk and her serious face warmed into a smile. 'Thanks for all of that. I think we'll get along well. I mainly asked you to come here so I could make sure you are who you said you are, and that you're not bonkers. And of course to check you're committed to your career and fully invested in your future. It's easier to tell face to face than it is on the phone.'

Finn was startled. Her words were so similar to what Jade had said earlier that for a moment he was lost for words.

'I haven't offended you, have I?' She didn't sound as though she cared too much one way or the other.

'No. Not at all.' He explained about the dog home check he'd been entrusted to do, and Eleanor burst out laughing. 'Your fiancée sounds very sensible. People lie through their teeth when they're trying to get something they want. They'll say anything.' She steepled her hands and looked at him properly.

'It must be interesting living in an animal sanctuary. My mother used to keep alpacas.'

'Right,' Finn said. 'Was that for the wool?'

'I think she got the first one to protect her hens. Alpacas dislike foxes almost as much as hen keepers do, but then she realised she'd need two – apparently you need to keep them in pairs – and so she ended up with a few, and she did sell the wool, yes.' She paused. 'She doesn't have them any more. She's ninety-eight but she has great memories and she's sharp as a tack. I told her about your spaghetti theft incident. She hasn't laughed so much in years. So I thank you for that.'

Finn relaxed for the first time since he'd arrived. He knew it was going to be OK. And it was. They breezed through the paperwork after that, and then Eleanor looked at her watch.

'I have a lunch appointment, Finn, so I must fly. But I'll be in touch about the exhibition.'

'Would you like me to leave these canvases here?'

'No, no. I'll let you know when I need them. Good to meet you. Keep painting. Speak soon. Yah?'

Finn refuelled his car and grabbed a meal deal, which he ate parked in a layby before phoning the couple about the home visit, who said they'd be very happy to see him in the next hour or so.

They sounded great on the phone. And when he tracked down their little house on the north side of Salisbury, Babs and Andrew Mason seemed just as nice face to face. They didn't seem bonkers and their little garden was fully fenced. Finn's intuition told him that Jade would like them too. They clearly loved dogs as much as she did. They had a rogue's gallery of previous dogs they'd owned adorning the walls of their lounge.

'We always get their portraits done,' Babs explained as she told him a little about each one. 'The white Highland Terrier was called McKenzie. He lived to the grand old age of seventeen. We still miss him, don't we, darling?'

Andrew nodded seriously.

'And that little brown border terrier – she was a minx, wasn't she, love? She was a rescue as well though, so we forgave her. You can never tell about their background so you need to be forgiving.'

'They're great portraits,' Finn said. 'Almost photographic.' He peered in to look at the artist's signature.

'They are, aren't they? They're done by a friend of a friend. She's an accountant by trade, but she does these in her spare time. She's very talented. But she doesn't have much confidence. We always pay her more money than she asks.'

Finn agreed that she was very talented. He'd done a few animal portraits for Jade for her sponsorship packs and animals weren't easy to master. His hadn't been proper portraits either – they'd just been sketches. He wondered if all artists were the same. Filled with self-doubt about their abilities.

He left Babs and Andrew the contract to read and told them to get in touch if they had any more questions, but that as far as he was concerned they'd passed the home check with flying colours. They were delighted and Finn got a sense of what Jade must feel all the time. A deep sense of satisfaction. It was very rewarding being an animal matchmaker.

He was on his way back home when he had a phone call from his father. Ray phoned him so rarely that Finn thought something might be wrong, so he pulled over to answer it.

'Hi, Dad. Is everything OK?'

'Everything's fine with me, lad. I was wondering the same about you. You haven't called me in two weeks.'

'We spoke on Wednesday, didn't we?'

'A week ago, Wednesday, we spoke. Not this one just gone.'

Finn realised his father was right. He hadn't called because it
had been the day he'd spoken to Caitlin Neale and he'd needed
to tell Jade about that conversation before he mentioned it to
anyone else. He still hadn't told Jade. A part of him was still
trying to process it. Or maybe he'd just buried it. He wasn't sure.

'Sorry, Dad. We've been a bit busy.' He told his father about
the meeting he'd just had with Eleanor Smythe and the contract
they'd signed. 'So I now have an agent,' he finished.

'That's grand, lad. I'm made up for you. I really am. Dorrie
will be too when I tell her. Dorrie,' he yelled. 'Our Finn's just got
himself a top-notch artists' agent. That's grand news, isn't it?'

Finn could hear Dorrie's bubbly voice in the background.

'She sends her congratulations,' Ray said, coming back to
the phone. 'She also wants to know if there's any news on the
wedding? Have you set a date yet? You're not going to just spring
it on us, are you? She said she'll need plenty of time to choose an
outfit.'

'Funny you should mention that as it happens. I do have
some news.'

'Hang on a tick. I'm going to put you on speaker. Save
repeating everything. There you go. Dorrie's listening now too.'

Finn told them about the possible double wedding and
heard Dorrie's squeals of excitement. 'Oh, a double wedding.
How fabulous. Isn't that fabulous, Ray. Everything doubled up.'

'We haven't definitely decided on the double wedding,' Finn
cautioned. 'So keep it to yourselves for now. We haven't said
anything to Ben yet. So if you speak to him, not a word.'

'Not a word,' Ray said. 'We can keep a secret, don't you
worry.'

Finn knew that was true. His father had always been tight
lipped. Suddenly he wanted to ask Ray if he knew that Bridie
hadn't really gone back to Ireland. If that had just been a line

he'd told Finn so he didn't feel as hurt. Had he been trying in his own clumsy way to protect him from a dreadful truth? Bridie hadn't loved either of them and she'd just left because of that. Had Bridie and her whereabouts been the biggest secret Ray had ever kept?

It was on the tip of his tongue to ask his father now. To let it all come pouring out and demand that he be told the truth. But questions like that were best asked face to face. That had been a repeating refrain all morning. People could say anything on the phone. It was easy to lie if you didn't have to look someone in the eye to do it.

Finn made a split-second decision. He would ask his father. But he would go up to Nottingham and do it face to face. He could tie it in with a trip to tell them about the wedding plans.

'I've got to go, Dad. I'm in the car. But Jade and I are seeing Sarah and Callum tomorrow about all things wedding. And as soon as I know more I'll let you know. I might even come up and see you. If Jade can spare me for a few days.'

'That would be grand, lad.' Finn heard Dorrie's murmur of agreement in the background. 'It will give us something nice to look forward to.'

9

Jade wholeheartedly approved of Finn's plans to see Dorrie and Ray. 'I do feel guilty that I stole you away from them,' she told him as they got ready to go to Sarah and Callum's for supper the following evening.

'You didn't steal me away. We're hardly in another country.'

'I know but we might as well be, what with me being so tied to this place. If you still lived in Nottingham you could see more of them.'

'To be honest, even if I was there, I wouldn't see Dad that much. He's always had an active social life and now Dorrie's on the scene he's even busier. It would be me who'd be sitting around twiddling my thumbs. You don't fancy closing up this place and coming with me, do you?' He raised an eyebrow.

'No. Not unless you want me to come.' Jade felt a jolt of indecision. 'I mean, it's possible. I'm sure I could get a couple of days' cover. Sarah and Dawn might do it between them.'

'No, it's fine. Really I just wanted to check in with you.'

Jade thought she saw a fleeting look of relief in his eyes.

'Finn, if I ask you something, do you promise to tell me the truth?'

'Of course.' Now he definitely looked worried.

'Do you really want a double wedding? You've been a bit quiet lately and I wondered if you'd been having second thoughts.'

'I haven't.'

'You would tell me, wouldn't you? It's not too late to say we've changed our minds.'

'Of course I'd tell you.'

Finn hoped she wouldn't ask if anything else was bothering him because he couldn't lie to her and say it wasn't.

Then in the next breath she did ask. 'Finn, you'd tell me if anything else was bothering you, wouldn't you?' She had her back to him. She was applying lippie in the mirror. She rarely wore lipstick.

Finn took a breath. He needed to tell her the real reason he was going to see his father. He couldn't keep putting it off. He hesitated and at that exact moment, a text came through on her phone, and she reached for it and got sidetracked.

'That was Sarah.' She turned from the mirror. 'Just asking if we could pick up a pint of milk on the way. Callum used it all for the custard he was making and didn't tell her.'

Saved by the bell, Finn thought as she went on without a pause. 'I'll tell her it's no trouble. We need to stop on the way and pick up some wine anyway. Who's driving? Or shall we get a taxi back?'

'I'll drive. I think one of us needs to keep our wits about us. I don't want us waking up tomorrow and finding we've agreed to have our wedding ten metres under water or on a roller coaster at Thorpe Park.'

'I can't see Sarah wanting to get married underwater, but a

roller coaster, yes. That would be right up her street. You're right. One of us definitely needs to be stone cold sober. Are you sure you don't mind?'

'I don't mind one bit. Did you say Callum's cooking? What's he making?'

'Thai curries. Don't worry, he's making a meat one as well as a vegetarian one for me.'

Finn felt his mouth water. Callum's dad was a top Scottish chef with his own restaurant in Dundee and although Callum hadn't taken it up as a profession, he was equally talented. His food was wonderful.

Finn had been wary that Callum might object to him being on the scene when he'd first met him, but the guy was really nice. He was totally OK with the fact that Finn was in Sarah's life only because of Ben, and Ben got on really well with Callum too.

Half an hour later they were walking up Sarah's crazy paving path. The back door was open and the heady scents of lemongrass, chilli, garlic and ginger drifted out into the summer evening.

'Come in, come in.' Sarah, effusive as always, ushered them in to the lounge and took the wine and milk Jade was holding out.

'Thanks so much. What do I owe you for the milk?'

'Don't be daft. Something smells amazing.'

As she spoke, Callum popped his head around the kitchen door. 'Hey, guys. I'll come and be sociable in a tick. But I'm at a critical stage.'

'Do you need a hand?' Sarah asked.

'Och, no. Might need a beer though.'

'Coming up.' She blew him a kiss and turned back to Jade and Finn. 'Guinness and wine, you two?'

'I'm driving,' Finn said, 'so something soft for me.'

'Keeping a clear head so you don't agree to anything too crazy on the wedding front?' Sarah guessed correctly, and they all laughed.

While Sarah organised the drinks, Jade and Finn sat on the old comfy sofa.

Jade had been surprised when she'd first met the flame-haired giant that was Callum. He wasn't Sarah's usual type, but now she'd got to know him she really liked him. He was gentle and unassuming with a dry understated sense of humour, and he and Sarah clearly adored each other.

It was odd being in the house with no Ben, although there were traces of him everywhere. A game was out on the floor next to his school rucksack and there was a dinosaur sock draped across the back of an armchair. A new painting of a colourful parrot that was clearly Mr Spock lay on the dining-room table. Sarah had pointed it out to Finn before she went into the kitchen. 'Ben's latest. He was very keen you should see it.'

'It's great,' Finn had said. 'His art's really coming on.'

'So how's things with you guys?' Sarah came back with their drinks. 'Any exciting news to report?'

'We have actually.' Jade glanced at Finn and he looked startled. 'Your contract?' she added. 'Or have you forgotten about that already?'

'Course not.' He told Sarah about it. 'I've signed with the agent and with a bit of luck she'll be able to sneak a couple of my paintings into the exhibition. There are some other more established artists there.'

'She won't be sneaking them in – she'll be showing them off proudly,' Jade contradicted him fiercely. 'What are you like, Finn? You should be proud of your work.'

He flushed beneath their joint gaze. 'I am. Of course I am. And I'm delighted about the contract.'

For a while they discussed the pros and cons of having an agent and every now and then, Callum popped in and joined in the conversation.

'I've got some exciting news too, as it happens,' Jade said on one of the times he was in the room.

'You're pregnant,' Sarah shrieked. 'I knew there was something different about you. You're glowing.'

'I'm *not* pregnant.' Jade snapped out a swift denial, although the idea of being pregnant was actually not that unwelcome. 'Although I am expanding.'

Both Sarah and Callum looked utterly mystified and she left them dangling for a good few seconds before she caved and told them about buying the field next door to Duck Pond Rescue.

'But that just means you'll end up with even more flaming animals,' Sarah said, shaking her head. 'I thought the idea was to rehome them, not keep them.'

'It is. But we definitely need more space. The hens used to be in the yard but they've taken over half the dog field now and OK, I know I shouldn't take on so many, but it's really hard to say no to ex-battery ones when I know they'll just go for dog food if I don't. And frankly if you've got ten hens, another ten don't make much difference.'

'Clearly that's not true,' Sarah argued. 'Or you wouldn't need more space.'

'They do help to pay for themselves.' Finn came to her rescue. 'Because we sell their eggs.'

Sarah laughed. 'Good point. Although I bet that field will cost more than a few egg sales.'

Jade told her about the deal she'd got and Sarah nodded slowly. 'That's not bad. OK, I'll stop nagging. I know it's pointless nagging you when it concerns animals. Besides, it's a good investment. Land always is. Have you rehomed that crazy parrot yet?'

'No. It's not easy to rehome a parrot that swears. You need the right person. I'd hate him to just be a novelty factor in someone's back room until they got bored and then he'll be shut in a cage for life and ignored. He likes seeing lots of people.'

'Sounds like a good excuse to keep him to me.' Sarah narrowed her eyes. 'Like you kept that mouse-murdering black cat and that rug on legs, Mickey, you said no one else would want.'

'That was true in Mickey's case,' Jade said, completely unrepentant. 'Besides, we love Mickey, don't we, Finn? He's a character.'

'He is that. Although he does ruin our TV viewing by barking his head off at inappropriate moments.'

'I think he improves it.' Jade smiled and explained. 'We were watching this crime drama a few weeks ago and Mickey took a dislike to this totally innocent-looking guy on the screen and started barking furiously. We were mystified. Mickey did it every time he appeared. We thought maybe he'd taken a dislike to the bloke's beard. But then it turned out the guy was the baddie.'

'It's true,' Finn said, backing her up. 'We thought it was a coincidence at first. But it's happened four or five times since then. Mickey starts barking when he sees a particular character, and then we find out they're a master criminal. He always gets it right. We don't even need to watch the end.'

'I'm assuming they haven't got a gun and an evil laugh,' Sarah asked, intrigued. 'Or a white cat on their laps like the Bond movies.'

'No – there doesn't seem to be any rhyme or reason to it.'

'How about a black car? Have you noticed that baddies on crime dramas always drive black cars?'

'Don't think so,' Jade said, laughing, 'but we'll keep an eye out.'

Callum interrupted the conversation by coming to tell them dinner was ready. They sat outside in the garden to eat it, making the most of the long July evening, with a citronella candle burning on the table to see off the mosquitos. They all helped to carry out dishes of delicious-smelling Thai curries and fragrant rice, with serving spoons so they could help themselves.

'I'm surprised you're not expanding yourself if you get fed like this all the time,' Jade told Sarah a few minutes later. 'This food is amazing.'

'We don't eat like this all the time.' Sarah beamed at Callum. 'Although we might once we're married, eh, love?'

'I'm happy to cook any time. So long as you don't mind waiting for your scran some nights.'

'Yeah, that's the drawback,' Sarah said. 'Cooking food like this takes ages.' She filled up their wine glasses. 'Anyway, on the subject of weddings, we should talk shop. Are we on the same page as regards venue – do we want a church or another venue? Summer or winter? Big or small? Joint honeymoon?'

'Joint honeymoon!' Finn looked startled.

'I was joking about the joint honeymoon,' Sarah quipped. 'Just to see if anyone was listening.'

'I haven't got strong feelings about getting married in a church,' Jade said. 'I don't know about the rest of you.'

They all shook their heads.

'One-stop wedding venues aren't bad value, these days,' Callum said. 'We went to one not that long ago, didn't we, pet?'

Sarah nodded thoughtfully. 'Yes, it was a friend at work. They did everything there, even stayed there the night before. They're good for guests too. No traipsing about between different places. The ceremony and the reception are all in the same place. You can even stay in them for your first night – before going off on your separate honeymoons afterwards,' she added hastily. 'We're probably going to have a minimoon. Just a weekend somewhere. Then maybe have a longer holiday later with Ben.'

Callum reached across the table to put his hand over hers, nodding in agreement.

'Minimoon sounds a good idea to me.' Finn glanced at Jade. 'But I don't mind if we spend that at the cottage. Maybe get a bit of cover and just go for days out so we don't need to leave the animals at night.'

'Wow, he really loves you, doesn't he?' Sarah said, before slapping her hand over her mouth. 'Sorry, did I say that out loud? Too much wine already.'

Jade laughed. 'It's OK. And it's true. You're spot on. Love me, love my sanctuary.' She looked at Finn, feeling a deep sense of love welling up in her. 'It can't be easy marrying someone who has a blinking great millstone around her neck.'

'I don't see it like that at all,' Finn said quickly. 'I'm as committed to that collection of waifs and strays as you are,' and she saw in his eyes that he meant every word. Then he lightened his tone and added, 'Now, if you had sixteen kids it might be a different story.'

Everyone laughed again and the banter resumed.

By the end of the evening they had thrashed out a lot. They would have an August wedding, which gave them a full year to arrange it. They would look for a wedding venue that was nice but not mega bucks. The first thing to do was to draw up a guest list and decide on a budget.

Jade knew she and Sarah would definitely be on the same page about that. The sky had slowly darkened so they went back inside for coffee. While Finn helped Callum load the dish-washer and clear up the kitchen, Sarah and Jade sat beside each other on the sofa.

'When we were little I used to dream that one day we might have a double wedding,' Sarah said, meeting Jade's gaze.

'You never said anything.'

'That's because you always swore blind you'd never get married. You said you were going to live in the middle of nowhere with a cat and a dog and maybe a goat.'

'Crikey, did I?'

'And then it came true,' Sarah said, 'to the power of ten. Apart from the goat. I don't think you've got any of them yet, but I bet it's only a matter of time.' She widened her eyes. 'Seriously though, I'm really glad you met Finn. I'm really glad you're as happy as I am, Jade. And I can't imagine a more lovely day than us tying the knot together. I really can't. Ben is going to be over the moon when we tell him.'

'I know. It's going to be fabulous. Do you think we can arrange to have some animals there at our wedding?'

'If you want to.' Sarah gave her a sweet smile. 'I'm sure there must be animal-friendly venues if we shop around.'

Jade swallowed a sudden ache of emotion because Sarah wasn't a mad-crazy animal lover like she was, but she'd have put up with it for her friend's sake. 'It's OK. We don't need to have animals. It might get too complicated. Anyway, it'll be nice to have a day off from them all. But thank you. You're the best friend ever.'

She saw the warmth in Sarah's summer-blue eyes. 'You are too, Jade. I'm thrilled to bits you're up for this. And we'll make sure our wedding day is the best day of our lives.'

'I'll drink to that,' Jade said, and they clinked glasses.

10

Finn decided to go up and see Ray and Dorrie midway through the following week.

'If you're sure you don't mind?' he said, checking in with Jade just before he left. 'I could phone them instead.'

'No, you should go and see them. You haven't been for ages. I've got plenty of help. Some of the schools have already broken up, but there will be even more soon. I'll have an influx of animal-mad kids to worry about then.'

'Yes, that's true. Maybe I should wait a fortnight and take Ben. Although it might be tricky persuading him he'd rather see his grandad than stay here with the animals.'

'You can take him next time. There'll be plenty of time in the holidays.'

'OK. Good plan.' Finn picked up the small holdall he'd put by the front door. He always travelled light. 'I'll only stay a couple of days and I'll phone you as soon as I arrive. So you're not worrying.' He kissed her and Jade smiled.

'Am I that transparent?'

'Only to me.'

She did worry about him, Jade thought as his taillights drew out of the main gate. She bent to stroke Mickey, who knew something was going on and had been watching the proceedings with anxious eyes.

'It's OK, boy. He's coming back.' Jade knew she was reassuring herself just as much as she was reassuring her dog.

The downside to love – if there was one – was that it made you worry about people. When it had just been her and the animals it had been easier. Since she and Finn had been a couple, her love had grown deeper and deeper. She loved everything about him. The way he insisted on bringing her a cup of tea every morning in bed, the way he snored gently when he was dropping off to sleep, but shut up instantly if she touched his shoulder. The way they shared their innermost thoughts. The way he read her every expression easily, even though she still had trouble seeing what was going on behind those inscrutable grey eyes. Finn was much harder to read than she was.

She loved the way he always had her back. She would have trusted him with her life. She had never felt like that about another human being. And it was wonderful. She knew she was going to miss him. Even if he was only away for a few days.

Luckily, she didn't have time to miss him for long because she didn't get the quiet morning she'd expected. A couple of young volunteers arrived in reception to see Mr Spock. He'd become quite a draw because of his talkative nature. Jade smiled at them as they chattered away to him and pretended not to hear when they encouraged him to say 'I love bums', which was his latest favourite phrase.

The couple who Finn had home checked in Salisbury arrived to collect the Jack Russell cross they'd reserved and it was heartwarming seeing them go off with her, tail wagging madly.

Jade's next visitor was a worried-looking teenager with a ponytail and the sides of his head shaved. Dawn brought him into reception.

'This is Zack. He's asking if we can rehome a flock of geese. I said we don't have the space. But he insisted he speak to you.'

'We're really desperate.' Zack stepped forward nervously. 'Or I wouldn't ask. We've had some of them since they were tiny chicks. They're very tame. They're not attack geese. Nothing like that.'

'Why are you giving them up?' Jade gave him her coolest gaze. 'Did you not realise how long they'd live? Birds are a major commitment.'

'They're not mine. They're from my school's farm. The farm has to close because the school's lost the funding for it. Cutbacks.' He spread his arms and gave a helpless shrug. 'They've got homes for some. Me and my sister have got a couple, but that's the most we can have in our back garden. We live on an estate, see, and Mum says the neighbours won't like it. And Dad's muttering because one of them already ate his favourite goldfish.'

'How many are there? Geese, I mean, not goldfish?'

'Eight left,' Dawn supplied helpfully. 'You've got nowhere for those, though, Jade. Unless they go in with the hens, but we're pretty full on that front and geese need to be near water.'

'Well, yes, that's true, but...' Jade hesitated, thinking of the field she planned to buy. There was plenty of room for geese there. But she hadn't told Dawn about that yet in case she jinxed it.

'Leave me your details, Zack. I'll get back to you if there's any chance. But Dawn's right. We don't have much space.'

Zack put his palms together as if in prayer and took a few

steps backwards, bowing his head as he went. 'Thank you. Even if you could just take a couple it would be amazing.'

As he exited reception, Dawn glanced at her. 'You're going to say yes to a couple, aren't you?'

'I didn't say it was definite.' Jade bit her lip. 'I said I'd think about it.'

'Fair comment.' Dawn looked as though she was about to say something else but thought better of it. It was probably some warning about taking on too much. Jade knew Dawn had her best interests at heart. She was kind, sensible and protective – the kind of mother Jade would have chosen, if you could choose your mother.

She barely had time to pause for breath when a smartly dressed, clean-shaven man came in. At first, Jade didn't recognise him because she'd only ever seen him in old outdoor clothes and he was so out of context.

Then it hit her. 'Farmer John! Gosh, you scrub up well. I mean... I hope that didn't sound too rude. I hardly recognised you for a moment.'

'No. I've just been at my solicitors. Er – look, Jade. I'm afraid this isn't good news so I'll get straight to the point. I've got a buyer for the farm. It's a property developer, but they're not happy about me selling that field off to you. I'm really sorry, but I'm going to have to renege on our deal.'

Jade felt a coldness slide down her back. 'But why? What difference does it make to them? There's plenty more land for their houses.'

'Something to do with access requirements.'

'But there's plenty of room for access too. You said there was.'

'I thought there was – but they say not.' He shrugged and looked embarrassed. 'I've argued till I'm blue in the face, but they're not having any of it. And they've made me a good offer, Jade.'

'I see.' Her brain whirred madly. 'What if I up my offer? Would that make a difference?'

'I'm afraid not. They said they'll buy all of the farm – or none of it. And they won't budge. I really am sorry.' He was turning away. He was clearly anxious to go. She called after him before he reached the door.

'Which developer is it? Maybe I could speak to them. Appeal to their better nature.'

He made a sound somewhere between a grunt and a snort. 'You could try. It's Rural Developments. I've been talking to one of the negotiators.' He felt around in the top pocket of his shirt and found a business card. He came back to hand it to her. 'Here's his number.'

'Thanks,' she said quietly. 'I'll give him a call.'

'Good luck.' His face reddened but he sounded like he genuinely meant it.

Jade had to suppress a yell of frustration as she watched him hurry across the yard towards the exit gates. Bloody developers. Who did they think they were, bulldozering in and trampling over deals that had already been made? So much for a gentlemen's agreement. She wondered how much they'd offered Farmer John to make him backtrack so unequivocally. Or maybe, as he'd said, it wasn't about the money – but more about the fact they were being so dogmatic about it. 'It's our way or the highway.'

Well, there had to be some wiggle room there surely. Especially if she told them she had an animal sanctuary right next door to them. Jade paced restlessly around the small reception, disturbing Mickey who was in his basket, watching her through half-closed eyelids. He wasn't used to seeing his mistress agitated.

'What do you think, boy?' she asked him. 'Shall I try appealing to their better nature?'

Mickey wagged his tail uncertainly and shifted in his basket, revealing what looked like one of Finn's black socks under his tail.

Jade hooked it out. Oops! Finn was always complaining that he could never find a complete pair of socks. No wonder when Mickey was such a terrible thief. He seemed to prefer Finn's socks to Jade's too. They were probably smellier.

'Maybe they're like you, Mickey, and don't have a better nature,' she said, stroking the dog's head. Not that she blamed Mickey for being a thief. He'd been brought up in a house where his owners didn't believe in toys for dogs apparently, so he'd always had to find his own entertainment.

'Or if that doesn't work, I could point out that the more space there is between us and the houses the better. That way the residents won't be able to hear dogs barking and cockerels crowing – never mind the geese honking.' Jade knew she'd already decided that two of the geese could go in with the hens, even if she didn't take all of them. She could ask Finn to dig out a pond. Geese were great protectors. It would stop her worrying about foxes so much.

Mickey went back to sleep. Jade sat back in the office chair and twirled around.

Surely the more space there was between them, the better it would be for the residents of the houses they planned to build.

Maybe the developers wouldn't care about that. She wanted to tell Finn that he'd been right about the access after all – maybe he'd have some ideas. But she guessed he'd still be driving as he hadn't messaged to say he'd arrived yet.

She glanced back at the name on the card Farmer John had given her, Declan Stone. Stone was an apt name for someone who worked in property development. She wondered what he was like. Young? Old? An ambitious go-getter or just used to getting his own way? From what Farmer John had said, he was stubborn. Or maybe that was his employers. She went back to the big appointments diary that was on her desk. There were no home checks this afternoon. No scheduled visits – at least none she'd remembered to put in the diary – and Dawn probably wouldn't mind dealing with unscheduled ones if she asked her.

Maybe it would be better to call round and see Mr Stone. It was easier to brush someone off on the phone, but if they were standing in front of you it was far harder. And Jade could be very persuasive.

Having decided there was no time like the present, Jade went to find Dawn.

'I need a massive favour.'

'Does it involve geese?' The older woman winked.

'Nope. It's just to keep an eye on Mickey and reception for a couple of hours if you don't mind? I need to go and see someone, but I shouldn't be that long.'

'Of course I will.'

'Thank you.' Jade squeezed her hand. 'I don't know what I'd do without you. I wish I could pay you more.'

'You pay me quite enough. Besides, you know I don't do this for the money.'

Jade thanked her and hurried into the cottage. Having decided to go, she wasn't sure what to wear. What did you wear to go and see a dogmatic unreasonable dictatorial property developer who was issuing ultimatums? Maybe he wasn't any of those things.

Yes, he was, or he wouldn't have shoved her aside so easily

when Farmer John had told them she existed. And he'd definitely issued an ultimatum. Our way or the highway.

She cursed them under her breath. Nevertheless, it was probably unwise to go in all guns blazing. Much as she'd have liked to. She might get further with a softly softly approach. With this in mind, she picked her outfit carefully.

A three-quarter sleeve, high-necked navy-blue jersey dress that said *feminine, upmarket, professional*. Court shoes with kitten heels. A leather satchel bag that was big enough for her to take along some of the sanctuary paperwork. She'd packed a couple of adoption packs of her cutest animals. She wanted to make it clear she was a reasonable, level-headed businesswoman who provided a valuable service to the community, not an eccentric animal lover who collected other people's cast-offs – even if she did veer more towards the latter on occasions. It was the same outfit she wore when she was on a mission to get sponsorship from local businesses. It had always served her well.

A touch of make-up completed the look, and Jade left her long hair down but tidy. Then she studied her reflection in the mirror and smiled. Farmer John wasn't the only one who scrubbed up well.

Five minutes later, she was in her Land Rover heading towards Rural Developments. Their headquarters was in Salisbury and Declan Stone would be there for the afternoon. She'd called his office earlier and checked with the person who'd answered the phone.

'Watch out, Mr Stone,' she said under her breath as she drew into the company's car park twenty-five minutes later. 'I'm coming for you.'

Rural Developments' headquarters was in the middle of an industrial estate, in the middle of a built-up area, Jade discovered. That was ironic when Declan's card showed beautiful houses surrounded by fields. She parked and found the entrance which led her up a narrow flight of stairs to a door with a brass plaque.

She walked in and found herself in a small reception area. A woman behind a computer glanced up. 'Can I help you?'

'I'm here to see Declan Stone.'

'Is he expecting you?'

Jade smiled at her. 'No. But it's about a possible sale on the south of Salisbury. I think he'll want to see me.' She doubted he would, but it might get her in the door. 'I'm happy to wait.'

'Can I have your name, please?'

'It won't mean anything to him, but it's Jade Foster.'

Five minutes later, a man opened a door that led off the reception and Jade got her first look at Declan. He was younger than she'd expected. She guessed a similar age to her – twenty-six or twenty-seven. He was expensively dressed with a hint of cool. He had dark hair, serious blue eyes and a nice smile. In her head she'd made him a smarmy salesman in a cheap suit – but he wasn't.

'Come in. Please.' He ushered her through to an office that was plusher than the reception and gestured her to one of the two visitors' chairs. 'Will you sit down? How can I help?'

Jade introduced herself and told him what she wanted.

He looked at the adoption packs for long enough to show her he wasn't completely disinterested, then listened politely until she'd finished explaining the situation before he offered her a coffee.

Disarmed, Jade accepted, and he got it himself from a machine in the corner of the room and brought it back to the table. She hadn't expected that either. She'd expected him to phone through and ask the receptionist to do it.

'Thank you.'

'You're welcome. And I appreciate your situation, truly I do...'

She sensed the 'but' coming.

'But we are in a difficult position too. Access is a big issue. Without it we can't get planning.'

'So, that's it then? You're not prepared to honour the agreement I already had with John Lawson.' She looked him in the eyes and he held her gaze.

'I didn't say that.' He sighed. 'Look, I do want to help. We're not unreasonable here at Rural Developments and we do want to fit in with the local community. We don't want to kick off on a bad footing with neighbours.'

That was probably true. They wouldn't want to be fighting their way through numerous objections. They'd want a smooth ride. Or was that just her being cynical? Maybe all this softly

softly stuff was just a build up to letting her down gently. She braced herself and then he surprised her again.

'I've a suggestion, Jade. Can I call you Jade?' He waited for her to nod. 'Why don't I come out and see you at Duck Pond Rescue? You could show me the piece of land in question and I can have a look at the situation. We could surely come to some kind of compromise. How does that sound?'

'That sounds great. Thanks. When can you come?'

'I could probably come tomorrow afternoon if that's convenient. I'll need to check my diary and maybe shift a few things around. But that's not an issue. This is important to you, isn't it?'

'It is, yes. Very important.'

'Right then. I'll call you. Is the mobile number the best one to catch you on?'

'The signal isn't always great. So try the landline if it doesn't work.'

'I'll do that.' He stood up, indicating the meeting was over, and they shook hands.

Jade left the building feeling a lot more positive than she had when she'd arrived. OK, so it wasn't a done deal, but it sounded as though she was in with a chance. It had been good of him to suggest coming over so quickly. He was obviously serious. And a nice guy.

As soon as she was back out in the car park, Jade glanced at her phone. Finn had sent her a message about ten minutes ago saying he'd arrived safely in Nottingham and that he looked forward to catching up later.

She texted back a thumbs up emoji and a row of kisses before heading towards her parking place.

* * *

Declan Stone watched discreetly from an upper-floor window as Jade crossed the car park and got into a dark green Land Rover Discovery. When he'd first heard about the animal sanctuary next door to the farm Rural Developments wanted to buy, he'd envisaged Ms Foster as some batty old woman.

And when Jess, their receptionist, had said she was here to see him, he'd mentally prepared himself for a battle. He had not been expecting the very attractive girl who'd walked in. The professional part of him had instantly been hit by her obvious confidence and an air of *don't mess with me*, but the man in him had been drawn to her great looks and beautiful eyes. Old and batty, Jade Foster was definitely not. Hot was a much better description. Except that there was also an air of cool unavailability about her. She had that aura of *don't touch* that some women gave off – usually ones who were married and moral.

She hadn't been wearing a wedding ring. Although that could have been an engagement ring on her left hand. No matter. Declan had never been put off by the fact women were married. He wasn't up for commitment anyway. He was far too young. The thrill of the chase was where it was at for him.

Women who had *don't touch* tattooed across their foreheads had always been irresistible to Declan.

He'd guessed the reason she'd come as soon as Jess had told him she was here, and he'd been ready to tell her, regretfully, but firmly, that there was no way they could change the deal he'd just agreed with the farmer. It just wasn't possible. He'd decided before he'd seen her that he'd let her down gently and then close the door firmly behind her and hopefully he'd never see her again.

But as soon as Jade had stepped into his office, he'd changed his mind. Not necessarily about the deal – although there was some room for manoeuvre on it – but the fact that he didn't want to see her again. He very much wanted to see her again. And not in a business sense. He wanted to get to know her better. Arranging to go over and meet her on home turf was a good move. He could check out the lie of the land. In more ways than one.

* * *

Finn got a huge welcome from Dorrie when he knocked on the door of his father's end-terrace house in Nottingham.

'Finn, it's wonderful to see you. Ray's just this second popped out to get a pint of milk. I told him he'd miss you if he went now, but he insisted, the daft bugger. He doesn't listen to me. He shouldn't be long. Come in. Come in.' Between sentences she swooped in and pecked his cheek.

He was struck – as he always was – when he met the petite blonde sixty-seven-year-old by her vibrant energy. She was still chattering happily as she gestured him ahead of her to the living room opposite the kitchen at the back of the house.

'Sit down, dear. Can I get you a hot drink? Tea? Coffee? Or would you prefer something cold? I think we might have a can in the fridge – Guinness, isn't it?' She rubbed her hands together and shot him a beaming smile, and Finn, who wasn't used to being fussed around, realised he liked it.

'A Guinness would go down really well,' he said, sitting on the sofa and letting himself relax into the warmth of her company. He was starting to feel a tiny bit guilty that he'd come up here on a fact-finding mission, which he knew wasn't going to be popular – at least not as far as his father was concerned – and not just to tell them news about the wedding, which was what they were both expecting.

Dorrie disappeared to get his drink and Finn's gaze

wandered around the little room. It looked the same as it always did, although possibly with less dust and there were no dead flies on the windowsills. His father was tidy but he didn't notice details like that.

There might have been a slightly larger flat-screen TV, but the old-fashioned sideboard was the same. It was crowded with framed photos. There were a few of him in his younger days, and some of him and Ray, but there was also a big one of Ben in a gold frame that Finn had got him for Christmas. There was a new photo there now too, he noticed. It showed Ray and Dorrie sitting at a table somewhere, possibly in a pub, smiling into the camera.

She came back into the room with his Guinness in a glass and a mug of tea. 'Have you eaten, dear? I've got a bit of Stilton pie in the kitchen. It's homemade.'

'I'm good, thanks. I stopped for a bite at the services. Although it does sound delicious.'

He already knew Dorrie was a dab hand at cooking and had noticed his father had put on a few pounds since they'd been together. Mind you, he'd given up smoking since they'd met too – and for that, Finn was eternally grateful.

Dorrie, who was a feeder, was not to be deterred. 'How about just a small slice then?'

Finn's mouth watered and he was about to backtrack when the front door banged and he heard his father clearing his throat as he came down the hallway.

'Is he here then? I thought I saw his beaten-up old banger lowering the tone of the neighbourhood. Oh, hello, lad. Didn't see you there.' He winked as he stood in the doorway and Finn got up and went across.

They weren't really a hugging kind of family but he patted his father's arm and Ray beamed at him. 'Did you have a good journey? You haven't brought the lovely Jade then?' He glanced around the room as though he was expecting her to materialise from behind the sofa.

'You know she can't get away, Dad. Not unless we get in some cover.'

'Which is why we should make more effort to get down to you,' Ray commented. 'We've got more time as well, haven't we?'

'It's fine, Dad. It's only three hours.'

'Three hours on a good day,' Dorrie said. 'I bet it took you longer than that today. Everyone going on their summer holidays.'

'Four with a stop. But I really don't mind. And it's a lot easier to drive than it is to do it by coach.'

'We appreciate it, don't we, Dorrie? How's my grandson?'

For a while they talked about Ben and their plans for the rest of the day. Ray had booked a table for them all at the Cock and Bottle for dinner and then tomorrow they'd have dinner in – Dorrie was happy to cook, but they'd have lunch out if he liked the sound of that. There was some new art exhibition in town that Dorrie thought he might like. It was worth a visit while he was here. He could stay as long as he liked. Pointless driving four hours for a whistlestop tour.

Wow, they'd really pushed the boat out, Finn thought, feeling guiltier than ever but also pleased they were going out later. He could offer to drive if he didn't have any more beers, and he could pay too.

It would be easier to talk to his father when he'd downed a couple of pints and was nice and relaxed. Also, they would be on neutral territory at the Cock and Bottle.

12

Nevertheless, Finn felt his stomach crunching with tension as the three of them walked into the Cock and Bottle that evening, just before seven, and were shown to a table in the restaurant part of the pub by a smiling waitress.

Talking about the past – especially the bit that included his mother – had always been a definite no-no in their family. This was all uncharted territory. Ever since he'd spoken to Caitlin he'd been torn in two. Half of him had wanted to shove the past right back in the Pandora's Box and get the lid on and sit on it. Bury it deep where it had always been and avoid any more emotional turmoil. Because turmoil summed up exactly what had been going on in his head since that phone call.

The other half of him had wanted to open it wide, whatever the consequences were. He needed to know what had happened. He needed to know what his father knew. Had Bridie really said she was going back to Ireland or had that been what Ray had decided to tell him? The need to know was like a burning hot coal within him.

Once he knew the facts, he could talk to Jade too. He was

sure he could find a way to tell her what had been going round and round in his head lately, explain why he'd been slightly distant. Trust was hugely important to both of them.

'What's on your mind, lad?' Ray's voice cracked into Finn's thoughts and he looked up.

'Sorry, I was miles away.'

'That's obvious. I've asked you what you wanted to drink twice and I'm still none the wiser.'

'I'll stick to orange juice. But it's OK. I'll get them.'

'Pint of Guinness for me then, and a white wine for Dorrie. Cheers.'

Finn escaped to the bar. The Cock and Bottle was a popular pub not far from the River Trent. It had wooden tables, comfy seats and was full of light. It did good food, but was also big enough so you could usually get a table, which was why his father and Dorrie favoured it.

It was a far cry from the spit and sawdust old working men's club with its tatty seating that Finn and his father had frequented in the past. Finn could see why Dorrie wouldn't have wanted to go there.

He set up a tab and took the drinks and some menus back to the table.

When they'd all ordered and were settled again and had established there might be a fair wait for the food, which was all cooked to order, Finn decided that now was as good a time as any.

'I spoke to Caitlin Neale the other day, Dad...'

'Oh, aye.' Ray's face tightened and his eyes shadowed a little. It wasn't much but Finn, who'd always been adept at reading faces, knew that despite his father's apparently casual words, he wasn't keen on having this discussion.

'Did she say owt interesting?'

Dorrie leaned forward, putting her elbows on the table and her chin on her hands. She clearly knew who Caitlin Neale was and Finn's impressions that it was Dorrie who was driving this excursion into the past, not his father, were reinforced.

Finn took a deep breath. 'She did say something that shocked me a bit. She said Bridie had never gone back to Ireland, which was what I'd always thought had happened.'

'Aye.' The word was noncommittal and Finn felt as though the whole world had stilled and gone silent and there was just him and his father in a locked gaze moment, staring at each other across the table. No one else existed.

'Did you know that, Dad? Did you know she hadn't gone back?'

'I did know.' Ray sighed deeply, took a slug of his pint and stared at the table. 'But not at the time. It was true what I'd told you. I thought she'd gone back to Ireland. Fled to her family. That was what I thought.'

Finn closed his eyes. He felt as if the past was like shifting sands in his head. Being rewritten, taking on a different narrative, one that was alien and confusing.

'So when did you discover she hadn't gone back?'

'It was a few years later. I don't know. Maybe five – you were about ten or eleven when I got a phone call from her.'

'From Bridie? From my mother?'

'Aye, from Bridie. But she had no right to call herself your mother. Not then, Finn. Not as far as I was concerned. She'd abandoned you without a word. Vanished without trace. Left us to get on with it. She didn't care about us.'

There was a hard edge of pain in his voice. Finn could hear it, even after all these years. He fought with himself not to react. This was not the place. Maybe this hadn't been such a good idea to talk here. Maybe there was no such thing as neutral territory – not with a subject as explosive as this.

Sound had rushed back in again – he could hear the buzz of chatter from the tables around them, the smells of food from the kitchen. If anything, these things were intensified now, not deadened. He became aware his father was speaking again.

'I was trying to protect you. You were settled down, Finn, doing well at school. The last thing we needed was Bridie coming back into your life. Stirring it all up again. Least said, soonest mended. That's what I thought.'

'Did she say she wanted to see me then? Was that why she phoned?'

'She wanted to visit. Yes. And I said she couldn't. I told her you thought she had died. And it would be too much of a shock if she just rocked up on the doorstep large as life.'

For a second, Finn didn't think he'd heard right. It was a while before he could formulate a sentence. 'But you *didn't* tell me that. I *knew* she was alive. All those years you let me think she didn't care, Dad. Why would you do that?'

'Because it was for the best, Finn. I had no way of knowing she wouldn't disappear permanently again once she'd seen you. I couldn't risk it.' Ray's voice cracked. His face was white. 'She'd already broken your heart once. And mine.'

It was too much to take in. Finn shoved back his chair from the table, the legs scraping on the wooden floor. He couldn't stay listening to this. His head was spinning and he felt sick. He needed to get out.

He heard Dorrie's voice calling after him, but he didn't turn. He couldn't bear to be near his father a second longer.

He was back in his car before he realised he couldn't just leave the two of them sitting there either. Well, he could, but he wasn't going to. A tiny thread of sanity was working its way into his brain. Like an earworm that wouldn't be banished. Despite the shock of it, there was some grain of truth in what his father had said.

What if Bridie had come back and then she'd vanished again? Perhaps that would have been worse. He'd always known on some level that his father had been as heartbroken as he'd been when Bridie had left. Ray had never said this out loud. But neither had he ever badmouthed her. Ray wasn't the type of man to do either of these things. He was the type of man who got on with it. And he'd got on with bringing Finn up alone.

Finn had come to understand that this was unusual. There were lots of single-parent families at his school, but it was always the dad who had left. None of his mates were being brought up by single fathers. There was one boy who'd lost his mum to a car accident, but he had a stepmum and a stepbrother – and he'd told Finn on more than one occasion that he wished he hadn't.

Finn had grown up to realise that Ray was something of a one-off, and the older he'd got the more he'd come to value this as something precious.

But he still couldn't bring himself to go back into the pub and so he stayed where he was as the light slowly dimmed and long shadows of dusk began to fall across the carpark.

Eventually, it was Dorrie who came out to him. She knocked on the driver's window and Finn lowered it slowly.

'I know you must be hurting like hell, my love. But your dad's hurting too. He only did what he thought was best for you.' She hesitated. 'Will you come back inside or shall I tell Ray to come out? Would you prefer it if we got a taxi back home?'

He met her anxious eyes. 'There's no need for a taxi. I'll take you both home. Of course I will.'

It was an awkward journey, with Dorrie sitting silently in the passenger seat and Ray in the back but with his head turned slightly so that every time Finn glanced in the rear-view mirror he didn't have to meet his son's eyes. When they arrived, Finn was tempted to say he'd find somewhere else to stay, but Ray pre-empted him.

'I know you'll be thinking you don't want to stay under my roof and I don't blame you, but it's too late to drive back down south.' He paused. 'I really am sorry, Finn.'

'I know you are.' Finn climbed out and stretched his limbs, which felt stiff from sitting in the car for so long. His stomach rumbled and he realised he was hungry too.

'At least come in and have something to eat,' Dorrie added. 'You must be starving. We are.'

'We cancelled the food,' Ray said in explanation.

Again, Finn hesitated. He didn't want to go inside and eat with them. He still felt too betrayed and confused. But he knew they couldn't leave it like this. If they did then this rift would grow bigger and bigger between them. And he had questions. So many questions.

It was time he knew the whole truth, and Ray must think that too, or he would never have prompted them onto this path. He would never have sent that news article. He must have known this might be the outcome.

Inside the house, Dorrie bustled about heating up Stilton pie before serving it up to them in the back room. 'I'll leave you boys to it,' she said, closing the door behind her.

When she'd gone, they ate in silence, with plates on their knees, Finn in the armchair where he'd sat earlier and his father on the sofa opposite. Finn found his appetite had returned enough to eat every crumb, but his father got halfway through his before putting down his knife and fork and pushing the plate to one side.

'Ask me anything you like now, Finn. And I'll tell you the truth.'

13

Finn looked at his father carefully. He still looked pale and it seemed as though new lines of strain had appeared around his eyes – even tonight.

'OK. Why now, Dad? Why did you decide it was time to tell me the truth now? Because that was what you were doing, wasn't it – when you sent me that news item. You were prompting me to ask.'

'It was Dorrie. She thought you should know. And I won't deny I've wondered that too, Finn. Several times across the years. It's got more difficult as time's gone on. As you might guess.'

'So that's why you sent the news item. You thought if you did that I might start the conversation and you wouldn't have to.'

'Aye. I'm a coward, lad, I know.'

That was something his father had never been, but Finn couldn't bring himself to acknowledge that yet.

'Did Gran and Grandpa know she came back?'

'No, they didn't. She never contacted them. Or if she did they never told me. And Finn, I just want to get something straight.

Bridie wasn't coming back to us. She'd got a new life set up. She'd...' He hesitated, his northern accent thickening a little as he got more emotional. 'She'd got married ta another man, soon after she left us. She'd moved on. I guess – I guess...' He put his head in his hands. 'I thought she might want ta take you away from me. Apply for parental custody – you know – and she might have won because mothers had all the rights in those days, and as you know, although my name was there in black and white on the birth certificate, we never had got married. I couldn't bear ta lose you too. That's why I lied. To you and ta her. I was scared if I let her see you, she'd want to take you.' He let out a deep breath and Finn let out a deep breath with him.

He had no doubt he was hearing the whole painful truth now and although he didn't condone what his father had done, he was at least beginning to understand it.

'I'm telling you now because Dorrie said I didn't have the right to keep that kind of secret forever. She thought maybe I should write it in a letter to you, Finn. At least give you the option of whether you wanted to go looking for Bridie, now you were a man – a father yourself. And old enough, you know, to make your own decisions.' He met Finn's eyes again. 'But I'm not much of a letter writer.'

There was a pause as Finn digested all of this. His father fidgeted, picked at a loose thread on the arm of the sofa. Then after a while he cleared his throat and spoke again.

'There's something else you need to know, lad.'

Finn doubted his father could say anything that would shock him more than he was already. 'Go on.'

'When Bridie phoned up asking to arrange that visit, she told me why she'd left us.' He closed his eyes, and now his cheekbones were very tense, his jaw locked tight, and it was a while before he could speak again. When he did, his voice was calm, almost detached. 'She'd been having an affair with a man she called her childhood sweetheart. She'd met up with him again in England. She said he was her soulmate. And she told me she was pregnant with his bairn.' Ray opened his eyes again and blinked a few times and Finn saw to his horror that his eyes were full of tears.

As if slowly becoming aware of this too, Ray swiped at his face, like he was swatting away a fly, and shook his head. 'That's it. You know it all.'

Despite himself, despite his own shock and pain, Finn's overriding feeling was compassion. He was in no doubt that carrying this awful secret must have been burning away like acid in his father's heart for years. The pain that sharing it gave him was awful to witness. He got up swiftly and crossed to the sofa.

'Dad, Dad, it's OK.' He sat beside his father and rested a hand on his shoulder. 'It's all in the past. All done with. All done.'

Ray felt rigid and stiff beside him and Finn knew in that moment that if he pushed it any further – tried to hug him or comfort him with any more words – he might break. So he just sat, quite still where he was, with his hand on his father's shoulder, and for a few seconds he could feel Ray trembling as he struggled to contain his emotions.

He wasn't even sure how long they sat there, but eventually Ray stopped trembling, sniffed, then fumbled for a huge white handkerchief in his jacket pocket and blew his nose with it. 'I'm sorry,' he said again. 'I'm so sorry I didn't tell you all this before.'

'You've told me now. That's what counts. You've told me now.'

* * *

At Duck Pond Cottage, Jade had just gone to bed. Against her better judgement, and because she was missing Finn, she'd let Mickey go upstairs with her and he'd taken full advantage and was now stretched out on the bed beside her.

'This is our secret, right,' Jade told him, stroking his shaggy head and uncovering a brown eye. 'And it's not going to be an everyday thing, OK?'

Mickey thumped his tail twice on the duvet in agreement – or at least Jade hoped it was agreement – and snuggled in close so the length of him was against the curve of Jade's body. It felt nice having his warmth beside her. It took the edge off the faint disappointment she felt that Finn hadn't phoned. Out of sight, out of mind, she presumed; typical man.

Not that he needed to phone, she reminded herself. He'd only been gone a day, and the whole point was that he was spending some quality time with Ray and Dorrie. But it would have been good to have told him about Farmer John retracting his offer and about her meeting with Rural Developments, and the further one tomorrow. It would have been good to know his thoughts on the whole scenario.

She should probably have texted and told him what had happened, but it had been such a busy day. Anyway, she could deal with Rural Developments. She didn't need any help. This way, with luck, she could just tell Finn the whole story when he got back from Nottingham.

And the whole story would be – hopefully – 'Farmer John changed his mind about selling me the field, but luckily I managed to persuade the developer it would be in their best interests to sell me it, so all's well that ends well.'

Jade wasn't at all sure this was going to happen but for now she wasn't letting any negativity or doubt spoil her happy vision.

She fell asleep to the sound of Mickey's snoring, which was

louder than Finn's and didn't stop when she touched him on the shoulder.

What with the prospect of meeting Declan Stone tomorrow and Mickey's snoring, it wasn't the best night's sleep she'd ever had, which meant Jade overslept. Usually her eyes snapped open just before six and she was up and about by ten past, but on this Wednesday she didn't wake up until nearly twenty to seven and she felt bleary eyed.

Mickey was still asleep beside her. 'Why didn't you wake me?' she scolded him gently. 'Now everyone's going to have a late breakfast.'

The cockerpoo wagged his tail at the word breakfast, yawned, sat up and began scratching himself.

'You'd better not have fleas,' Jade said, even though she knew he'd been dosed the previous month. July was always tricky for fleas.

Everyone was going to have a late breakfast, Jade thought, gulping back an instant coffee and skipping her usual toast. She didn't mind not eating, but there were eight dogs, plus Mickey, five cats, plus Diesel, who'd probably caught his own breakfast by now, two horses, several hens and one verbose parrot who would all be wondering where their benefactor was.

Breakfast and mucking out took the best part of an hour and a half at Duck Pond Rescue, although it was slightly easier in the summer because the horses were out at grass this time of year and didn't need much feeding. Jade did put fly sheets on them in the summer, though, which helped to keep them from being bitten too much. Recently she'd had a couple of teenage girls – Thea and Ann-Marie, who were best friends – who'd come in to help exercise them.

Jade was painfully aware that without exercise both her horses were in danger of getting too fat. Rosanna, a 15-hands thoroughbred cross, who'd been at the sanctuary the longest, went lame if she had very much exercise. Light riding or lead rein walking was best for her. She was a sweet girl, but not a very good proposition for rehoming because of this. Jade was hoping someone might come along who was looking for a companion horse for one that would otherwise be kept alone – this did happen occasionally.

The other horse, Cocoa, was an elderly cob and his previous owner had given him up when he'd got too old for her to compete on, saying she didn't have the space for a horse that wasn't earning his keep. Jade had never been able to understand how anyone could give up an animal just because it had entered its golden years, but it happened a lot. Senior dogs and cats, past their sell-by date, and sometimes requiring ongoing medication, often came in to rescue too, and she knew that some of them would never leave. This was another reason she needed extra land. Not all animals were rehomable, and Jade had a mission to give the ones that would live out their lives at Duck Pond Rescue a comfortable and peaceful retirement.

The teenagers, Thea and Ann-Marie, were both really nice girls who adored animals and shared Jade's sentiments about heartless owners, who were only interested in young and healthy animals. Neither of them would ever be able to afford their own horses, but they loved helping out with Rosanna and Cocoa, and Jade was grateful for their help.

Jade got a WhatsApp from Finn about ten, which said he'd just woken up. She felt slightly guilty about that. Finn must have been totally exhausted to have needed such a long lie-in. She had always been a lark – getting up with the dawn even before necessity had forced the issue, but she'd never considered that Finn might actually like the odd lie-in. He never had them here.

Again, she marvelled that she'd met a man who seemed

totally happy to fit around her life because running an animal rescue centre wasn't a job, it was a vocation. Finn never complained or even questioned the fact that their lives revolved around the feeding, cleaning and rehoming rituals of the sanctuary. They couldn't go away for as much as a day without having to get cover. It was not easy by anyone's standards.

She messaged him back, telling him to make the most of it. She got a smiley face back and a 'catch you later'.

Hopefully he meant on the phone, Jade thought as she got on with the business of the day. She'd also got a text from an unknown number which turned out to be from Declan Stone, asking if 3 p.m. would be a convenient time for him to call.

She texted back and said it would. With luck there would be a volunteer around to cover reception while she walked down with him to look at the area she was hoping to buy, and if there wasn't, she'd lock up for half an hour or so.

True to his word, the property developer arrived bang on time. A shiny black Range Rover Sport with alloy wheels drew into the yard and parked outside reception, and Jade watched Declan Stone emerge. He was carrying a briefcase and he paused to look around him.

His Range Rover, which was almost new, reflected the afternoon sun like a gleaming sculpture of black glass, and Jade was reminded of what Sarah had said.

'Baddies always have black cars.' She'd been talking about crime dramas though, not real life. Jade cursed her overactive imagination and gave herself a little shake as she went outside to meet him.

14

'Good afternoon, Mr Stone. Thank you for coming.'

'It's my pleasure. Please call me Declan.'

'Declan.' She smiled at him. 'I don't want to take up too much of your time. Shall we get down to business?'

'That's why I am here.' She caught a flash of white teeth. Or maybe that was just the contrast against his tanned skin. He didn't look as though he spent much time indoors and she was pleased to see he was wearing sturdy boots. Of course he was – hadn't Farmer John said he was one of Rural Developments' negotiators? He must be out surveying land all the time.

As they walked across the yard, Diesel strolled across in front of them and Declan remarked, 'That's supposed to be lucky, isn't it? A black cat crossing your path.'

'Let's hope it is for us.'

'It obviously is for him – I'm presuming he's escaped.'

'No, he has free range of the place. He was the first cat I ever rehomed so I decided to keep him.'

'Shame, I might be in the market for a cat.'

'Seriously?' Jade shot him a sideways look. For some reason

he hadn't struck her as an animal kind of person, but you never could tell. Maybe she'd misjudged him. 'I could show you our cats,' she suggested. 'Maybe after we've discussed the other bits and pieces.'

'Cool. I'd like that.'

Jade felt herself relax a little. There was a part of her that had been dreading this visit. But she was starting to think it was going to be all right.

Declan commented on every enclosure they passed, usually favourably. It reminded Jade of when she'd first shown Finn around and the observations he'd made. Thankfully the sanctuary was a lot more up-together than it had been back in those days. She was very relieved about that. She didn't imagine Declan would have been too impressed if he'd discovered he was going to be building new houses next to an eyesore.

They passed the pink caravan and the picnic table and a short while later were crossing the hen field and had arrived at the boundaries of Jade's land. Jade paused to lean on the five-bar gate and hoped the hens who were all heading over at top speed wouldn't be too much of a nuisance.

These hopes were soon dashed when one of the braver birds swooped in for an experimental peck at Declan's trouser legs.

'Ouch.' He bent to brush her away and Jade suppressed a giggle as he danced around out of the hen's reach.

As he straightened, he caught Jade's expression and frowned. 'Did you think that was funny?'

She was mortified. 'Um, no, sorry. I wasn't laughing. I was – er...' She halted when she saw the amusement in his eyes.

'I had you going there, didn't I? You should have seen your face. It's OK. My parents kept hens when we were growing up. I'm well used to their antics. I'm guessing this lot see you as food giver, don't they?'

'They do. Yes.' She smiled in relief.

'All the same. It might be safer if we stood on the other side of this gate?'

For someone wearing a smart suit, he was much more nimble than she'd have guessed as he leapt over the five-bar gate.

She followed, and to her embarrassment stumbled as she landed on the rutted ground the other side and would have fallen if he hadn't put out an arm to stop her.

'Thanks,' she murmured, grabbing it, and feeling embarrassed. 'I'm not normally so clumsy.'

'No problem.' Just for a second there was something in his eyes. Something that wasn't professional, but it was gone so quickly she might have imagined it.

'Why don't we walk around the boundary you were hoping to buy?' Declan said, so they did just that until they were standing at the treeline that led down to the road.

She pointed out that the trees made a natural border and Declan nodded in agreement.

'I do see what you mean. But I need to show you something.'

'OK.'

They continued walking towards the road that bordered both the farm and Duck Pond Rescue and once there, Declan stopped and turned to her.

'The difficulties we have, Jade, are all to do with access. You see how the road curves around on a bend just up there?' He pointed as he spoke. 'We can't put an access to a housing estate on a blind bend. It's deemed too dangerous. And if you were to buy the land up to the point you'd like, our access would be right on that blind bend. Do you see our difficulties?'

Jade felt her heart sink as she nodded. She could see exactly what he meant.

There was a long pause and she wondered why he'd bothered coming to see her at all. Maybe he'd just wanted to show her that Rural Developments weren't being unreasonable. They were just being practical.

'So, you're telling me that what I want is impossible. Is that right?'

'Not impossible. But I wanted you to see for yourself how the land lies – if you'll excuse the pun.'   .

She waited, not daring to hope. 'There is one possibility,' Declan went on. 'I'd need to speak to the powers that be. It's a bit above my paygrade. But it might work if we kept the same access but then rerouted the road away from your property instead of going straight into the estate. If we did that you could still buy most of the land you want and everyone would be happy.'

'Is it possible to do that?'

'Possible but more expensive. It would be quite a hard sell. And we may have to charge you more than you were hoping to pay. What was that?'

She told him and he didn't quite suck air through his teeth but he did look surprised. 'I see. Hmm. That's not to say it would be a definite no.' He met her gaze steadily. She was aware of the seriousness of his blue eyes. 'I'm going to try for you, Jade, because I can see it means a lot to you. But I can't make any promises.'

'Thank you.' Impulsively, she touched his arm. 'It does mean a lot to me.'

'OK, then that's what we'll do.' A brief smile lit up his face. 'Maybe you could show me those cats now?'

'I'd love to.'

* * *

Softly softly catchee monkey, Declan thought as they walked back across the hen field towards the yard. When she'd touched his arm back there he'd been so tempted to return the gesture, but he didn't want to go in too heavy. She reminded him of a roe deer. Beautiful, but wide eyed and ready to flee at the slightest wrong move.

Yet he already knew there was more than one side to Jade Foster. He had no doubt at all she'd fight for what she loved. And that was definitely her animal sanctuary.

'So is there a Mr Foster?' he asked as they walked. 'I'm guessing you don't run this place on your own.'

'You're guessing right. My partner helps. He's away at the moment. I also have quite a few volunteers.'

'I bet you do. It must be a magnet for animal lovers.'

'Yes, it is. I'm really lucky. How long have you worked for Rural Developments?' It was a deft change of subject.

'A long time. It's my grandfather's company. I always knew I'd go into the family business. My dad's the general manager, but he's the kind of dad who thinks kids should make their own way in life, so I had to work my way up through the ranks. I did a business degree first, so I know about the business side of things. I also had to do some legal training, and believe it or not I've done all sorts of jobs on site too – I was a brickie for a while.'

'You never were?' He had her attention now. She was looking at him in amazement.

'It's true. It was a surprise that he let me go to uni at all. My dad's an advocate of the school of hard knocks. So's my grandpa. Which isn't so surprising. My grandfather started the company from scratch in Northern Ireland.'

'Wow, so you're Irish? You don't sound it.'

'I'm half Irish but I grew up in England.'

They'd arrived back at the yard and their conversation was

interrupted by a blonde-haired middle-aged woman, heading towards them with purposeful steps.

'Jade, sorry to interrupt but Aiden's here and I'm not sure which animals you wanted him to look at. Do you have a second?'

'Of course.' Jade glanced apologetically at Declan. 'Aiden's my vet,' she explained, 'so I'm going to have to go, but Dawn's my right-hand woman. I'm sure she'd be more than happy to show you the cats.'

'The cats?'

'You said you might be in the market for a cat?'

'I am. Yes. That'd be grand. Thank you.' He berated himself for that throwaway comment. He was definitely not in the market for a cat – but he would go and look. He could find some excuse to pull out later.

* * *

Jade went to greet Aiden, who was waiting for her outside reception. She felt hugely relieved. Declan was a nice guy. She didn't think there was going to be an issue at all with getting the field, although it did look like the cost would go up.

'Morning, Jade.' Aiden, who'd always dressed like an old-fashioned gentleman farmer, in tweeds and green wellies, had a more relaxed look since he'd met Kate, his new girlfriend. Kate was a stunner and she'd obviously had a hand in changing Aiden's look. Today Aiden had a light brown fleece over an expensive shirt. He'd swapped the green wellies for trail boots.

'Morning, Aiden. Thanks for fitting us in. Your first patient's Mr Spock. Apparently he's got a cough, although I must admit I haven't heard it. A few of the volunteers have been worried, though. So I thought maybe you could look while you're here.

The other patient's a cat that's a bit off colour in the hospital block.'

'No problem.' They went into reception and Jade saw to her chagrin that Mr Spock was out of his cage. The piece of paper she'd left sellotaped to the door saying to leave him in today must have fallen off.

'Don't worry, he's easy to catch,' she told Aiden. But these proved to be famous last words.

Like all living creatures, Mr Spock had superb 'vet radar' and he led them a merry dance around reception, flying from one end of the room to the other but never landing anywhere for more than a few seconds.

After ten minutes, Aiden said, 'I think it was James Herriot who said if you can't catch your patient, there's not much wrong with it. Shall we go and see the cat first and let him settle?'

Just as he spoke, Mr Spock alighted on top of his cage and started preening. Aiden, who was closest, pounced but in the process he tripped over Mickey's basket, stumbled and lurched into the cage so it tilted and the whole lot teetered to the left and then tipped over. Somehow Aiden ended up on the floor too. It was chaos. Sandpaper, parrot toys and bird poop littered the floor.

Jade leaped to Aiden's side. 'Oh, God. Are you OK?'

'I'm good.' Aiden picked something unmentionable out of his hair and winced from his position on the floor. 'Sorry. I lost my footing. Where did the bloody parrot go?'

Jade looked around them. Mr Spock was back on the window beside reception. 'Bloody hells bells,' the parrot said cheerfully, and before either of them could speak, he added a string of ruder expletives and finished with a cough.

'Did you hear that?' Jade said.

'Yes, but that's a human cough. Parrots don't cough like us.

They have different respiratory systems. They don't have a diaphragm.'

'Of course they don't.' Jade clapped her hand over her mouth. It had been a while since she'd done her vet training, which she'd never completed, and a memory of a distant lecture was surfacing. 'I'm so sorry, Aiden, I've dragged you out on false pretences.'

Mr Spock 'coughed' again and Jade glanced back at Aiden, who had just climbed to his feet and was righting the bird cage.

'I reckon he's heard someone with a cough,' Aiden muttered. 'He's mimicking. That's all. Judging by all the – er – swear words he knows, he's quite a good mimic.'

'He is.' Jade felt her face flaming. 'I'm so sorry.'

'Don't worry. I'm sure we'll laugh about this one day.' Aiden gave her a crooked smile. 'But please don't tell Kate. Or I'll never hear the end of it. She already thinks I'm accident prone.'

'My lips are sealed,' Jade promised, privately thinking Kate might be right. It wasn't that long ago that Aiden had been head-butted by a goat, had knocked himself out in the process of escaping, and had ended up spending a night in hospital with suspected concussion.

'Are you sure you're not hurt?' she asked solicitously.

'I'm good. Let's go and see this cat, shall we? It's probably a safer option.'

* * *

Finn couldn't remember a time when he'd felt so emotionally wrung out. He and his father had stayed up talking deep into the night. They'd finally got to bed sometime around 4 a.m. and despite being convinced he wouldn't sleep, Finn had dropped into an exhausted slumber sometime around five thirty, which was when he'd have usually been waking up.

The next thing he'd been aware of was bright sunshine pouring into the room and when he'd rolled over and reached for his phone, he'd been shocked to see it was ten fifteen.

For a while he'd lain in bed, listening to the sounds of the house. He could hear someone moving around downstairs in the kitchen and the buzz of muted chatter. Maybe that was what had woken him. He could also smell toast – that might have woken him too. For a few seconds he stayed wrapped under the duvet in warm blissful ignorance and then the memory of last night came crashing back into his consciousness.

After Ray had told him Bridie had left because she was pregnant with another man's child, Finn had felt knocked sideways. He was torn in two. It was no surprise that Ray had kept this whopper of a secret – he could see that had been done out of fear.

But the fact he had a sibling out there – a brother or sister – who he'd grown up not knowing felt like a body blow too. After he'd acclimatised to the shock of his past being rewritten, one overriding feeling had risen out of the chaos.

He'd known he wanted to meet them. Bridie and whatever family she had now. He wanted to see them. Even if it was only once. He knew there was a possibility they wouldn't want to see him. Bridie might not have told any of her family she had an older son. When Ray had told her on that long-ago day that Finn thought she was dead, she might have decided to leave the past alone. To focus on her new family. In fact, the more Finn thought about it, the more likely this seemed.

If he were to turn up in Bridie's life now, he'd probably be a major bombshell. These churning thoughts that had kept him awake into the early hours started to churn again and Finn blinked away the pain. He had a searing headache. He needed to get up and find some painkillers.

Besides, he had to go downstairs and face his father and Dorrie – she had made herself scarce last night, and he wasn't sure she hadn't gone back to her own house a few doors up from his father's. That had been diplomatic of her.

He hadn't even told them about the double wedding yet – at least that was a nice non-confrontational subject they could chat about.

He also urgently needed to speak to Jade. He felt terribly guilty that he hadn't already told her what was going on.

15

Closing time at Duck Pond Rescue varied with the light. In wintertime Jade closed when it got dark, which meant not long after four thirty on the shortest days, but in summertime she left the main gates open longer, and often sat in reception to catch up on paperwork.

Tonight, it was just after 8 p.m. when she enticed Mr Spock back into his cage with a slice of banana and half a tomato, two of his favourite treats. She should have thought of that earlier! She hoped Aiden was all right.

She gave Mickey his tea in the cottage and then decided to call Finn from reception. They'd had a landline in the cottage once, but she'd had it disconnected because it was the same number as the one in reception and rang all hours of the day and night. Most people either didn't know or didn't care that Jade was the sole proprietor of Duck Pond Rescue and much as she was happy to be on twenty-four-hour call, even she needed to sleep sometimes.

She settled in her comfy office chair and speed-dialled Finn's number. It rang so many times she thought it would go to voicemail, but just as she was about to disconnect and try again, he picked up.

'Jade. I've missed you.'

'I've missed you too. But you sound like you needed the break. I can't believe you didn't wake up until gone ten. Did you have a late night or something?'

'Very late.' His voice sobered and even on the phone she could hear his anxiety. Suddenly she was on full alert.

'Finn, what is it? Is everything OK? Your dad's all right, isn't he?'

'We're all fine. Don't worry. No one's ill. But I do have a lot to tell you. Is now a good time?'

'Of course it is. Go for it.'

She heard him take a breath and then let it out with a slight shudder, which worried her even more. Finn was the epitome of calm. He rarely got ruffled about anything.

'OK. It's a long story. Last night Dad told me some things about my past – it turns out my mother's disappearance wasn't as straightforward as I've always thought.'

'Go on.'

'Well, I guess one of the most important things is that she never went back to Ireland.'

'But that's what your dad told you.' It wasn't really a question. They'd talked about their childhoods quite a bit when they'd started dating.

'You got it. The truth is that my mother lives in England. Possibly in Southampton, and I think she always has.'

By the time he'd got to the end of the story, Jade's head was reeling almost as much as his must have been.

'Oh, my goodness, Finn, that must have been such a shock. Do you know why your dad decided to tell you all this now?'

'It was Dorrie's influence. They'd talked about it, you see, and Dad told her the truth. She was the first person he'd ever told. It's not like it was common knowledge or anything and I was the last to know. Not even my grandparents knew, but you know how Dorrie has a way of getting people to tell her things.'

'I imagine she's very easy to confide in.' Jade had only met Ray's partner a couple of times but her impressions of Dorrie were that she was warm, discreet and also a little bit bossy. A powerful combination.

'I'm glad she did persuade Dad. At least, I am now I've got over the shock.'

'*Have* you got over the shock?'

'Maybe not entirely. But I'm getting there.' There was a slight pause. 'I did have a bit of advance warning. Dad sent me a news item a few weeks ago about estranged families reuniting. It got me thinking about the possibility of tracking down my mother.'

'You never said. Why didn't you tell me?' The words were out of her mouth before she had a chance to edit them, and Jade knew she must sound hurt. She was a bit hurt. 'Is that why you've seemed so preoccupied lately?'

'Yes. No. OK, maybe, and look, I'm sorry I didn't say anything at the time. I was worried it might stir up too many emotions for you, because you've closed the door on your past. I...'

'Finn. My past is totally irrelevant to yours. I'd have supported you in whatever you chose to do. And this is a massive thing in your life. I thought we shared the big stuff. Didn't you trust me?'

Finn could hear the edge of hurt in her voice and he felt terrible. 'We do share it. And of course I trust you. It wasn't that.'

'It obviously was. Or you'd have told me.'

She broke off this time and he wished he was with her. Wished he hadn't told her this news on the phone. But that would have meant keeping it a secret for even longer while he went down the trail of finding his mother and any other family he might have, and he knew he couldn't do that. He'd already left it longer than he should.

She'd gone so silent he wondered if she'd disconnected the call.

'Jade, speak to me.'

'I'm still here.' Some of the usual warmth had gone from her voice.

'I'm so sorry I didn't tell you. I should have done. I wasn't sure it was going to come to anything. So I decided to investigate a bit. I thought maybe there was nothing to find and if there wasn't then – I'd... I'd have worried you unnecessarily.'

'You don't need to apologise. It was a shock, that's all. So what do you plan to do now?'

She still sounded a bit cold, but there was nothing he could do about that from up here. His impulse was to leave immediately and rush back down to Wiltshire, talk it through until things were right between them again, but there was too much unfinished business in Nottingham. It was clear that last night had been emotionally devastating for Ray too. They'd both said things they didn't mean. They'd both hurt each other. And Finn was desperate to repair that. If he walked away now while the wound was still so open and raw he knew he'd regret it.

'I don't want it all to be buried again, Jade. I want to know all there is to know while the subject's uppermost in mine and Dad's minds. Then maybe we can leave it alone and shut the lid on it.' He hesitated. 'I think I'd like to find Bridie too if I can – I want to talk that through with Dad first too. It affects him just as much as it affects me.'

'And Ben,' Jade said softly.

'Yes, and Ben. He may have another set of grandparents, and uncles and aunts. Or the whole lot of them may want nothing to do with me. I need to find out before I say anything. Would you mind not saying anything to Sarah until I've done that?'

'I won't say anything to Sarah. It's not my secret to tell, is it.'

She sounded bleak and he remembered the last occasion she'd said those words to him. 'It's not my secret to tell.' Except that time she'd been talking about the fact she'd known he was Ben's father before he had.

'You won't have to keep it a secret for long,' Finn reassured her now. 'I don't think I'll be up here long. I just want to calm things down with Dad. I'll probably come back on Sunday or Monday.'

'OK. Sure.'

'Is that really OK?'

'Of course it is. Do what you need to do, Finn. Everything's fine here.'

'I love you.'

'I love you too.'

As Jade disconnected, she realised she hadn't told him about the problems with the field and the access and the fact that her land purchase now had a giant question mark hanging over it. But that all seemed trivial in comparison to his bombshell news.

Declan hadn't got back to her, although she supposed it could take some time to sort out. She guessed there would have to be surveys and things and from what he'd said, correspondence with the Highways Agency. Besides, just because Declan only had to get approval from his family, that wouldn't necessarily make things any easier. As Jade knew from experience, working with families could be a lot tricker and more complex than working with people to whom you weren't related.

She admired Declan for going into the family business. But Jade had always known her mother's empire wasn't for her. Elizabeth was a tough, pragmatic powerhouse of a woman, who could manoeuvre and manipulate people with the skill of a very successful salesperson.

Jade was a sensitive introvert and had always felt happier in the company of animals than being with her own kind. The one thing she had always been certain of was that she was not going to be running any hotels.

This had not gone down well. Jade's refusal to go into the family business had been a bone of contention for a long time between her and her mother.

Jade had regretted her part in this ongoing conflict when her mother had died from a fatal stroke. Not so much that she hadn't done as her mother had wanted but more the fact they'd had so many arguments about it. Sometimes Jade wondered if the conflicts between them had actually contributed to her mother's premature passing, and there was a part of her that would feel forever guilty.

For a while she stayed where she was in reception. It had been greyer today and it had just started to rain. She could hear the patter of it on the old stone roof and raindrops chased each other down the windowpanes.

Mickey had fallen asleep in his basket. Diesel was curled up asleep in the visitor's chair. Even Mr Spock was quiet on his perch. There wasn't so much as a mimicked cough from the bird. Jade felt an ache of loneliness. Finn might only be 170 miles away but it felt like he was on the other side of the planet.

16

Thursday and Friday passed in a blur of activity and Jade was pleased it was busy because it stopped her thinking so much about Finn's news and how sad she felt that he hadn't shared it with her sooner. She could have supported him if she'd known. A problem shared was a problem halved.

She rehomed four ex-battery hens to a couple who'd just bought a smallholding in the area. It turned out the woman's cousin was also thinking of keeping hens and she promised to pass on Jade's number.

There was still no word from Declan Stone. When Jade was walking the kennel dogs with Dawn on Saturday morning, she asked her how he'd got on with the cats.

'I don't think he saw one he liked,' Dawn told her, 'although he did say he'd keep in touch. Seemed an OK chap. Was he just looking for a cat? He looked more like an estate agent than a rehomer.'

'I think he was on his way to work.' Jade still hadn't told Dawn about her land purchase. She was so anxious not to jinx it.

At midday, Zack, the teenager who'd wanted to rehome the geese, called by.

'I was wondering if you'd had any more thoughts about taking the couple we've got at home,' he asked. 'Only my dad has given me until tomorrow as the deadline. After that...' He made a slicing motion across his throat and looked pleadingly at Jade.

'You can bring them here,' she told him, 'but there's a condition.'

'What is it? Anything.'

'You'll have to dig out a pond for them.'

Zack's blue eyes lit up. 'I'd be happy to. Where?'

'I'll show you.' Jade took him up to the hen field and showed him the place she had in mind in the lower corner. 'Do you have any mates that can help you? It's quite hard graft.'

'I do. Thanks. I'll get hold of a few people.'

'You do that, and I'll supply the shovels and the pond liner and the other things we'll need.'

'I'm so grateful. When can we get started?'

'I'd say straightaway if the deadline's tomorrow. The geese are going to need a pond before they can come over. Oh, and there is one other condition.'

'What's that?'

'My godson, Ben, is going to want to help. He's seven so I'm not sure how much help he'll be, but he'll be over later and there's nothing he likes more than getting filthy. Are you OK with that?'

'I am. Totally.'

They exchanged a smile and Jade decided she liked this young man. He had the same light in his eyes as Ben did when he talked about animals. The same light that she felt when an animal had captured her heart. She often saw it in teenage girls, but rarely the boys, who were usually more interested in chasing after the teenage girls.

Sarah brought Ben over as promised just after lunch. 'Finn's not back yet then?' she observed, looking around for his car.

'No, he's still in Nottingham. He decided to stay a few days longer. It's quite a long way, isn't it, so if he's going to drive all that distance it makes sense to have plenty of time up there. Make the most of seeing Ray and Dorrie while he's there. He'll probably come back tomorrow or Monday.' She knew she was over explaining because she couldn't tell Sarah the reason he was really staying up there, but luckily her friend was distracted and didn't notice.

'I brought Ben a change of clothes, like you said. He's very excited about digging out a duck pond. It's even trumped our double wedding and he was fairly excited about that. But now it's duck ponds.' She laughed. 'I didn't think you had any ducks.'

'We haven't. It's for some geese we've got coming.'

'No wonder Ben loves it here. There's never a dull moment.'

'Tell me about it.' They smiled at each other. 'Where is he anyway?'

'In reception teaching Mr Spock a new word. We should probably intervene. It's not likely to be polite.' Sarah rolled her eyes. 'Digging out a duck pond sounds like a good diversion, although I think he's going to be disappointed the occupants aren't here. Are you free for a bit? I want to run some wedding plans past you.'

'Of course I am. I want to talk to you about some stuff too. Shall we get the pond diggers going and sneak into reception for a coffee?'

Twenty minutes later, having made sure everyone had started digging in the right place – Ben had a miniature shovel and a determined expression – Jade and Sarah were in reception with freshly made coffee and some coconut macaroons Sarah had brought.

Jade bit into one, letting the rice paper melt in her mouth and the sweetness of coconut fill her senses. 'Oh my God, these bring back memories. We always had these on midnight feasts.'

'I know. That's why I got them. Although I reckon they were bigger in those days.'

'Everything was bigger in those days. All chocolate bars have shrunk as well as getting more expensive. And packets of crisps used to be enormous compared to the ones they sell now.'

'Or maybe it's just we were smaller then,' Sarah said with a sweet smile. 'And now we're all grown up and on the verge of getting married – how's that for a cool segue into weddings?'

'It's impressive,' Jade said as Sarah rummaged in her bag and drew out some leaflets.

'I've got the details of some venues. I know you can look at them online but I always think it's better to have the actual bits of paper in front of you. Then you can compare them side by side. I've done a spreadsheet too that compares costs, distances from here, facilities for guests, photo opportunities, that kind of thing.'

'Blimey, I'm even more impressed,' Jade said, feeling a stab of guilt because she hadn't done anything. She'd barely even thought about weddings since they'd had the dinner. She'd got totally sidetracked, firstly with Farmer John's backtrack and her visit to Rural Developments and then by Finn's bombshell news.

'I've got more time than you,' Sarah said, interpreting her guilty expression. 'At least I have until the schools break up. Eek, ten days to go, so I thought I'd crack on while the going's good.'

'He can come here in the holidays,' Jade said instantly. 'That'll help, won't it?'

'Yes, that's true. You'll probably see more of him than I will.'

They both laughed as Sarah laid out three brochures on the desk.

'One's an old mill,' Sarah said, 'and the other two are hotels. The mill is really picturesque. I can imagine us standing by the water for the photos, the river meandering behind us through the idyllic Wiltshire countryside and a pair of doves flying up into an azure-blue sky.' She closed her eyes dreamily.

'That sounds like a quote from a brochure.'

'It is a quote from a brochure. Their brochure.' Sarah laughed. 'Since when have I been one to use words like azure? It does sound good though.'

'It sounds brilliant. Do they guarantee the azure bit?'

'No. I'm afraid not. Although they can supply the doves. There's a list of links of all the things mentioned in the brochure.'

'I'm not sure if I'm happy about doves being used at weddings. What are the other two like?'

'The hotels are both in Dorset. One of them's the place where our friends got married. So we've been there already. It was really nice. That one's the cheapest venue too.'

'But it doesn't have a meandering river and an azure sky?' Jade teased.

'No. Nothing like that. It's rural. But...' She paused. 'The other hotel in Dorset is up on a cliff in the isle of Purbeck overlooking Old Harry Rocks. The photos would be amazing there. They're not actually a specialist wedding venue. But they do have a really good reputation.' She pushed the brochure across to Jade. 'Look at their mission statement.'

Jade read it aloud. 'We're here to help you make your dreams come true.' She paused. 'The Bluebell Cliff Hotel. I think I've heard of that. Someone's mentioned it to me recently. I think it was Aiden. I'm pretty sure he took Kate to stay there for her birthday. There's actually a restored lighthouse in the grounds that they use for special occasions and they've got a world-class chef as well, according to Aiden.' She sighed. 'It'll definitely be out of our price range.'

'Surprisingly it's not. Not if you consider what they offer. And we don't have to go for the world-class chef. We can have our own caterers. It says that on the brochure.'

Jade could hear the excitement in her friend's voice. 'I'm guessing this one's your favourite, too.'

'Yeah, I think it is. It looks amazing. We obviously need to see what Callum and Finn think. And we'd need to go and look at them all. It might be interesting to see what Aiden thinks too. He's a born romantic, isn't he?' Sarah's eyes were shining. 'It's really exciting, isn't it?'

Jade nodded. It was hard not to get caught up in Sarah's excitement despite all of the other things swirling in her head.

They were interrupted by a knock on the door.

'Come in, you bugger,' said a high but quite distinctive voice. A parrot's voice.

Jade looked round in alarm. Mr Spock was sitting on top of his cage and as she looked at him, he threw back his head and said it again, louder. 'Come in, you bugger.'

'Oh, good grief, who taught him that?' she muttered, getting up to open the door.

'I think I can guess.' Sarah groaned. 'I'm really sorry. Can you unteach him?'

'Come in, you bugger,' Mr Spock screeched at the top of his voice as the door opened slowly. A tall woman, who could have passed for Halle Berry, but who had white corkscrew curls that looked amazing against her brown skin, came in hesitantly. She was beautifully dressed and carrying a cat basket. She looked at Jade and Sarah. 'Is this Duck Pond Rescue?'

'It is, and I'm the proprietor. Jade Foster.' Jade got up from the desk. 'Please ignore the parrot.'

'Oh, I see.' The woman glanced around, spotted Mr Spock and looked relieved. 'I thought for a minute there... um...' She chuckled and then put the cat basket down and Jade saw a flash of white fur through the grille.

'This is my neighbour's cat, Snowy. He's looking for a home. I said I'd bring him in.'

'Is your neighbour no longer able to care for him?' Jade asked.

'She died last week. I've been taking care of him since – as Laura, the daughter, can't. She's got allergies.'

'I see. Well, that's kind of you to bring him. We'll need to just do some paperwork if you don't mind. Would you be the person who's able to do a transfer of ownership form?'

'I guess I can. No one else wants poor Snowy.' She sighed. 'I'm Ursula. Ursula Hargreaves.'

'I'll nip up and see how Ben's getting on while you're doing that,' Sarah said. 'And I'll have a word with him about that parrot.'

* * *

Ursula Hargreaves was a sweetie, Jade decided as they did the paperwork on Snowy. In her experience, most people who dropped off an animal disappeared as soon as they humanly could, never to be seen again. Whether it was guilt, or the pain of goodbye, or a mixture of both was hard to tell – and Jade tried not to judge – but Ursula was not like this at all.

She came down to see where Jade settled Snowy in the cattery and she looked with interest at all the other cats in situ.

'I think you people do amazing work,' she told Jade. 'I can't take on the commitment of an animal just now, but I've always wanted to volunteer in a place like this. Do you take volunteers?'

'We certainly do. There's lots of ways you can volunteer. I need dog walkers, event organisers for fundraising, people to sponsor animals, even if you can just afford a one-off donation it would help.'

'I'd love to volunteer. I've always wanted a dog, but I still work full time.'

'What do you do?' Jade asked more out of politeness than any real curiosity.

'I work for Wiltshire council. I'm an ecologist. It's a great job but it means pretty long hours and the odd weekend away. It wouldn't be fair to keep an animal. Even a cat really. I've got quite fond of Snowy since my dear old neighbour died but I'm away next weekend so rehoming him seemed the best option.'

'Of course. I do see.'

'Many of my weekends are free though. So if I could help at all...'

After they'd settled Snowy, Jade introduced Ursula to Dawn so they could talk about volunteering and the informal schedule they had on a whiteboard in reception. Then Jade went up to the hen field to check out 'Operation Pond Dig'.

They'd done a surprising amount. Thanks to the recent rain, the ground was softer than it would usually be in mid-July.

Zack and his team of volunteers had dug out about half of the pond. Sarah and Ben were sitting on the ground slightly off to one side. Ben was filthy from head to toe, Jade saw, no surprises there then, and it looked like Sarah was telling him off.

Jade heard Ben say, 'It wasn't me,' as she got closer. His face was mutinous. 'I haven't even seen Mr Spock for a week.'

It was always hard to tell whether Ben was lying. He was basically honest but he wasn't above bending the truth if it suited him. A little like his mum, Jade thought wryly.

'Hi, how's it all going?' she said as the teenage lads, who'd been studiously ignoring the exchange between Ben and Sarah, stopped work and either leaned on or put down their shovels when they saw her.

Zack stepped forward. 'I think we're almost there. What's happened to the parrot?'

'Someone's been teaching him swear words,' Jade said, trying not to smile. 'Which can be embarrassing when visitors come to call.'

Zack smirked. 'That is pretty funny. What kind of swear words?'

'I don't even know any swear words, Auntie Jade,' Ben shouted across. 'I only taught him to say bum. Promise, promise and cross my heart. Hope to die. Bum isn't rude, is it? It's part of bodies. Bodies aren't rude.'

Sarah got up slowly, shaking her head. 'I don't know if I believe him or not. But I've tried.'

'It's fine. It really doesn't matter.' Jade caught Ben's gaze. He wasn't doing the wide-eyed look he sometimes did when he was trying to pull the wool over her eyes. He did actually look quite affronted.

Sarah would probably never see it as clearly as she did, but Ben was a complete chip off the old block. Sarah had always been a maverick, who'd push boundaries to their limit and thought nothing of breaking rules that didn't suit her. Jade wasn't a bit surprised that Ben was the same.

'Lots of people teach Mr Spock things,' Jade said now, 'and it's possible we misheard him, isn't it, Sarah?'

'Hmmm.' Sarah snorted. 'Maybe!'

'So, shall we leave these hardworking guys to it? I've got some news I want to tell you too.' She might not be able to share Finn's news about his past, but it would be good to talk to someone at least about Declan Stone.

17

Sarah was gratifyingly indignant when, back at reception, Jade told her the full story.

'Flaming arrogant developers trampling over people. Just because they've got deep pockets.' Her freckled face coloured up. A sure sign her emotions were running high.

'Although this one does seem pretty reasonable, as it turns out,' Jade said quickly. 'He came over the day after I went to see him and he explained all the ins and outs of everything, and he's promised he'll do his best to get them to change the access routes so the entrance to the proposed development could still be in the same place, but then the road will curve back round on itself, which means I can still buy my bit of the land.'

'He hasn't got back to you though, has he? So he might just have been paying lip service to it all.' Sarah drumrolled her fingers on the reception desk.

'I don't think he was. He seemed pretty genuine.'

'Huh. He might seem genuine, but I wouldn't bank on it. Bank being the operative word. You should work on the assumption that' – she pointed a finger at Jade – 'you are a lovely, generous animal-loving good person. And he' – she frowned – 'is a ruthless, grasping, property-developing baddie. I bet he's got a black car, hasn't he?'

'Black Range Rover.'

'I rest my case. What did Finn say?'

'I haven't had the chance to tell him yet. We've only had a couple of short phone calls since he's been away. He doesn't want to be speaking to me for hours – not when he's with Ray and Dorrie,' she added quickly in explanation.

Before Sarah could comment, there was another knock on the door.

'Come in, you bugger,' Mr Spock piped up, and Sarah shook her head. 'Blimey, you're going to have to gag that parrot. We're definitely not mishearing anything!'

From the other side of the door came peals of laughter, and Thea and Ann-Marie, the teenagers who came in to look after the horses, strolled in, looking pleased with themselves.

'I can't believe he learned that so quickly,' Thea said. 'It's hilarious.'

'So it was you who taught him,' Sarah berated them. 'Flaming heck, I've just torn Ben off a right strip for teaching him bad words.'

'Oh, no.' Ann-Marie, who was the most sensible of the two, looked stricken. 'Sorry. Yes, it was us. It was just a bit of a laugh. We didn't expect him to pick it up so soon to be honest. That is one smart parrot.'

'We'll teach him something different,' Thea promised. 'He'll soon forget he's learned that.'

There was a little pause. Then, into the silence, Mr Spock yelled, 'Come in, you bugger,' at the top of his voice and cackled.

'Good luck with that,' Jade said.

There was another brief silence before Sarah broke it by

laughing. 'I suppose it is quite funny. But I'm going to have to apologise to Ben.'

* * *

Jade didn't lock up until later than usual. Mostly because of the pond diggers who'd worked like troopers and finished not only digging the pond, but getting the liner in it too, just before dusk fell.

Filling it up with water was quite a job because although they had a field water supply, the hose wouldn't quite reach so they used buckets and a chain of people to do the filling. Any volunteers left on site helped, and Jade saw to her surprise that Ursula Hargreaves was one of them. She and Dawn seemed to be getting on like a house on fire.

It was heartwarming, watching her join in with the others passing buckets of water along the chain to get the pond filled. As Jade glanced up towards the slight slope of the hen field, she saw a line of people of all shapes and sizes silhouetted in the sunset across her land. And all because two geese needed a home. She swallowed a lump in her throat. People were so amazing.

Jade knew even before Zack asked her again that she was going to say yes to whatever geese were still left at the school. It would have seemed crazy not to say yes after they'd done all this work. It would be a push if they didn't have room – but fingers crossed they would get the extra space and then there would be plenty of room.

By eight thirty, everyone, including an absolutely filthy Ben and Sarah, who'd also joined in, had finally gone home. Jade was just locking up the main gates when a black Range Rover Sport drew up outside them and parked.

She paused. She only knew one person with a car that flash, and sure enough, a few seconds later, Declan climbed out.

'Hi, sorry to call so late. But I'm really glad I caught you. I've got news and I wanted to tell you as soon as I could.'

'Thanks – that's kind of you.' Jade felt her heart do a little jump of hope. He didn't have a bad news face on.

'Is it OK to come in? Were you just going out?'

'No, I was just finishing up here.' Jade started to unbolt the gates.

'I'll wait for you,' Declan said. 'I don't want to interrupt.'

'It's fine. I don't have anything else on. Apart from getting some supper. I'm starving.'

'Tell you what. Why don't I stand you some supper? I've only just finished work too. I want to show you some proposals and it'll take a little while. But if we do it over supper then we can kill two birds with one stone. Sorry – bad metaphor for an animal rescue.'

Jade was about to refuse. But then Declan smiled at her disarmingly. 'Bring your partner along too. We can all chat it through.'

'He's not here at the moment.' She hesitated. Oh, why not? Declan seemed harmless enough and he knew she had a partner. And he was right, it would kill two birds with one stone. However inappropriate the metaphor was.

'Give me ten minutes to get changed,' she told Declan, 'and I'll take you up on that.'

Declan gave her another smile and headed back to his car before she could have second thoughts and change her mind.

Another ten minutes wouldn't hurt. He'd been waiting for three quarters of an hour already up the road. He'd seen the chain of people in the field and then he'd waited for them all to go again, before he'd stopped 'casually' by.

He'd sat in his Range Rover, flicking idly through the paper-work. He'd produced a set of drawings himself, and he was working on getting them past his father, which wouldn't be that straightforward because it would be considerably more expen-sive than the company's original plan.

His plan as far as Jade went was to get her to believe he was totally on her side, and happy to fight her case with his family, even though it was going to result in a level of extra expense. That he was prepared to put himself out for her, because he liked her.

All of these things were true. He was on her side, and he did like her. And it might be possible to sway his old man, although his grandfather would be the real stumbling block. Grandpa Nick was a hard-headed businessman and he hadn't built up a very successful development company by wasting money and pussy-footing around upset neighbours.

Declan would need to put in a lot of legwork, and he needed to make that clear to Jade too. He could do it, but he wanted something in return. There was no sign of a live-in boyfriend either. Maybe that was just a line Jade used to stop people thinking she lived alone out here. Maybe that was why she wore the ring too. Declan hadn't given up on making their relation-ship a bit more personal.

He smiled to himself as he saw Jade come out of the front door of her cottage and head towards the gates. She'd got changed, as she'd said, and was now wearing skinny jeans and a smart jacket. She'd let her hair down, and my God, she had gorgeous hair.

He jumped down from the driving seat and went to meet her.

'Shall we go in my car? Save you getting yours out.' He saw the hesitation in her eyes. 'It's up to you, but I don't drive like a madman, and I'm not a total weirdo.' He grinned. 'At least I don't think I am. You'd have to ask my friends to be sure.'

She laughed then, and he knew he'd passed stage one of her trust test anyway. That was good. He was very much looking forward to spending the evening in her company. He hadn't expected she'd agree to dinner, but now she had it was the icing on the cake. A much more appropriate metaphor.

* * *

In Nottingham, Finn, Ray and Dorrie had just finished eating supper, ham hock and leek pie and mash, made and served up by Dorrie. Despite the fact Finn knew Jade had been jolted by his news, he was glad he'd made the decision to stay. Now Ray had finally decided to break the years of silence, it seemed he couldn't stop talking, and Dorrie, bless her, was being endlessly supportive, even though a lot of the story must be difficult for her to hear.

'I met your mother at the goose fair in 1990,' Ray was saying now. 'She was working on one of the rides. Her family were something to do with the fair – I think it may have been an uncle who part owned the ride – I forget the details, but that's where we met.' He looked at his hands. 'Bridie was everything I was not. Exciting, streetwise, very clever, even though she'd missed out on a lot of formal education. She was a wild child. She always said exactly what was in her head, even if it caused offence. Whereas I was Mr Boring. I took after my father. I was a plodder, happy to toe the line, happy with my lot, happy to work in the mine like my dad had done before me, and his dad before that. They say opposites attract.' He glanced briefly at Finn, but he didn't meet Dorrie's eyes.

'I guess it wasn't just Bridie I fell for. It was the whole package. The excitement of the fair, the glamour of her. She was very pretty, and I was flattered because she'd singled me out over all my mates. I couldn't believe she'd chosen me. We lived in such different worlds.' His eyes misted and it was a while before he continued.

'When I look back, I think she fell for me because I was so unlike anyone she'd ever met. I wasn't bad looking back then. I was older than her, of course, and I had money to spare.' He blew out a breath. 'The goose fair was the highlight of our year.'

'I remember lads talking about it when I was at school,' Finn said. 'We all had theories about why it was called the goose fair. Wasn't it something to do with geese being sold there back in the mists of time?'

'Aye, I think so.'

'It was,' Dorrie murmured. 'If you go back a few hundred years, thousands of geese were driven to Nottingham from the Lincolnshire fens in the east of England – they used to protect their feet with a mixture of tar and sand so they could do the fifty-mile journey. The chicks from the spring were ready for the pot for Michaelmas Day.'

'Aye, that sounds familiar,' Ray said, looking at her with respect. 'That must have been a sight – all those geese milling about.'

'But we never went to the goose fair when I was a boy, Dad. You said you preferred Skegness. I always wondered about that because Skeggy was so much smaller.'

'And now you know why. The place held too many memories.'

Finn nodded. He'd never questioned it when he'd been small. He'd never questioned any of his father's choices. He suspected this was because he was cut from the same cloth as his father – until he'd moved down to Arleston and fallen in love with Jade, he'd always done pretty much what life and society had expected of him. He'd never stepped outside of the straight tracks his family had trodden.

It was strange hearing that his mother hadn't been like that at all. That she'd been part of a showman's family, someone who'd travelled around the countryside with one of the biggest fairs in the world. Although Finn had romanticised her as a child, reinventing her as some beautiful princess, he'd never imagined her as what she actually was. Being a showman still felt romantic somehow. Knowing he had showman's blood running through his veins, even though before tonight he hadn't known that, both unnerved and excited him.

'I'll make us another pot of tea,' Dorrie said, getting up from the sofa. 'Or would you boys like something stronger? I think there's some cans of Guinness.'

'Tea's fine,' Ray said, and Finn nodded his agreement.

'Did you ever go back to the goose fair after Bridie had left us?' Finn asked when Dorrie was out of the room.

'I went once, the year after she left. But she wasn't there. I didn't really expect her to be. Like I said, back then I believed she'd gone back to Belfast anyway.' He paused. 'When she phoned me up that time, wanting to see you, when she told me she'd left us because she was pregnant, I asked her about the childhood sweetheart. I thought it must be an Irishman, because she was brought up in Belfast. But it wasn't, Finn. The guy was English. Apparently his father had worked in Belfast in the seventies and Bridie and the lad went to school together. Bridie was in love with an Englishman. Or should I say an English boy. They were both fourteen when his family took him back to England.

'I think maybe Bridie had a thing for Englishmen. I think

that's why she fell for me. I think maybe I reminded her of him in some way.'

'Did you ever know his name?'

'No. She wouldn't tell me. She probably thought I'd want to settle a score. After all, he had stolen her from me – from us...' He blew out a long sigh. 'I should stop talking about it. It's giving me a headache. And it's not fair on Dorrie.'

'I'm fine with you talking about it, my love.' Dorrie came back into the room with a tray. 'Your boy deserves to know his heritage, his birthright. Every man does.'

She put the tray on the table and as she did so, Ray put his hand on her arm.

'Thanks.' His voice was husky. 'I don't deserve you.'

'Oh, yes, you do.' She perched on the arm of the sofa where he sat. 'You deserve the best of the best, Ray McTaggart. You're a good man.'

'I've got the best. I've got you.'

That was something he was completely in agreement with, Finn thought as he watched the look of love that passed between them. Dorrie was the best thing that had ever happened to his father. And he was so glad of it.

18

Jade had expected Declan to take her to the Red Lion, because it was the closest eatery, and they'd headed in that direction, but he drove straight past it.

'We can do better than that,' he said when she called him on it. 'There's a nice little country pub I know. It's not much further and it does way better food.'

Jade didn't feel entirely comfortable with this. She was beginning to wish she hadn't agreed to come, but she could hardly demand that Declan turn round and take her home again. That would have felt like an overreaction, so she kept quiet, looking out of the window as the darkening countryside flashed past.

Besides, she did trust Declan to behave professionally, because he'd behaved impeccably so far, and there was no reason she could think of that would make him change.

It still felt slightly wrong though when they drew up in the car park of a pub called The Stag's Head a few miles further towards Salisbury. She decided she would just have a very quick snack – possibly a starter if they did them – and then insist she needed to go home. She had to get up at the crack of dawn and couldn't have a late night. She was sure Declan would understand that.

A few moments later they were inside the pub, which had a selection of stags' heads dotted around its lounge bar and was what Jade and Finn would have described as a green wellie kind of place. This was code for upmarket and overpriced, and mainly frequented by city dwellers who got paid megabucks and/or had trust funds, and weekended in their country houses.

'We haven't booked but we'd prefer the restaurant, please,' Declan told the waitress who came to greet them.

'I'll see if we've got a table, sir.'

'I'd be quite happy in the bar area,' Jade added.

'It's fine – we have a table in the restaurant.' The waitress smiled at her. 'That'll probably be quieter too – I think the bar's very busy.'

'Thanks.' Declan glanced at Jade. 'Is that OK with you? We'll need to be able to hear ourselves speak.'

She nodded, feeling uncomfortable once more, but unable to argue with his logic.

Jade picked up the leather-bound menu the waitress had brought back to their table. Not a snack in sight, although she supposed she could have a starter. The only vegetarian option was watercress soup, which didn't sound very filling. But that would have to do.

'I can recommend the mushroom risotto,' Declan said, leaning across the table. 'Are you vegetarian? If not, the fish is good here too. And Chef's always happy to add and subtract ingredients. They cook everything from scratch.'

'I am vegetarian.' Again, he'd surprised her. 'Is it that obvious?'

'Educated guess. I wouldn't have thought a woman dedicated to saving animals would also be happy to eat them. Although I guess some with less integrity might be.' He snapped his menu shut. 'I'm going for the mushroom risotto myself.'

'Are you vegetarian?'

'I am if it's tasty.'

'I'll join you,' Jade said, making a split-second decision. She was pretty hungry, and if she was going to wait for him to finish a main course, then she might as well have one too. Mushroom risotto was one of her favourite things but she rarely had it because it was a faff to make, and Finn didn't like mushrooms. Finn was a confirmed meat eater and rarely ate much vegetarian food.

As soon as the waitress had taken their order and Declan had talked Jade into a glass of white wine – 'You might as well as I'm driving' – he got out a folder and laid it on the table between them.

'I know you're not here because of my charm and good looks,' he said with a smile in his voice, 'so let's get down to business, huh?'

He glanced up, and fleetingly she caught his gaze. There was something about him that was attractive. It wasn't a looks thing though. Maybe it was his slight air of self-deprecation. It was the same thing that had attracted her to Finn.

He was nothing like Finn. She reminded herself that he was her adversary. She imagined what Sarah would have said. Sarah didn't trust anyone until she'd known them for at least a year and had interrogated them thoroughly. Unless she was drunk, in which case all bets were off. She remembered the conversation they'd had this afternoon when she'd told Sarah about Declan.

'You are a lovely, generous animal-loving good person. He is a ruthless, grasping, property-developing baddie. With a black car.'

Jade smiled despite herself, and then realised to her embarrassment that Declan was watching her.

'Something I said?'

'No. I was miles away. Sorry. You were going to show me something.'

He pulled out some official-looking drawings with lines, numbers and measurements on, and laid them in front of her on the table. 'These are just drafts, but they're indicative of what we can do. I wanted to run them by you before I take them to Grandpa Nick. Make sure you're happy with what I'm proposing before I show him. Likely as not I'll just get the one chance to persuade him to change the plans. He's a tricky old sod.'

Jade looked at the plan, which showed Duck Pond Cottage and its land as well as Farmer John's land and the boundaries between them.

'This is the access point we're planning.' Declan put his finger on the drawing, which had a clearly marked access point in the field directly beside her property. 'As you can see, the original road goes straight from there, which means we need the land that directly abuts yours – i.e. the field you want to buy – but as I mentioned before, if we keep this access point but curve the road immediately away from your property, you could have most of the land you want. The proposed new road is the one with the dotted line.'

Jade studied the drawing for a few seconds. 'That does look good.'

'And see here' – Declan moved his hand across a little so it was very close to hers – 'this is the new boundary for the development. It would be good for you in another way too because the closest house to your land would have to go over a few metres. Does that make sense?'

'It does make sense.'

'Great. That's settled then.' He gathered up the drawings to slide them back in the envelope, accidentally touching her hand in the process but seemingly unaware that he had. 'Ah. Actually.' He paused. 'I'll leave you a copy of this – you might want to look at it again. I'll leave you a copy of the originals too. For comparison's sake.'

'Thanks.' She shifted the envelope he gave her from the table to her bag and sat back in her chair. For the first time since she'd met him, she was aware that Declan might have an ulterior motive for helping her. Her spider senses were kicking off. There was also a touch of her ex about him. Antonio, who'd been her last serious partner before Finn, had been a predatory womaniser and although Declan had done nothing to suggest he was the same, Jade was beginning to get an inkling he might be.

She decided straight talking was best. She gave him a direct look. 'Do you have a partner, Declan? Girlfriend, wife, significant other?' She could see his ring finger was unadorned but that didn't mean anything these days.

'I'm currently single. To be honest, I've only recently separated from a long-term partner.' He looked pained for a second. 'I won't lie. It wasn't an easy parting. Acrimonious would be an understatement. I've no plans to jump back into the fray. Once bitten, twice shy and all that.'

'I see. I'm sorry to hear that.'

What was it about him that made her have to constantly reevaluate her opinion of him?

Declan waved a hand. 'It's in the past. Best forgotten. Anyway… looks like our food is here.'

He was right. The waitress had arrived with two steaming fragrant plates of risotto decorated with chives and what looked like curls of crispy parsnip. Jade felt her mouth water as its delicious scent hit her nostrils – she was very glad she hadn't settled for soup.

'Can I get anybody any more drinks?'

Jade put a hand over her glass as Declan glanced at her. 'Not for me.'

He shook his head. 'I'm fine too, thank you.'

The food was, as he'd said, delicious, and for a while they ate in silence. Maybe it was the food and wine. Or maybe it was the gentle ambience of the pub, which was busy but not noisy – the tables being far enough apart not to be able to hear anyone else's conversation too clearly – but Jade felt herself begin to relax.

Declan was good company. He kept her entertained with building anecdotes, some amusing and some more serious.

'There was one site where we dug up some human bones,' he told her. 'The police had to come out and I thought there was going to be a full-scale murder investigation for a while – which would have spelled disaster for the development. Thankfully the bones turned out to be very old. In the end they dated them to be from around AD 200. Turns out we'd stumbled across an old Roman burial site. They said that at least one of the bodies was someone well-to-do because he was in a stone coffin. The rest were in wooden coffins and only the rusted-out nails were left.'

'What happened?' She stared at him in fascination.

'They had to be moved, of course. Some guys from the local archaeology trust turned up, and the bones were rehomed, so to speak.'

'Wow. Never a dull moment.'

'Exactly. But I'm guessing it's the same in the animal-rehoming world.' He batted the conversation back to her. 'Tell me some things about your work, Jade.'

She told him the story of the geese and the teenagers digging out the duck pond and the chain of people who'd filled it with water using buckets. 'I love the way that people pull together to rescue animals. It's heartwarming.'

'It really is.' He leaned across, touched her arm. 'You're amazing. You put me to shame. I don't do anything outside of work.'

'Well, if you ever want to come and volunteer for us, you'd be more than welcome,' she said.

'I'll give it some serious thought. Would you like a dessert?'

Jade realised the waitress was back at their table to collect their plates.

'I can highly recommend tonight's cheesecake,' she said on cue. 'It's lemon and ginger.'

'Oh my God, my favourite. Yes, please...' Declan broke off. 'I mean, sorry. Jade, how do you feel? I feel like I've taken up enough of your time. Your call?'

'I'd love to try the cheesecake too.'

It was close to eleven when they finally left The Stag's Head. So much for having a quick snack, Jade thought as Declan opened the passenger door for her before going back round to the driver's seat and climbing in. When she'd tried to give him her half of the bill, he'd told her not to worry, it had been put on his business account. In view of the extra amount the land was now going to cost her, Jade had let that one go.

But it had been a worthwhile evening. They had covered a lot of ground and it was good to know he was on her side. She was beginning to have very rosy thoughts about Rural Developments.

She was so relaxed she must have dropped off on the way

back because the next thing she knew the vehicle had come to a stop and Declan had turned off the engine.

'We're back, lovely Jade,' he said, and she blinked sleepily as she looked at the dim outline of his face.

'Blimey, I must be more tired than I thought.'

'I consider it a compliment that you trusted my driving enough to fall asleep. I'll see you to your door.'

'No need. I'm only a few steps away from it.'

'I insist. No gentleman abandons a lady without making sure she's home safe.' He glanced up and down the dark unmade lane and at the weeping willow that shrouded the duck pond on the opposite side of it. 'You never know who is around.'

Then he walked beside her to the front door of Duck Pond Cottage and waited patiently while she got out her keys.

'Thank you,' she murmured as she unlocked and pushed open the door.

'The pleasure is all mine.' Before she knew what was happening, he swooped in and kissed her. A peck, but it was definitely aimed at her lips, not her cheek. And he was right on target. She was aware of his breath on her skin, his eyes close to hers.

Startled, she shrank back from him. 'Er, no... Declan. I think you've got the wrong end of the stick. I'm...'

'Night, Jade.' He was already turning away, as if nothing untoward had occurred. 'I'll be in touch about the plans. Sweet dreams.'

Shivering slightly from the unexpectedness of what had just happened, Jade went in and closed the door firmly, then waited with her back to it, until she heard the Range Rover pull away. Mickey came to greet her, wagging his tail, and she bent to stroke his head.

'Bloody hell, Mickey, why did I not see that one coming?'

Mickey gave a soft humph of agreement and wagged his tail some more.

Sweet dreams, Jade thought as she put the deadlock on the door and went deeper into her cottage, were probably not on the agenda. She felt unnerved and somehow ashamed. Had she led him on somehow? What had she done or said to make him think she'd be up for a goodnight kiss?

19

Jade contemplated messaging Sarah. Was ten past eleven too late? She swore under her breath. Sarah rarely went to sleep much before midnight. A quick WhatsApp message wouldn't hurt. If Sarah's phone was off she wouldn't be disturbing her anyway. She was now wide awake, adrenaline coursing through her veins.

Had he meant to do that? He must have meant to do it. Why had she let down her guard? Why hadn't she stuck to her strategy of just having a starter? Why had she had a glass of wine? Why had she laughed with him? Had she encouraged him? Had she made him think it was a date?

She messaged Sarah.

> Are you awake? Need to talk.

Then she went into the kitchen and made herself a camomile tea.

Sarah called her on WhatsApp before she'd finished making

it. 'You're in luck. You caught me before I turned my phone off. What's up?'

Jade outlined the events of the evening, and apart from a couple of hmms and mmms, Sarah didn't interrupt until she'd finished. 'Tosser,' she said then. 'What is it with predatory men? That they think they can just dive in and have a grope.'

'He didn't do that.' Jade was afraid she'd overegged the situation. 'He just gave me a peck.'

'On the lips,' Sarah clarified. 'Lips are out of bounds for anyone but lovers. That's the rule. He knew that, Jade. He was just trying it on.'

'Do you think he was?'

'Of course he was. He knows you've got a partner, doesn't he?'

'He does, yes. I told him Finn was away.'

'I rest my case. Did you say you fell asleep in his car? Are you sure he didn't drug you?'

'I don't feel very drugged. No, I'm just tired.' She paused. 'Do you think I gave him the wrong impression, Sarah? I'm worried I must have somehow given him signals I was interested in him. I mean, he did say he was single. But he also said he wasn't looking for another relationship.'

'That's even worse.' Sarah's voice was heated. 'So what was he after exactly? If you ask me, he was testing the waters. If you'd shown any sign of responding to his kiss, he'd have been in the front door, hanging up his coat and hotfooting it up your stairs.'

Jade groaned. 'I've been an idiot. I let my guard down with him. I shouldn't have done. Up until that point it was a successful evening. He'd drawn up some new plans so I can still buy the field. He said he wanted to make sure I approved before he showed them to his grandfather – got an official yes.'

'It sounds to me like he was on a different kind of fact-finding mission tonight. He wanted to check if he could see his way clear to getting in your knickers. Not to put too fine a point on it.'

Jade swore under her breath. 'Do you think that means he's not going to try and get the plans changed after all? Now he knows that's a no-go.'

'I think you'll probably find out the answer to that very soon, honey. When's Finn back?'

'Tomorrow, fingers crossed.'

'Did you say he doesn't know anything about Rural Developments gazumping you?'

'That's right. I was going to tell him when he got back.'

'It might be best not to tell him about tonight,' Sarah said thoughtfully. 'It probably won't help if Finn goes up there and starts shouting the odds.'

'I know. And I feel terrible about that. It's one of our things – we don't have secrets – and now somehow we've got one. Arghhhh. How did I get into this situation?'

'You didn't. You haven't.' Sarah yawned. 'It will all look a lot better in the morning. Everything looks better in the morning. Besides, for all we know, that Declan chappie was just trying his luck, and it won't affect anything. He'll still be professional. You said he was professional up until that point, wasn't he?'

'He was. Totally.'

'Fingers crossed then.' Sarah yawned again. 'Let me know. And by the way, if you ever need any more ponds digging, let me know about that too. We've hardly had a peep out of Ben all evening and he went to bed half an hour early. He's very keen to come back and see the geese as soon as possible.'

'He's welcome any time.'

They said their goodnights and Jade went slowly up to bed

with Mickey at her heels. She hoped Sarah was right about Declan's professionalism. But only time would give her the answer to that.

* * *

It didn't take long for Finn to repack his overnight bag on Sunday morning, although Dorrie refused to let him leave without a full English breakfast inside him.

'Does your young lady let you cook bacon in her kitchen?' she asked him curiously as several rashers sizzled and spat in the pan.

'She does.' Finn sniffed the air appreciatively. 'She doesn't eat it herself, obviously, but she always says it's up to me what I eat, as long as I don't wreck her frying pan.'

'It's wonderful you can agree to differ, even when your opinions on something are total opposites. It makes for a healthy relationship.'

'It does.' Finn looked around his father's small kitchen. 'You two obviously talk about difficult subjects too – I mean, judging from the last few days.'

'Yes, we do. I don't think there are many secrets between me and your father.' Her bright blue eyes met his. 'I hope you didn't mind me stirring up the past, Finn. Persuading Ray to tell you what had happened. I hope my interfering's not been too painful.' She put down the spatula. 'I'm sorry if it was. I sometimes regret my big mouth.'

'I'm glad you "interfered".' He mimed the quotation marks in the air. 'If that's what you want to call it. I don't know what the outcome will be, about finding my mother, obviously, but I am definitely going to try. It's good to know Dad's OK with it too.'

'And we're both thrilled about the wedding. That's something we can definitely all look forward to.'

Ray appeared at the kitchen door. 'That smells good, my love. Morning, Finn. Thought you'd be gone by now.'

'Not without breakfast he won't. Morning, Pumpkin.' Dorrie blew him a kiss. Finn felt a warmth stealing through him. He'd never expected his dad to find a new partner, certainly not one as decent as Dorrie. Someone who wanted the best for him as well as herself. So often his dad had warned Finn there wasn't such a woman, and that if he wanted companionship he'd be better off with a dog. Ray had been so jaded about the whole subject of relationships and marriages and now that Finn knew how badly Bridie had hurt him, he could see why. It said a lot about his father's integrity that he was prepared to forgive Bridie now for the sake of their son.

But it was heartwarming to see how much Dorrie had changed things. How happy and easy around each other they seemed to be. He hoped he and Jade could stay the course too. He couldn't wait to see her now. To tell her properly about the past few days. It was so much easier to speak face to face about emotional stuff than it was to talk on the phone.

* * *

Finn had texted to say he'd be back mid-afternoon on Sunday, with luck, and Jade had been both really relieved and had felt a stomach crunch of anxiety. She couldn't wait to see him, but she was also painfully aware they needed to talk – not just about him finding his family but about the whole field thing.

It was 4 p.m. when his old Toyota drew into the yard, and Finn got out with the strap of his overnight bag slung over his shoulder. Jade was in reception, talking to Zack and his father.

The two of them had just brought over ten geese in a travel crate. She excused herself and went to meet Finn. Heedless of the volunteers who were milling about, she ran over and hugged him, and he hugged her back, almost lifting her off her feet.

'Hey, what a welcome. I take it you've missed me.'

'I have. I have. Was it a good journey? Did you have lunch?'

'Yes, and I didn't need lunch. Dorrie made me one of her breakfasts. What are you up to? Shall I just go and put this in the house?'

'That'll be great. I've got to sort out some geese.' She looked into his beautiful grey eyes and felt the tiniest twinge of guilt. Crap. She hadn't even wanted that kiss from Declan, and Sarah was right. She definitely couldn't tell Finn about it without causing all sorts of trouble. She rushed on. 'It's been relatively quiet for a Sunday. I think it's the Wimbledon final today.'

'Yeah, Dorrie mentioned that. I'll get changed and come back.'

'Come back?'

'To give you a hand with the geese?'

'Ah. Yes. Thanks.'

Mickey trotted out to say hello and Finn bent to stroke his head before striding into the house.

A few minutes later, Finn, Zack and his father and Jade were in the yard again, discussing the best way to get the geese up to the field.

'In the car's probably easiest,' Finn said. 'Shall I go ahead and then I can open the gates as you come. That way, we shouldn't lose too many hens while we get them in. I assume they're going in the hen field.'

'They are.' Jade dragged herself back to the business in hand. 'OK, let's do it.'

'Don't geese need a pond?'

'We sorted that out yesterday,' Zack told Finn enthusiastically.

'I don't know. I go away for five minutes and everything changes.' Finn winked at Jade. 'Have we taken in any other waifs and strays you haven't told me about?'

'A lovely white cat called Snowy. He shouldn't take long to rehome.' She smiled at him, and Finn felt some of the stress he'd been feeling lift from his shoulders. He might not be as besotted as Jade was with animals, but he loved her, and he loved this place. Even though he'd grown up in the sprawling metropolis of Nottingham, he knew his heart belonged in the countryside. Seeing the landscape slowly change from built-up grey to the patchwork of green and brown fields of the Wiltshire countryside as he'd driven home had felt like a balm to his soul.

'Right then.' Finn looked at Zack's father. 'Are you all right to take your car off road? Or do you want to transfer the crates to mine?'

'I'm good with off road. Zack can point me in the right direction.'

'Great.' To Finn's relief, Jade didn't seem as cool with him as he'd feared she might be. She was acting like her usual beautiful self.

Half an hour later, Operation Geese Rehome had been accomplished. Finn, Jade and Zack had introduced the ten geese to their new surroundings. As well as digging out a pond, Jade had put up some temporary fence panels around a smaller section of the field so that the geese and hens could see each other but not intermingle.

The four humans were standing on the hen side of the fencing, watching the geese mill about. A few curious hens had already come over to see who the intruders were.

'This way they can see and smell each other while they get

used to the idea of sharing their space,' Jade said. 'I figure a more gradual introduction is better than a sudden head on. It's less confrontational.'

Finn nodded his agreement. 'Confrontations are never good.'

Watching the geese reminded him of what Dorrie had said about the origins of the goose fair. Not that any of this lot would ever see a pot. They'd be able to live out their lives in blissful freedom.

'Penny for them?' Jade asked.

'I'll tell you later.' He glanced at Zack and his father, and Jade nodded. Now he was home he was keen to tell her everything, and he could see from the expression in her eyes that she needed some alone time with him too.

'I think I might lock up early tonight,' she said, confirming she was on his wavelength.

20

Sunday was usually the night Finn and Jade watched cosy crime dramas, curled up on the sofa together, with Mickey keeping a watchful eye on the TV to see if he could spot any baddies to bark at. But tonight after they'd finished supper, neither of them suggested switching the television on, although they did retire to the little back room.

Finn sat in the old armchair where he'd always sat before he'd known Jade as well as he did now, and Jade sat on the sofa so they were looking at each other's faces instead of side by side.

Jade had opened a bottle of wine and now she poured them both a glass and left the bottle on the round wooden coffee table between them.

'I want to know about everything that happened in Nottingham,' she told him, handing him his glass and taking a sip of hers.

Finn took a deep breath and bit by bit he told her it all, filling in as many details as he could remember. From the fact that his parents had met at the goose fair in Nottingham to the shock discovery that Bridie's childhood sweetheart had been in

England all along, which was why she still lived in England now.

'Caitlin, who's her sister, thinks they got married, but she couldn't tell me his name. They haven't been in touch for years by the sounds of it. Dad couldn't tell me his name either. I think he may have known it once, but he's blotted it out.'

'It's not something he'd want to remember, is it? Oh, Finn, how awful for your dad, finding out she'd already started a new family with him when she left you both.'

'Yes, I know. And I do get why he wouldn't let her see me. He must have felt so hurt and betrayed. I was angry at first. I felt like he'd stopped me from growing up knowing my mother, but it wasn't like that. They weren't married. He was scared she'd come back to take me away from him.'

'Bless him.' Jade leaned across and put her hand on his arm. 'Our parents have a lot to answer for, don't they, but we don't realise that they were dealing with stuff too. My mum always told me my dad ran for the hills when he found out she was pregnant. But for all I know he might have come back too.' She sighed. 'In my case there's no way of knowing. Anything that happened in the past died with my mum.'

'Is there no other way of finding out? Any other relatives you could ask?'

'No. Mum's parents died when I was about eight. I don't even remember them, but they were quite elderly then so they must have had her late in life.'

'Would you want to find out if you could?' Finn held his breath, knowing that her answer was really important because it somehow gave credence to what he wanted to do.

'I don't know, to be honest, Finn. I mean, I've thought about it, obviously, across the years. I've wondered if maybe my father wasn't as terrible as Mum made out. Maybe he just took fright and ran. Although that doesn't explain why he never came back again. Or never paid her any maintenance. After all, they *were* married. It doesn't really stack up.' She shrugged. 'Maybe he's dead.'

'Yes, I wondered that about my mother occasionally.'

'But if she is alive, you're keen to meet her and your half sibling.' Jade finished the sentence for him. 'How did Ray know the baby she was carrying wasn't his?'

'He said they'd had separate beds for a little while, so the timing was off. Would you mind if I met them?'

She looked startled. 'Oh, Finn, of course I wouldn't mind. Did you really think I might?'

'I don't know.' Had he? 'I thought that maybe...' He broke off and ran his hand through his hair. 'I was worried it might stir things up for you. Bad memories.' It seemed petty and short sighted now. Especially when she was looking at him with such surprise on her face.

'Your past is yours,' she said, reaching for the wine bottle and pouring them both another glass. 'It has nothing to do with mine.' Her hands were perfectly steady, he saw. Her voice composed. 'I get that you must have a million questions you want answers to – I would if it were me. And if you've got a chance to find out those answers, of course you want to try.'

'I'm so sorry, Jade. I should have told you sooner. In the beginning when I first realised there might be more to know than I'd thought, I wasn't sure what I wanted to do and it seemed pointless stirring things up if I wasn't going to do anything. And I felt similar when I went to see Dad. I wasn't sure he'd want to talk about it. It's been buried for such a long time. It was Dorrie's idea to tell me apparently. She felt I had a right to know the truth.'

'Good for Dorrie. Do you know why? Did she have a similar thing going in her past?'

'I don't know.' He felt a pang of regret. 'I was too wrapped up in my own stuff to ask her. Oh, crikey – maybe you're right.' He glugged his wine. 'I've been pretty selfish all round, haven't I?'

'No. No, I didn't mean that at all.'

He got up from the armchair and went and sat on the sofa beside her. 'Can you forgive me?'

'Finn, it's OK. It really is. There's nothing to forgive. I get it.' She leaned against him and he put his arm around her. 'It must have been a lot to take in.'

'It really was a lot.' He hugged her close, wanting to cry. He'd cried a few times lately. He'd cried more about the fact his mother had cropped up again – even if only in his head – than he'd cried when she had gone from his life.

He told Jade this now. 'Would you really not mind if I looked for her?'

'Of course I wouldn't mind. I'd support you whatever you did.' Her beautiful dark eyes were full of compassion, and Finn had never loved her more. For a little while they sat close together, without speaking, listening to the sounds of the house. Mickey's gentle snoring, the faint buzz the fridge made when it went into a defrost cycle in the kitchen. The creaks and clicks and stirrings of the old cottage as it settled for the night.

It was Finn who finally broke the silence. 'Are you OK? This has all been about me, and I haven't asked about you and we haven't spoken properly for days. Me being selfish again.'

He stroked her hair.

'Finn, you are not selfish. Never.' Jade could hear the emotion thickening her voice. It was so rare to see Finn totally vulnerable like this, all his emotions stripped bare, and she felt almost overwhelmed with concern for him and the longing to make him feel OK again.

'I'm good. I'm fine, although I do have things to tell you. But they can all wait until morning.'

'No, they can't. Tell me now.' She felt him shift beside her. 'I want us to be able to start tomorrow with a clean slate.'

'OK. Well, we've had a setback on buying the field.'

'Really?' He sat up straight again but still with an arm around her shoulder.

'Yes, you were right about the access.' She told him about Farmer John calling to tell her she'd been gazumped by Rural Developments. She told him about her visit to Declan Stone and the compromise she thought they had struck about them moving the layout of the access road. She hesitated to tell him about last night when Declan had manipulated her into going out to dinner with him. She wasn't even sure now that Declan had manipulated her – maybe she was being oversensitive about that. Reading things into it that weren't there. She hadn't imagined that kiss though. She took a deep breath and met Finn's eyes and knew in the next heartbeat that she couldn't tell him.

Not now. Not after he'd just laid himself so emotionally bare to her. After all, it wasn't as if anything had actually really happened. Declan had made a pass and she hadn't responded. End of story. She thought about what Sarah had said about Finn going round and punching Declan's lights out. It was a scenario she could imagine all too well, especially at the moment when he was stirred up emotionally enough. Thumping Declan certainly wasn't going to help anything.

'I'm hopeful we can get an agreement from Rural Developments,' she said instead. 'Declan's going to let me know as soon as he has confirmation.'

'Fingers crossed.' Finn turned his head to look at her. 'It's a pity the land next door has to be developed at all. But I guess it's inevitable. There's building going on everywhere at the moment, isn't there?'

'Yes. I think that's down to the government. They've got targets. One and a half million houses to be built every year for goodness knows how long. I suppose they've got to build them somewhere. On the bright side, hopefully at least some of the people who buy them will want to rehome a cat or dog.'

'That's another thing I love about you, Jade. Your unerring ability to look on the bright side.'

She smiled and closed her eyes for a second, because his glowing assessment of her made her feel even more guilty.

'Hey, it's late,' he said. 'You look worn out. We should get to bed. It's all right for me, I've had a few lie-ins lately, but you never get the chance. How about if we swap things round tomorrow? I'll get up early and do the breakfast rounds, and you can have a lie-in for a change?'

'We can play that by ear. I'll probably be awake anyway, and I can't just lie in bed and let you do all the work.'

'Yes, you can,' Finn said, catching hold of her hand and kissing it. 'In fact, I insist.'

21

Jade got her lie-in the next day, or more accurately she pretended she was still asleep long enough for Finn to bring her a cuppa in bed.

As he clunked the mug down on the bedside table, she opened her eyes.

'I'm awake.'

'Maybe I ought to get back in bed then and we can carry on from where we left off last night?' He winked, and she smiled and sat up.

'Or maybe I should just get up as usual, Finn. Really. I'm wide awake anyway. You know what my body clock's like. I might just as well get up and help you. But I really do appreciate the gesture.'

They both smiled then and drank their tea in bed and then they got up and slipped into the routines of the day, which now included a bunch of noisy geese, who were making their presence known. Luckily they were quite a way from the house.

As Jade fed dogs and cats and cleaned out kennels and catteries, snatches of the Saturday evening she'd spent with

Declan kept popping into her mind. The times his hand had touched hers when he'd been pointing out things on the plans, the laughter they'd shared, her falling asleep on the journey back, and then finally that unwanted kiss.

It had been a little like a date in some ways, although that had certainly not been her intention, but was it possible she'd given off signals and he'd misinterpreted them?

Maybe she had played a part in him getting the wrong end of the stick? She didn't think she had. She'd told him she had a boyfriend. Even so, she kept searching her memories, looking for clues, and ended up feeling discombobulated and uneasy.

She couldn't be sure she hadn't inadvertently led Declan on. The thought unsettled her. One thing she was sure about was that she would put him very straight next time she saw him. Perhaps it would be better if Finn was the one who dealt with him from now on.

Not that Declan had been in touch since Saturday night. In fact, Declan was conspicuous by his absence.

The following week passed without a word from him and Jade found this both a relief and a worry.

'I'd say it was a good sign,' Sarah said when Jade phoned and gave her an update. 'He's probably realised he's got no chance with you, and he's backed off. Good job.'

'I hope you're right. Do you think I should contact him?'

'No. I don't. He could be the kind of bloke that regularly tries it on. Maybe kissing clients he fancies his chances with is standard practice for him and he's moved on.'

Sarah sounded so cheerful that Jade felt cheered too. 'Yes, you could be right.'

'Just forget about him. He's bound to be in touch sooner or later about the plans. Have you said anything about him to Finn?'

'I haven't said we went out for dinner. Which means I feel guilty about it, doesn't it?'

'Yes, but you really shouldn't. You haven't done anything wrong. Anyway, enough of him. What did Finn say about the wedding venues?'

'He liked the Bluebell Cliff Hotel the best. What about Callum and Ben?'

'Callum loved that one too, and Ben was persuaded when I told him there were guinea fowl there, although he wasn't so keen when he found out they were on the menu.' She sighed. 'I probably shouldn't have told him that bit. He'll want to rescue them all.'

Jade knew how he felt, but she was more resigned to the realities of meat eating than Ben was. She realised Sarah was still speaking. 'It sounds like we're all on the same page then. Shall we arrange a time to go there and have a chat with them? Could you get Dawn to cover for you for an afternoon? We were thinking if we went in the week it would be less busy.'

'I'm sure Dawn would be happy to help. Is Ben coming with us?'

'He's not that keen to be honest. And I don't want to force him. He said he'd rather go to his mate Darren's for the afternoon than look around stuffy old buildings.'

Jade could imagine him saying that.

'OK, I'll ask Dawn which days she can cover. Wednesday or Thursday are best for her usually. She sometimes has her grandchildren on a Friday in the holidays.'

'OK, in that case maybe next Wednesday or Thursday could work? I'll check with Callum.'

'I'll check with Finn too.'

'How exciting,' Sarah said. 'Once we get the venue organised it's going to feel really real, isn't it?'

* * *

They booked an appointment for the following Wednesday. The Bluebell Cliff Hotel was in a spectacular location, perched on top of a Dorset headland, overlooking the English Channel. The headland was part of the world-famous Jurassic coastline. The beautiful golden sands of Studland Bay lay to the north and Swanage Bay lay to the south.

It was an hour and a half in the car from Duck Pond Cottage, but Sarah and Callum had both insisted it was worth the drive.

Sarah picked them up at ten. It was already a beautiful blue-sky day with warmth in the air and Jade felt as though she was skiving, even though, as everyone pointed out when she mentioned it, she very rarely had a full day off from the sanctuary.

There was a holiday atmosphere in the car, helped by Sarah starting off a round of 'We're All Going on a Summer Holiday'. Everyone joined in, even Finn, Jade noticed with satisfaction, because he always insisted he was tone deaf. He certainly didn't sound tone deaf to her.

By the time they reached the ruins of Corfe Castle, which was close to the Bluebell Cliff and one of the south coast's most spectacular landmarks, they were all in really good moods.

'Have you ever been up there?' Callum asked Sarah as the jutting pillars of grey Purbeck stone, high on a hill, came suddenly and spectacularly into view. The eleventh-century castle, built by William the Conqueror, was impressive, even in ruins. Now owned by the National Trust, it was a major tourist attraction.

'Yes, Jade and I went up for a picnic when we were teenagers. Do you remember, Jade? You had that ratty old Mini and we had a puncture on the way back?'

'It was worth it though,' Jade said, thinking back. 'The view from Corfe Castle is stunning. You can see all the surrounding countryside.'

'That's right. We pretended we were ladies from King John's court, drifting around the castle, issuing orders to our servants.' Sarah giggled and Jade joined her. It was rare to see Sarah in this mood – all loved up and happy. She forgot sometimes that before Ben had come along and Sarah had turned into a responsible mother and for a long time a single parent, she'd been a reckless wild child, always up for an adventure.

Sarah had suggested they go to Corfe Castle at night and climb up the hill, rather than go in the conventional entrance during the day. Jade had persuaded her the daytime would be just as much fun. And it had been, in spite of the puncture.

'We should all come again,' Sarah suggested as they drove past. 'Bring Ben.'

'Aye, I'd love to,' Callum said.

'Same.' Sitting beside Jade in the back, Finn squeezed her hand. She laid her head against his shoulder.

They should do more things like this. It was so easy to get tied up with the routines of Duck Pond Rescue that sometimes she forgot there was a beautiful world just on their doorstep.

Ten minutes later, Sarah pulled into the gravel car park of the Bluebell Cliff Hotel and they got their first view of the venue. It was a long, low, white-painted art deco-style building with a flat roof. Above their heads, a lone seagull squawked as it soared across the sky.

As Sarah had said, there was a disused lighthouse in the grounds, separate from the hotel, which had been refurbished to a luxury standard and was available to hire out for special events. From what they'd seen on the brochure, it was only big enough for one couple to stay there at a time. Jade wondered if either of them would stay there for their first night.

Being here, standing outside in the car park, breathing in the sea air, and the scent of roses and lavender which must be growing close by, made getting married feel incredibly real.

A few minutes later, they were inside a foyer that smelled sweetly of vanilla air freshener, and a bubbly receptionist with a name badge that said 'Zoe' had asked them to wait while she contacted Clara King, the manager, who would show them around.

Clara King, who was wearing a gorgeous pale lilac suit, turned out to be just as bubbly and nice as the receptionist.

'Before we start our tour, may I offer you a complimentary drink – or would you like to see around first, and have a drink later? I believe you have a reservation for lunch too, don't you?'

Sarah said that they did, and after some consultation, they opted for the tour first.

The Bluebell Cliff Hotel was beautiful, Jade decided as they were shown the restaurant, which had windows overlooking what she could see were extensive grounds, dotted with wooden picnic benches, wooden loungers, and was that a hammock in the distance? Lawns sloped down towards a fence, and beyond that they could see the strip of blue sparkle, which was the sea.

'We grow all our own veg here,' Clara told them. 'I'll show you our gardens when we go outside, but we'll check out our wedding venue first, shall we? You're in luck. We have a wedding here tomorrow so you can see it in all its full glory.'

She led them through to the back of the hotel and opened a door to reveal a large oblong room, full of light and flowers.

There were several rows of chairs, maybe five in each row, on either side of a wide aisle. At the end of each row of chairs were white candles in crystal holders with white ribbons trailing from them. A slightly raised stage, which was closest to them, was set up with a lectern. Tall vases of pink flowers were everywhere. They filled the room with their sweet scent.

'Wow,' Sarah said, eyes wide. 'Isn't it romantic?'

It was a rhetorical question. Jade knew they all felt it. She squeezed Finn's hand. He was looking around him with a sense of wonder. His usually inscrutable face was impressed.

Callum cleared his throat. 'In Scotland we'd say braw. It means excellent,' he added, although his explanation was unnecessary, Jade thought. It was obvious they all felt the same.

Beside them, Clara puffed up a little, like a proud mother hen.

'Our official honeymoon suite is in the lighthouse, although we do have another beautiful suite, here in the hotel too. It's a little more spacious and some people prefer it, and as you are two couples...'

* * *

After their tour, they had a scrumptious lunch in the restaurant, seated at a round wooden table in one of the window alcoves. Herbs grew in terracotta pots on the table and the sparkling cutlery was rolled up in white linen napkins.

By the end of their visit, they were all high on the atmosphere, and Jade knew they'd found their dream wedding venue. It was a little pricier but between them it would work. She couldn't believe they'd found somewhere so beautiful.

They'd provisionally booked their date for the following August with the ever-helpful Clara, paid a hefty deposit, and strolled back out to the car beneath a sky that was still blue.

'Even the loos were amazing,' Sarah breathed as they

climbed back into her car. 'Gorgeous toiletries and those little rolled-up hand towels.'

'My mother used to say you can always judge a venue by its loos. Relaxed luxury is the secret,' Jade said, aware of Finn's glance. She rarely talked about her mother.

'She was so right,' Sarah said as she reversed skilfully out of the car park, which was a lot fuller than it had been when they arrived. 'We've stayed in a few posh places, haven't we, Callum, but they have to be really good to get the loos right.'

'I can't believe you two are talking about loos.' Callum threw back his head and laughed. 'It's the food I'm interested in.'

'That's because cooking is in your blood, babe.'

'Fair comment.'

The banter continued much of the way home. Callum was still threatening to wear a kilt. They were still arguing about who would have the lighthouse suite. Jade thought Sarah should have it because she'd found the venue. Sarah thought Finn and Jade should have it because it only slept two and they wanted to be close to Ben in the main hotel.

In the back of the car, Jade squeezed Finn's fingers. She felt full of contentment. It was really happening. They had booked a venue. She was going to get married to the man she adored with the people she loved most in the world, Sarah, Ben and Callum. It felt amazing.

They got back to Duck Pond Rescue just after 5 p.m.

She'd had nearly a whole day off, Jade thought with a stab of guilt. It felt really odd.

'Some plonker's parked in my space,' Sarah said as she drew up behind a black Range Rover Sport outside the front gate.

'You can park by reception if I open the gate,' Jade said, recognising Declan's vehicle with a little twinge of anxiety. He was in it too, by the look of it. He must have only just arrived.

'It's OK, we should get back anyway. We've got to get Ben from Darren's.' She turned round in the driver's seat. 'It's been such a lovely day. I hope he doesn't spoil it.' She gave Jade a knowing look.

The last bit had been said in a stage whisper, but Finn looked at them both curiously.

'She doesn't mean Ben,' Jade explained. 'She means the guy in the car. It's the chap from Rural Developments.' She felt her face flush scarlet. Bloody hell, what bad timing.

'Would you rather I dealt with him?' Finn asked. 'Are you worried it's bad news?'

'It's fine, I can deal with him. You go on in.' Jade undid her seat belt. 'I'll take him into reception. I'm sure whatever he has to say won't take long.'

22

Jade felt her stomach clench as Finn took her at face value and walked ahead of her through the sanctuary side gate, and Sarah drove off in the direction of home.

She went to the driver's window of the Range Rover where she could see that Declan was doing something on his mobile phone. When he saw her, he slid down the window.

'Good afternoon, Jade. Good to see you again.' His eyes told a different story and Jade felt a sense of trepidation building.

'Is this a flying visit, or would you like to come in?'

'I'll come in for a sec.'

He followed Jade through the side gate. The main gates were already locked, Jade saw, and Dawn's car had gone. She had said she'd have to get back just before five so that was fair enough.

Jade unlocked reception and ushered Declan in.

'Please sit down.' She gestured to the visitor's chair. 'Would you like a coffee?'

'No. Not tonight.'

What was that supposed to mean? Jade looked at him uncertainly. Was he implying he'd have liked one when he was here before, or was she being paranoid? Reading things into the situation that weren't there?

He hadn't sat down either. He was standing very still in the middle of the small room. Behind him in his cage, Mr Spock was also very still. There hadn't been a peep from him since Jade had opened the door. That was unusual. She longed for him to break the silence with some silly saying – even a swear word would have done. Maybe the parrot could sense that Declan was bad news.

'So what's the outcome?' Jade asked, forcing a cheery smile onto her face.

'The outcome is that we are not able to sell you any of the land. The development will go ahead as per the original plans.'

'Er, can I ask why? I thought you said it wouldn't be an issue. That the access road could just be altered slightly. Did the Highways Agency refuse permission?'

'Nope.'

'Then what went wrong?' She felt a bit shocked. This was such a different Declan than the amiable, helpful man he'd been the other times she'd seen him.

'Rural Developments have decided they can't change the original plans.'

'Can't or won't?' Jade asked, feeling a surge of anger rising. There was something in his eyes she didn't like. Something hard and cold and unfeeling.

'Can't,' Declan said, and a little smile played around his mouth. There was no warmth in it at all. He shook his head and put on a mock apologetic expression as he shrugged and spread his hands, palms upwards.

'These things are always give and take, aren't they, and there was nothing in it for them. My company. No sweeteners, no advantages, no real reason to alter their plans...'

'Are you saying what I think you're saying?' She took a step towards him, feeling even crosser. 'Were we – was I – supposed to offer you some kind of sweetener? Bribe even.' She could feel her skin crawl at the flash of acknowledgement on his face, even though it disappeared almost immediately.

'You said that – not me.' He was smiling openly now. 'But if we're on the subject of sweeteners, you did get a pretty good dinner out of it, didn't you, Jade?'

'Come in, you bugger.' Mr Spock chose that moment to speak and it couldn't have been more inappropriate, Jade thought, before she registered a movement to her left and realised that Finn was standing just outside the door. Oh my God, had he been listening? How much had he heard of their conversation?

She looked at him. His face was blank, but she could see the iciness in his eyes. 'I thought I'd come and see how it was going?' Finn said in a voice that was dangerously calm. He shot a glance at Jade. 'You've been out to dinner with this guy?'

'Yeah,' Declan said. 'She loved it, didn't you, Jade. We had a right laugh before I brought her home.'

Jade closed her eyes, God, he made it sound so sordid.

'Is this true?'

'It was a business dinner, that's all.'

'Last Saturday,' Declan added glibly. 'We were out so late she fell asleep in the car. She was too tired to invite me in for coffee. Gave me a lovely goodnight kiss, though.'

Jade gasped. 'That's a lie.'

But the damage was done. Finn stepped into reception, strode across the room and punched Declan squarely on the nose.

He went down like a felled tree, and in that slow-motion moment of shock, the only coherent thought in Jade's mind was, thank goodness he didn't take the parrot cage down with him like Aiden had done. Mr Spock could have been hurt.

'Another one bites the dust.' The parrot launched into song, roused into action.

Declan was now curled up on the floor moaning, and his hands were covering his face. 'My dose. He's broken my bloody dose.'

After that, everything seemed to happen at once. Finn was trying to haul Declan up, presumably so he could punch him again. Jade was shouting at the top of her voice. 'Stop it. For God's sake, stop it.'

Declan was still moaning and Mr Spock, excited by all the action, was singing 'Another One Bites the Dust' at the top of his reedy voice.

Mickey, who must have come out of the cottage with Finn, was now growling and trying to get a hold on one of Declan's boots.

'Stop it,' Jade shouted again at Finn, who was still beside Declan, although if anything, he looked even more dazed than Declan did. All of a sudden, he let go of Declan and backed away. He looked as though he wasn't quite sure what had just happened. As if it was someone else, not him, who had floored Declan so efficiently.

Mickey let go too and looked at Finn as though waiting for further instructions.

Declan, as if aware that the danger had passed, struggled up into a sitting position, still holding his nose, which was blood-ied. He started muttering about assault and going to the police.

Mr Spock, oblivious to the human fiasco that was playing out in front of him, had got to verse two and had also gone up an octave.

Both men were red in the face. Jade could smell the testosterone in the air and feel the terrible mortification of shame. This was all her fault. She was responsible for this fiasco. She glared at Finn.

'I did not kiss him. He kissed me.'

'I'm glad you made the distinction.' Finn glared back at her. 'Or are you saying he forced you?'

'There was no forcing,' Declan objected, taking his hands away from his nose for long enough to look indignant. 'I don't need to force myself on my women.'

'I am not your woman,' Jade snapped at him. 'And I'm not yours either,' she said, glaring at Finn, who was looking faintly mollified. 'For goodness' sake, I can't believe what just happened here.'

Declan, taking full advantage of the fact Finn had backed off, clambered unsteadily to his feet. 'I'm going straight to the police. I'll have you up on an assault charge.'

'You need a witness for that,' Finn said, flicking him a contemptuous glance.

Declan stared at Jade. 'You'll both lie through your teeth then. Is that what you're saying?' He aimed a kick at the parrot cage and connected with the lower part of it, and Mr Spock stopped singing mid-song and made a sound like a hiccup as he lost his balance on the perch and lurched against the bars of the cage.

Jade took a threatening step towards Declan. 'Touch any of my animals again and I'll thump you myself.'

Declan backed away. 'You'll never get your land. We'll build all over that site, and we'll be there for months, making loads of mess and noise and more noise, scaring the living daylights out of every living thing for miles around. You're going to regret messing with us. I'm going to make damned sure of it.'

He stood in the doorway for a fraction of a second longer,

before turning and striding away towards the side gate. A few seconds later they heard him screech away on the dirt track outside.

Jade looked again at Finn, and they both spoke at the same time.

'That wasn't necessary.'

'What's been going on, Jade?'

He gestured for her to go first.

'Can we talk inside? I just want to make sure that parrot's OK.'

Finn turned abruptly away. 'Of course you do,' he said in a voice that was both weary and sad. 'I'll see you inside.'

Jade felt her eyes fill up with tears as he strode away. Partly shock, partly anger, partly sadness that the day, which had started so promisingly, had ended like this. She opened the door of the cage and held out a hand. After a few seconds of coaxing, Mr Spock moved onto her fingers. She gently drew him out and checked him over.

He submitted patiently and Jade was relieved that he was totally unharmed.

'Just a few ruffled feathers, hey, boy?' she said, returning him back to the cage and offering him a treat, which Mr Spock politely declined.

He put his head on one side and said quietly, 'Ding dong, the witch is dead.'

In any other circumstances, Jade would have smiled. But she didn't feel at all like smiling today. Shock was still numbing her brain.

She turned off the lights, locked up and into the cottage. She and Finn didn't often row. He wasn't often angry. Certainly she'd never seen any sign of violence in him. Even when Aiden had thrown a punch at him last summer, he hadn't retaliated. In fact, if anyone had asked her before today if Finn was a pacifist, she'd have said yes, he probably was.

So what had happened just now? Had Finn really thought she'd kissed another man or had Declan just goaded him into it? The way he'd spoken, the cockiness in his voice, had been enough to rile a saint. She and Finn had a lot of talking to do, but whatever Finn had thought, he surely hadn't been justified in hitting Declan.

OK, so she'd not told him about the dinner, but she hadn't lied to him. She hadn't been going behind his back. She still felt guilty as hell though.

She found Finn sitting in the lounge, doing something with a pack of peas and a tea towel.

'Are you hurt?' She moved quickly across the room.

'Yeah. I think I might have broken something in my wrist when I hit that muppet.'

'Let me see. Where does it hurt?'

'I thought you trained as a vet, not a doctor,' he objected mildly, but he moved the makeshift ice pack and showed her.

'I think you might have injured your scaphoid. You'll need an X-ray to be sure. And if you have broken it, it'll need treating.' She realised she was preaching to the converted. The resigned acknowledgement in his eyes told her he already knew.

'Yes, I know. When I was a first aider I saw a guy who'd done the same thing. That was after a fight too. Hopefully it's not broken. But I need to check. Painting's going to be out for a while if I have.'

Jade felt a wave of coldness as the enormity of that situation hit her. 'You can't stop painting. What about the exhibition?'

'Hopefully Eleanor will have enough of my work without me doing any more.' He blinked a couple of times. 'It serves me right. I shouldn't have hit him. I just saw red.'

She knelt on the carpet. 'Come on, I'll drive you to hospital.'

'Thanks.' He held the frozen peas against his wrist. 'I'll keep this on and keep my fingers crossed. Metaphorically anyway.' He managed a wry grin. 'We need to talk. But we can do that at the hospital. I need to know exactly what's been going on here, Jade.'

She felt another wave of shame. If she'd just told him everything before, none of this would have happened. She had a feeling it was going to be a very long night.

23

They discovered when they got to Salisbury A&E that the wait time to be seen by a doctor was running at around two hours. They took their seats in a room, crowded even on a Wednesday night, with people who had both visible and invisible reasons for being there, and they talked in low voices.

The enforced togetherness was probably a blessing, Jade thought, because otherwise she wasn't sure they'd have had such a difficult conversation. She wasn't sure which of them was the most mortified, herself for going out with Declan in the first place or Finn for hitting him because he thought he was protecting Jade. But at least they had a chance to properly talk. A chance for her to explain to Finn that Declan was in the wrong here. He'd knowingly overstepped the mark despite the fact Jade had told him she was spoken for, and then he'd deliberately overegged the situation to wind Finn up. Declan was not a man who liked to lose. Or one to be trusted.

She and Finn had time to properly apologise to each other, and to forgive each other. And she knew that part of the reason they could do that was because of the consequences of both their actions.

If Finn's wrist was broken, it had huge ramifications for him. No painting for the foreseeable future – his career might be over before it had begun. Jade felt terrible that she'd had a part to play in that.

They were finally seen two hours and fifty minutes after they arrived and Finn got his X-ray. Then there was another wait before they were ushered in to get the results. Jade held her breath. The lines of tension on Finn's face told her he was doing the same as they sat opposite the doctor, a slim, tired-eyed Asian man, who introduced himself as Dr Patel.

'You're lucky,' he said. 'It's not broken, just bruised. How did you do it?'

Finn told him. Jade could hear the embarrassment in his voice, but the doctor just nodded. 'It's not my place to judge. We see a lot of these breaks after drunken fights. People don't usually come in until the morning – that's when they realise it hurts.'

'I wasn't drunk,' Finn said. 'Which I guess is worse.'

The doctor didn't answer, just flashed them a rueful look. 'It'll feel better in a week or so. Take paracetamol if you need it. Drink plenty of fluids. Try and resist the urge to hit anyone else.'

They thanked him profusely and finally left the hospital around 2 a.m.

'I guess that's one of the reasons our NHS is in such a state,' Finn remarked as they got back in Jade's Land Rover. 'Self-inflicted injuries.'

'I think we've done enough beating ourselves up,' Jade told him firmly. 'Let's just draw a line under it and move on.'

He looked exhausted, and she felt exhausted too. The day had been an emotional rollercoaster. The joy of making plans to marry in the idyllic setting of the Bluebell Cliff Hotel to the stark crowded bareness of A&E. You couldn't get much more of a contrast than that.

'Is that how you feel about Rural Developments too?' Finn asked her as they drew out of the floodlit car park and onto the dark country roads towards home. 'Do you want to draw a line under it and move on?'

'Not exactly, no. I wasn't at all impressed with that little weasel's closing speech about developing the land. All that vitriol about making lots of noise and mess and scaring animals for miles around.'

'That's probably something he just said so he could get the last word. All building sites are noisy and messy. We're just going to have to grin and bear it, I guess.'

'Oh, no, we're not.' Jade shot him a look. 'They may have bought the land but they haven't got planning permission yet. He told me that much, and I'm going to do everything possible to make sure they don't. Declan Stone isn't the only one who can be difficult.' She felt a little surge of adrenaline. 'Don't worry, I'm not suggesting we have any more confrontations with the guy.'

'That's a relief. I don't think I'm cut out to be a boxer.' He paused. 'So what did you have in mind? Are you going to try and prove there's a species of rare bats resident in those trees?'

'That's one possibility.' She smiled, pleased he was on her wavelength. 'There's bound to be something I can do. I'm not sure yet.' She yawned. 'I'm too tired to think about it now. But tomorrow's another day. Declan Stone might think he's won the battle, but we're going to win the war.'

* * *

To Finn's relief, his wrist felt a little less sore the next day. He took painkillers as he'd been advised and Jade warned him to take it easy and not to lift anything heavy. He didn't plan to. The previous evening's events had shocked him. He'd never hit anyone before. He'd grown up an only child so he'd missed out on the rough and tumble of fighting with a brother and he'd never got involved in the frequent fights in the playground at school. He hadn't attracted the bullies because he'd been someone who didn't stand out from the crowd. He'd always been taller than average but not too skinny. He'd also been blessed with a quiet humour and wit that had meant it was easier to talk his way out of tight corners than to use his fists. This had served him well.

The strength of his emotions last night had also shocked him. The thought of that smarmy guy hitting on Jade when he wasn't around had made him see red. He'd always thought that was a myth too, the whole seeing red thing, but the adrenaline that had flooded his body last night had made thumping Declan seem like the only sane solution.

It was only afterwards, when he'd realised how close he'd come to ending up with such dire consequences – breaking his wrist would have been very bad – that he'd been really shocked. Remorse was in there too, but it wasn't nearly as strong as the instincts he'd felt to protect Jade's reputation, not to mention the plain old jealousy gene that had kicked in. He was ashamed of that but the shame, like the shock, had come afterwards.

Would he do it again? He hoped not, but he wouldn't have wanted to put it to the test. He was pretty sure that Declan flaming Stone would keep out of their way in future. The guy hadn't looked like he was suicidal, but there was no telling with some people.

Finn decided the best thing to do was keep some distance

between them. The idea of Jade fighting to stop the development, which had seemed pretty logical in the early hours of this morning, now worried him a bit. Maybe it would all blow over. Time was a good healer, and did anyone ever really stop developments from going ahead?

When he thought of protestors, the first image that sprung to mind was of people tramping through fields with placards or chaining themselves to trees or diggers. Did any of it ever really make any difference or did the developers just bulldoze their way over the locals' opinions?

He hated the thought of Jade going head to head with a development company that clearly had deep pockets and then being smashed out of recognition like the land they had purchased.

It would be better if he could get her to focus on something else. Something positive like their wedding plans, and the forthcoming exhibition, which was looming. It was on the third Saturday of September, seven weeks away. He still needed to finish some paintings for that. Not the ones they were displaying – they'd all been chosen and were ready – but if they sold, which Eleanor kept telling him was the whole point, then he'd need to have replacements ready for other buyers.

They were all going to the art exhibition. Finn, Jade, Ben and Sarah and Callum. It still seemed like a dream. But the occasional phone call from Eleanor made it real. Made Finn realise he could be on the brink of launching his career as an artist. Having an agent like Eleanor supporting his work was massive.

There was also, of course, the small matter of finding Bridie. Having set that particular hare in motion, Finn didn't want to give up on it. Since he'd come back from seeing Dorrie and Ray, he'd done nothing further to track down his mother. He hadn't even googled her name with the new location. Finding out that she lived so close – Southampton was less than an hour away from Arleston – had been a revelation. He wasn't sure why he'd done nothing else about tracking her down. Fear of what he might find, possibly.

* * *

As August got into its stride, bringing with it swathes of pink rosebay willowherb growing in the dog-walking field and impromptu blackberry and apple picking – it was a great year for blackberries – Finn began to stop worrying so much. As Jade had predicted, they had an influx of new volunteers because the schools were on holiday now, and it was brilliant to have Ben around so much. Ben, as Sarah often pointed out, would have lived full time at Duck Pond Rescue if he could.

Sarah and Jade had drawn up a guest list for their wedding and sent out 'save the date' cards for the third Saturday in August the following year. Ray and Dorrie were thrilled and had already booked their room in the Bluebell Cliff Hotel for the first night. Dawn was on the guest list, but she had said she was more than happy to come straight back after the wedding and stay over at Duck Pond Cottage so Finn and Jade could have at least one night away.

Jade hadn't mentioned the war with Rural Developments again, although Finn noticed she'd been researching things like 'protected species in the UK' and 'How wildlife can affect your next property development' on the computer in reception.

He didn't ask her about it, deciding that maybe one of his father's favourite sayings, 'Least said, soonest mended', did have some merits in certain circumstances, and life at Duck Pond Rescue jogged along peacefully. Animals came in and were rehomed at much the same rate. The summer was beautiful and he and Jade were happy. In some strange way, him hitting Declan had brought them closer because it had made them talk – really talk – about the things that were important. Finn was just starting to relax and think about searching for Bridie again when two things happened.

The first thing was that someone called Thomas O'Leary had come up on his Facebook feed marked as someone he might like to befriend, and when he looked into it he saw they had a mutual friend, Caitlin Neale – that was promising.

The second thing was that Jade said she wanted to introduce him to someone, who she said might be able to help in their quest to stop the development going ahead next door.

They were in the Red Lion, having margarita pizzas, at the time. It was one of the few Friday nights when they didn't have Ben and they'd just finished eating when Jade told him about the person she wanted him to meet. 'She works for the local council and she's also a volunteer. You may have seen her – she's a bit sporadic about volunteering because she has trips away quite often, but she's quite distinctive. Tall with dark skin and white hair. I think she's half-Jamaican. Her name's Ursula.'

'I think I know who you mean. Older lady? Likes cats? Posh voice.'

'Yes, that's the one. I first met her when she brought in her neighbour's cat for rehoming. The neighbour had died and the family couldn't keep him. Ursula said she'd have kept him herself, but she quite often has to go away on field trips apparently. His name was Snowy. We rehomed him quite quickly. He was very pretty. Anyway...' She shook herself, as if getting back on track. 'None of that's relevant. What is relevant is that Ursula is an ecologist.'

'And that's important because...?' Finn asked, although he had a feeling he knew exactly where this was going.

'Because Ursula knows all there is to know about planning and developments. Like for example...' Jade's eyes were shining with enthusiasm. 'All the endangered species that will stop a housing development from going ahead.'

'I see. So what has Ursula said about next door? Are there any endangered species on the site?'

'I'm not sure, but she's happy to give us some advice. Unofficially, of course, because she does actually work for the council who may or may not grant permission. The thing is, she's on our side. She's very sympathetic to the cause. I've told her all about Rural Developments and the muppets who work for them. One muppet anyway.'

'Okaaaay.' Finn drew out the word. He hoped Jade hadn't told Ursula about him hitting the muppet in question.

'I didn't mention the, er, altercation you had,' Jade said, reading his mind. 'I just told her in a general sense, you know, about how he'd made promises and then gone back on them when he realised I wasn't going to be part of the deal.'

'Right.' Finn nodded sagely. 'What did she say?'

'She said...' Jade broke off. '...I think I'll let her tell you that herself. She's meeting us for a drink.'

'What, now? Tonight? Is that why you were so keen to come out?'

'Yes, and I think I've just spotted her.' Jade leapt up from her chair. 'She's over at the bar, talking to Mike. You don't mind if I bring her over, do you?'

'Of course I don't.' Finn sat back in his seat as Jade headed across the bar. Jade was still obviously hellbent on fighting Rural Developments. So much for a quiet life then.

24

As Jade got back with Ursula Hargreaves in tow, Finn got up to greet them.

Ursula, whose corkscrew curls were up in clips tonight, smiled and held out her hand. She had twinkly brown eyes. 'Finn, I think we've seen each other at a distance, haven't we, but it's lovely to meet you officially.'

Finn added slim fingers to his first impressions as he shook her hand. She was also older than he'd thought, mid-to-late sixties, but something about the energy she exuded reminded him of Dorrie.

'It's great to meet you, officially, too. Can I get you a drink?'

'We've just ordered,' Jade told him. 'Mike said he'll get someone to bring them over.'

'Great.' They all sat down again.

'Jade tells me you work for the council.'

'That's right. I'm in the planning department. For my sins.' She laughed. 'Although it's quite a good job to be honest. Pays the bills. Gets me out and about a lot – which I love. I'd hate to be cooped up in an office.'

'Something we all have in common,' Jade said happily.

'But to get down to business,' Ursula began. 'I understand you're interested in the ins and outs of developments. Protected species surveys to be precise.'

'We're very interested,' Jade said. 'I understand bats are a protected species. Is that all bats or just certain types?'

'It's all bats and their roosts,' Ursula said. 'They tend to roost in old buildings. Are there any old buildings on the site you're hoping to purchase?'

'I don't think there are any old buildings on the bit we're after but there are loads of old buildings on the site as a whole. Does that mean that planning would be refused on the site?'

'Not necessarily, but if there were bats some works might have to be delayed. There are, for example, times when bats shouldn't be disturbed. Building work would need to be carried out either in April or between mid-September and the end of October when bats are least likely to be present.'

'So it wouldn't stop the work altogether then?' Jade said, disappointed.

'Not necessarily. Although you wouldn't want the buildings to be demolished, of course, which is what development companies are likely to want to do. The two main rules being that you can't disturb bats at certain times of year and you must leave them access to their roosts. The million-dollar question would be' – she leaned forward and rested her chin on her hands on the table – 'are there any bats in the buildings?'

'We don't know,' Finn said.

'We could have a look,' Jade added hastily.

Finn glanced at her, realising she must be planning to sneak over and have a look herself. So much for leaving things be then.

'What else is protected?' Jade asked Ursula, avoiding Finn's gaze. 'It can't just be bats.'

A barmaid brought their drinks to the table and put them down, and for a moment the conversation was halted.

'You're right. It's not just bats,' Ursula continued as soon as the barmaid had gone again. 'There are a few species that can't just be culled.' Her brown eyes grew thoughtful. 'Barn owls are a protected species. As are badgers and dormice, and certain reptiles. Are there any ponds on the land? Ponds are also the home of several protected species, although depending on the location these might be easier to preserve. Ponds are the homes of Natterjack toads – they're on the list as well, if my memory serves me correctly. And some newts.'

'There's bound to be a pond somewhere over there. This is quite a wet area.' Jade chewed her lip thoughtfully. 'So are you saying that any of these species would stop a development going ahead then?'

'Any of these species, if found on the land, may stop a development going ahead.'

'So if someone was to find, say, just one stray dormouse running around in the fields over there, even if they were just temporarily over there, and take a photograph of it running around somewhere prominent, then the whole development may have to be called off?'

'I think I'll pretend I didn't hear that question,' Ursula said, narrowing her eyes and shooting Jade a look of mock horror. 'But theoretically, yes. Although I'd say it would have to be more than a lone dormouse. Probably more of a family group.'

'Dormice are so cute,' Jade said reflectively. 'They've got big ears, haven't they? In comparison to the rest of their bodies, I mean.'

'That's right. The dormouse is one of Britain's rarest species,' Ursula said.

They talked on for a while about protected species and

Ursula told them how the dormice population had been increased lately, thanks to the work of conservation groups like the Wildlife Trust. 'The groups put out nesting boxes and monitor populations,' she said. 'They shave a little patch of fur from the heads of the dormice they're monitoring for identification purposes. They're doing great work. Now then, it's my round, I believe. Would anyone like another drink?'

While she went to the bar to get them, Finn caught Jade's gaze.

'You're really serious about this, aren't you?'

'Of course I am. How about you? Do you fancy coming on a dormouse expedition with me?'

Sighing inwardly, Finn nodded. 'I'll support you in whatever you want to do. You know that, Jade. But we will need to tread carefully. We can't go trampling on too many laws. We'd be trespassing for a start if we went wandering about next door. It's not like it still belongs to Farmer John.'

'No one's going to see us if we go in the dark. I'm an expert on rehoming animals, Finn. Relocating them from one place to another, making sure they're safe. It's what I do. It's what Duck Pond Rescue is here for.' She gave him a sweet smile, and Finn nodded again.

He couldn't exactly argue with that logic.

* * *

The following evening, when Jade was doing some research on dormice on the reception laptop, which she'd brought into the back room, Finn sent Thomas O'Leary a message.

He explained he was searching for Bridie Neale, who he understood now lived in Southampton, and that he'd be grateful if Thomas could give him any more information.

The answer came back more quickly than he anticipated. Thomas obviously signed in to his Facebook account a lot more often than Caitlin did.

> May be able to help, but let's speak on the phone. Then I can make sure you're not a bot or a scammer.

Thomas wasn't one to mince his words then, Finn thought as he typed in his number and pressed 'Send'.

His mobile rang about ten minutes later and Finn jumped out of his skin as he saw the unfamiliar UK mobile number. There was no Irish prefix like there'd been with Caitlin. He snatched it up, praying his one bar of signal would be enough.

'Finn McTaggart speaking.'

'Hey, Finn, how are ya?' The Irish accent was even stronger than he remembered from when he'd spoken to Caitlin.

'I'm good. Thanks for phoning.'

'What was your connection to Bridie then now? Did you say?'

'I didn't but I'm trying to track her down for my dad.' Finn trotted out the same spiel he'd said to Caitlin, unsure of who he was talking to. 'They were friends back in the early nineties when she was living in England. We always thought she moved back to Belfast in 1998, but Caitlin told me she stayed in England.'

'Aye, that's right, she did. She's still in England, far as I know.'

Finn hesitated. 'Do you mind me asking what your connection is to Bridie?'

'I'm her nephew. One of her nephews, I should say.' Thomas chuckled. 'There are a lot of us. I'm one of the ones who left the home country – most of them stayed in Ireland.'

Finn felt a stab of shock. So Thomas was his cousin, or half cousin at least, and by the sound of it there were lots more.

'Are you Irish yourself, Finn?'

'Half Irish. My dad's English.'

'And where are you living yourself, Finn?'

'I'm near Salisbury. Wiltshire.'

'Grand, same as myself. We're neighbours then.'

Finn felt another jolt of shock. It felt so weird to be talking to someone who was related to him. He'd had the same feeling when he'd spoken to Caitlin, but she'd been far away in Ireland. An untouchable aunt.

This was weirder because Thomas was right here in Salisbury. In touching distance, and he sounded like he was a similar age. He pulled himself back to the moment, remembering what his mission was.

'I don't suppose you happen to have a current address for Bridie?'

There was a pause on the line and Finn held his breath.

'Sure I do. But I should really ask her if it's all right to pass it on. What's your da's name?'

Finn's heart sank. So near and yet so far. Trust him to be in touch with a security-conscious cousin. 'It's Ray,' he said quietly. 'Ray McTaggart.'

'That's grand. Let me speak with Bridie, and I'll get back to you, Finn, so I will.'

'Thanks,' Finn said, realising the line had already been disconnected.

He felt like screaming. Maybe he'd have done better if he'd just told Thomas who he was, but he was still so wary of throwing a bombshell into a family that possibly didn't know of his existence. He decided he couldn't just come out with it. It wasn't fair.

At least Thomas had said he'd speak to Bridie. So she would know exactly who was looking for her. That was a good start.

He went to find Jade, who was still tapping away on the laptop downstairs. 'I think I just talked to one of my cousins.' He told her what had happened.

'Oh, Finn. That must be so frustrating.' Her eyes were gentle as she closed the laptop lid. 'I'm really sorry. Do you think he'll pass the message on?'

'I think he will, yeah. He's probably curious. He was curious enough to phone me anyway.' He gave her a wry smile. 'I was worried about the signal holding out for the whole conversation, but that was fine. Turned out to be Thomas who was holding out. Typical.'

'He's got your number though, hasn't he? So Bridie could actually phone you back.'

'She could. Yeah. Oh, God. I hadn't even thought about that. I'd better get my phone.' He ran back upstairs to get it and when he did, it nearly slipped from his hand, his fingers were so sweaty. If this was what tracking down your past felt like, Finn was no longer sure he wanted to do it. He closed his eyes. For the first time since he'd started on his quest to find his mother, he wondered whether he should just call the whole thing off.

Not that calling it off was as simple as all that now. If Thomas did get in touch with Bridie then she'd know exactly who was trying to find her. The whole thing was in Bridie's hands now, not Finn's. He'd rolled the metaphorical ball over the crest of the hill and there was no way he could stop it now. The outcome was in the hands of fate. Finn kept telling himself he was happy however it went. He had Ben and Jade and Ray and Dorrie. He would always be a winner in life, no matter what happened with Bridie.

25

This didn't stop Finn from being on tenterhooks for the next couple of days every time his mobile rang. But there was no return call from Thomas O'Leary. And no other unknown number tried to reach him. Or if they did, they didn't get through. For the first time since he'd lived at Duck Pond Cottage, he cursed the lack of signal.

Apart from the odd occasion when he had to make an important phone call like the one he'd once made to Eleanor Smythe, he quite enjoyed the fact that it was difficult to get hold of him. It made for a peaceful life. He and Jade WhatsApped or used Wi-Fi calling if they needed each other, and Ben did the same if he wanted to speak to him. So did Dorrie and Ray, these days.

But right now Finn just felt on edge.

'Do you think I should try calling Thomas again?' he said to Jade when the radio silence continued into another weekend. 'If Bridie doesn't want to have anything to do with me, I get it, but I really need to know.'

'I don't think it could hurt. Like you say, at least you'd know.

And it is possible that Thomas just hasn't done it yet. Or maybe she hasn't got back to him. Or maybe she has and he hasn't got back to you. It must be agonising.'

'It is.' He didn't remember ever feeling this edgy. He touched her hand. 'I'm sorry. I must have been hell to live with this last week. I haven't even asked how things are going with you? What's happening as regards dormice?'

'Not a lot, to be honest. There's no signs of any dormice activity next door. Or any bat activity, or badger activity or any other kind of protected species' activity, come to that.' She sighed. 'Ursula came over with me to check out all the possible habitats. And I know I joked about cheating and planting a few dormice, but I've discovered English dormice aren't easy to come by. They have a really long hibernation period, six months or more – that's where the name comes from, apparently, "dor" – meaning dormant. Anyway, it's not as easy as I'd hoped it might be to find a family that need rehoming.'

She smiled. 'I could probably get hold of some African ones – they're sold as pets. But no one's going to believe that they just happen to be living next door to us. Also... joking aside, I'm not sure how responsible it would be to relocate a family of dormice. What if they don't survive? That's not really what we're about, is it? Endangering a creature's life. We're here to protect them.'

'Even when it's for the greater good,' Finn said, and he felt a rush of love for her as he saw her startled expression. 'No, I guess it's not. So what next?'

'I'm not sure. Maybe you were right. Maybe we should just grin and bear it.' She put her head on one side. 'Or maybe I should think about relocating this place instead. Move somewhere there isn't going to be a housing estate built right next door.'

'Move the mountain to Mohammad, you mean?'

'Exactly that.'

He put his arms around her. 'We can't fight everything,' he said gently. 'Well, we can but sometimes if something's too hard it may mean it's not meant for us. My gran used to have this neat saying, "What's for you won't go by you." Meaning if something's meant to be, then it will happen.'

'I wish I'd had the chance to meet your gran.'

'I wish you had too. She'd have loved you.'

Finn knew he hadn't just told Jade about his gran's saying for her – it was for himself too. Maybe he wasn't meant to meet his biological mother. Maybe Ray had been right to keep them apart for all of those years, after all. He decided not to phone Thomas back. He'd give him another week or so.

* * *

'I have never heard such a load of defeatist, wet-blanket twaddle in my life,' was Sarah's opinion of the situation when Jade went over to see her for a chat about wedding cakes on Sunday afternoon. 'From either of you. I can't believe you're throwing in the towel so easily.' She tossed a couple of leaflets onto the table. 'I think we should go with Olivia Lambert at Amazing Cakes. She's the cake maker the Bluebell Cliff recommended. Her cakes look wonderful and she's got zillions of reviews. Anyway, about these dormice.' She gave Jade a searching look. 'Surely you're not giving up that easily?'

'What would you suggest? I can't get hold of any English dormice for a start.'

'You don't sound like you've tried very hard. They're native, aren't they? Why don't we just go and look for some? They must be about.' She scrolled through her phone and tapped on some screens. 'Here you go. Apparently you can find them in Sussex, Devon and Kent. They live in woodland. They're not hibernating in August, are they?'

'No, but they are nocturnal.'

'What difference does that make? We can go at night.'

Jade rolled her eyes in exasperation. 'So are you suggesting we rock up in some random woodland and pitch a tent?'

'*Yes*, I am. It says here they spend most of their time in trees. They're not even on the ground much. It can't be that hard locating a mouse that's tight roping along a tree branch, can it?'

Jade laughed despite herself. 'No. If you put it like that. Apparently when the Wildlife Trust are monitoring dormice, they shave little patches of fur from their heads for identification purposes. Ursula was telling me.'

'Even better. We can look out for a tight roping dormouse with a Mohican. Ben and I can come with you. Mission Mohican Dormouse. It'll be a great thing to do for his summer holidays.'

'You hate camping.'

'I know, but Ben would love it. All that nature and stuff. You can get Finn to look after the rescue for a couple of nights and you and I can chat weddings in our tent and Ben can keep watch for dormice and yell if he sees any. It'll be brilliant and—'

Their conversation was interrupted by Ben dashing into the lounge. 'Mum, Mum. I've found a hurt... Oh, hi, Auntie Jade. I just tried to call you. I didn't know you were here. Can you come? I've found a fox. She's not very well.'

Sarah and Jade exchanged glances. 'Slow down,' Sarah said. 'Did you say a fox? Where is it?' She shot Jade a look. 'It's a good job you're here. Aren't foxes dangerous? Ben, you mustn't go near it. You hear me?' Her son was already running out of the door again.

Both women leaped to their feet too. For the moment, Mission Dormouse was abandoned.

The orangey-red fox was at the bottom of Sarah's small back garden, half in and half out of a rhododendron bush. Jade could see its front end sticking out, its rear end concealed in the shrubbery. It was panting slightly and it regarded them with wary brown eyes but didn't attempt to move or run away.

'Ben, don't go too close,' Sarah called. 'Let your Auntie Jade deal with this. She's the one with the vet background.'

'I'm not too close.' Ben shot her a defensive glance. 'Anyway, she won't bite me. She trusts me.'

'How do you know it's a she?' Sarah asked as Jade stopped a little distance away and crouched down on the yellowing grass. 'Can you tell, Jade?'

'Not easily. I'd need to get a bit closer. Ben, lovely, I'm going to need your help. Would you have such a thing as gardening gloves in your shed?'

'I think so.'

'Can you get them for me, please, and also leave the shed door open?'

He ran to oblige and Jade glanced at Sarah. 'I think it's going to be tricky to catch this fox. It depends on how badly it's injured. But I'm hoping we can maybe herd him or her into the shed and find out. Is your garden fully enclosed?'

'I think so. I'm guessing it must have come in the side gate. Or over the back fence, although if it's injured that would have been quite difficult.'

'First things first.' Jade stood up slowly. 'I'll see if I can get a bit closer and have a look.'

Ben ran back with the gloves and handed them to her.

'Did you see the fox walking at all, Ben?'

'I did. She was limping at the back. She couldn't put her foot on the ground. Do you think it's broken, Auntie Jade?' His grey eyes were anxious.

'That's possible, love. I'm going to try and see. It would be really good if you and your mum could stand a little bit closer to the house, blocking the back gate. Then if she tries to run, hopefully she'll go towards the shed.'

They did as she suggested and Jade put on the gloves and went gingerly towards her prospective patient, speaking softly all the while.

The fox didn't move until the last minute and then she shot out, gave a small yelp, and stopped again before sinking down onto her belly, her straggly black-tipped tail lying on the grass. It was clear she couldn't go too far. There was a nasty gash on her side nearest to Jade and her back leg looked broken.

'I think she may have been hit by a car.' Jade backed off to give her some space. 'OK. I'm going to message Finn and ask him to bring the transporter over if he's not too busy. That'll be the quickest way to do it. If you guys are OK with that?'

'That would be great,' Sarah said. 'Can you tell if it's a she or a he?'

'Not really but more likely a she – they tend to be smaller, and she's tiny. Could just be young, of course.'

'Can you make her better, Auntie Jade?' Ben's eyes were hopeful. 'Like you fixed the broken wing on the red kite?'

'I think we're going to need a proper vet for this one. But I shall do my best,' she promised.

* * *

It took an hour and everyone's help to capture the little fox, transport her back to Duck Pond Rescue and settle her in the hospital block-cum-quarantine kennels, which luckily weren't in use at the moment.

Jade called Aiden, who was a personal friend as well as her vet, and he promised to call over in the next hour or so.

'Are you sure, Aiden? I feel bad calling you out on a Sunday.'

'I'm on call anyway, so you're in luck.' She heard his smile in his voice and true to his word, he arrived just after seven.

'She'll need to be tranquilised for me to have a proper look at her,' he murmured as Jade and Finn let him in. 'So I'll go and do that first. Can you give us a hand for two minutes, Jade?'

Half an hour later, Aiden had examined the now drowsy fox, which was a female, as Ben had guessed, and given Jade his assessment. 'She's lucky it's the back leg, not the front. That would have finished her. It's not a major break, and it should heal without too much trouble, if she's in a contained space, but the gash is nasty and prone to infection. So I'll stitch that up. I'd normally do that in a more sterile environment, but we can make do – and it'll probably be less stressful for her if she can recover here, rather than at the practice. We'll get some antibiotics into her too.'

Jade nodded.

'After that if you can feed her and keep her here for a couple of weeks, we can monitor it. Would you be OK with that?'

'Of course. That's why we're here.'

Jade helped hold their patient in the right place while Aiden worked. He was quick and efficient and Jade decided he was right. It was far less traumatic for the fox to be attended to here than being moved again.

'With luck and some care she'll heal fine,' Aiden said as he finished up.

'Ben will be so thrilled. He's already called her Carmelita – after a fox in a game apparently.'

Aiden shook his head. 'Kids, huh. How is Ben doing anyway?'

'He's as mad about animals as ever. He's going to be a zookeeper when he grows up apparently. At least that's the latest thing. He loves painting too, but he doesn't want to go to art college because he thinks he'd have to spend too much time indoors.'

'It's a bit early to be deciding that, isn't it?' Aiden looked amused. 'How old is he now?'

'Seven.' Jade smiled at him. 'I knew what I wanted to do when I was seven. Didn't you?'

'Nope. I didn't know I wanted to be a vet until I'd left school. It was my Uncle Seth who pointed me towards vet college.'

'We're all different.' She watched him packing away. 'How's life treating you, Aiden? How's that lovely girlfriend of yours?'

'Kate's good, thanks, Jade. We're both really well. We're off on holiday at the end of August. I'm taking her to Venice.'

'How romantic.'

'I hope so.' His eyes warmed. 'Can you keep a secret?'

'Of course.'

'I'm planning to propose to her there. On a gondola.'

'Oh, that's brilliant,' Jade said, thinking how typical of Aiden that was. He'd always been a totally idealistic romantic.

'Do you think she'll say yes?' He looked suddenly uncertain.

'I'm sure she will,' Jade said, thinking of the gorgeous Kate, who was a nurse at Odstock Hospital and was totally besotted with Aiden. She clapped her hands together, forgetting their surroundings for a moment, and Carmelita blinked sleepily.

'Ooops, I think we'd better leave her to recover,' she said. 'Thanks so much, Aiden. How much do I owe you?'

'Don't be daft. I've only been here ten minutes.'

'We both know that's not true! Come in for a drink then. Have you had supper?'

'I've had supper but a coffee would be lovely. Thanks for the "save the date" card for your wedding, by the way. Nice idea doing a double wedding.'

They walked back to Duck Pond Cottage and Jade thought how much had changed since she'd first met Aiden. When she'd set up the sanctuary, and asked him to be her vet, Aiden had had a bit of a thing for her. He'd even warned her off Finn when she'd first employed him. There had been a fair bit of rivalry between Aiden and Finn back in the days when Jade hadn't wanted a relationship.

Back in the days when she'd thought she'd never recover enough to be healed again. Like little Carmelita, she thought.

'Penny for them,' Aiden asked as they went into Duck Pond Cottage.

'I was just thinking how pleased Finn would be about you and Kate. Are we allowed to say anything to him?'

'I don't know. I don't want word getting out to Kate.' He put his fingers to his lips.

'Absolutely not. Then I won't say anything. I'll put the kettle on and nip to the loo.'

When she came back downstairs, Finn was slapping Aiden on the back and congratulating him. So Aiden had obviously changed his mind then. Jade smiled to herself. Times really had changed. While those two were never likely to be best friends, they'd clearly both moved on from the old days.

As they sipped coffee and ate some of the homemade cake Dawn had brought in, Aiden asked for news about the development next door. 'I heard a rumour the new owners had put in for planning permission.'

'Nothing's been approved yet,' Jade said quickly. 'How are the villagers reacting?'

'There are a few murmurings. I think they'd rather have had an arable farm than yet another housing estate.'

'Hear, hear,' Jade said, sneaking a glance at Finn. 'Fingers crossed they won't get permission.'

26

Ben was thrilled when he heard Carmelita was likely to make a full recovery.

'I saved her, didn't I, Auntie Jade?' he said as the fox got a little better each day.

It was now the last week of the summer holidays and other than when Sarah and Callum had taken him up to see Callum's parents in Dundee so that they could tell them the wedding news, Ben was at Duck Pond Rescue practically full time. Much to Finn's delight and Sarah's obvious guilt.

'Are you really sure you don't mind him being here so much?' she asked Jade every time she saw her. 'He's obsessed with that fox. I can't even tempt him away with the prospect of Mission Dormouse.'

They were standing in reception as they spoke and Mr Spock was entertaining a group of youngsters with a rendition of 'Here Comes the Bride, All Fat and Wide' in his thin reedy voice.

'I have no idea who taught him that,' Jade said, glancing at the parrot. 'But it's definitely getting old.' She lowered her voice.

'It beats him swearing his head off with all these kids about though.'

'True.' Sarah laughed. 'I can totally understand why Ben can't drag himself away from this place. It's all going on, isn't it?' She checked to make sure he was in the group of youngsters and hadn't sneaked off to see Carmelita, who was still in the hospital block in a kennel, with a big outside run. 'What is happening with the development anyway? Any news?'

'They haven't abandoned the idea, if that's what you mean,' Jade said reflectively. 'They haven't decided it would be much better to have a wildlife park next door and hand the whole lot back to nature, unfortunately. The plans have gone in for a development of seventy-five houses.'

Sarah gasped. 'I had no idea it was that many.'

'Me neither. They might not get them, of course. There's a lot of resistance from locals. Mike's on the planning committee and there's a worry there isn't enough infrastructure in place to build the number of houses they've put in for.'

'There isn't. It's hard enough to get a doctor's appointment as it is. Every time I phone up I get told I'm number sixteen in a queue.'

'Number sixteen!'

'OK, slight exaggeration. More like number six. But there's always a queue, and you can't just rock up and wait for an appointment like you used to be able to do. God knows what it will be like if we have another seventy-five houses built up the road. Are you sure you don't want to instigate Mission Dormouse?'

'I don't think we can.' Jade chewed her lip.

'How about toads? I'm sure there's a species of endangered toads. Chatterbox toads or something. David Attenborough mentioned them on some nature programme the other day. The male's got a distinctive mating call that females can hear up to a mile away.'

'They're called Natterjack toads.' Jade was touched Sarah felt as strongly as she did. 'But there are no ponds next door.'

'No pond. No problem. We know some very efficient pond diggers.' Sarah's eyes gleamed. 'We could do it in an hour – then get some cute little chatterbox toads and pop them over there for a holiday. We don't even have to get the toads. We can make recordings of their mating calls and play them.'

'It could be worth a try, I suppose. Don't worry, I haven't given up on stopping the development. I had an idea the other day. I need to talk to Ursula.' She broke off. 'Hang on, I've just spotted her in the yard with Dawn.' They both looked out of the window. 'Are you OK to answer the landline if it rings?'

'Course I am. It's the least I can do. I really ought to be paying you childcare fees. Like the rest of the mothers whose kids are here.' She winked. 'That's a good fundraising idea actually. You could charge kids to come here for summer camp.'

'They're already here.'

'Or you could take that parrot round to schools and entertain the kids. A one-woman entertainment show. You'd make a flaming fortune.'

'I'll definitely think about that one,' Jade said. 'I just want to catch Ursula.'

As she walked across the yard beneath the late-afternoon August sunshine, Jade felt happy. Despite everything that was going on, despite the shadow of the development that hung over them like a storm cloud, this was what she'd wanted. A place of sanctuary for animals, a place where a community pulled together. It got a little bit too hectic in holiday time – she was secretly relieved when all the kids went back to school – but most of them were brilliant, and she had a rule that youngsters must be accompanied by a responsible adult, and all visitors had to sign a waiver and agree to obey the rules of respectful behaviour around all animals. Some parts of the sanctuary were out of bounds to the public. These included the hospital and new arrivals block. But most of the kids who visited were great. Jade vetted them all personally before she let them near her precious animals.

'Hello, ladies,' she said as she reached Dawn and Ursula, and they both turned.

'Just the person I was hoping to see,' Ursula said, tucking a strand of white hair behind her ear and looking businesslike. 'I wanted to talk to you about something.'

'Ditto,' Jade said.

'Is there somewhere we can talk privately?'

'Round here?' Jade looked around her. 'Hmm, possibly not. We could go into the house.' As they walked in that direction, she remembered Finn was in there collating some adoption packs.

'Tell you what, why don't we wander over to the duck pond? It's probably relatively private over there.'

A few moments later, they had escaped through the side gate of the sanctuary and crossed the unmade lane to the duck pond. Sunlight shone through the weeping willow that stood like a sentinel, trailing long lime-green fronds over the clear water. A scattering of lilies huddled close to the bank, some of them still half open, showing creamy white flowers.

A pair of mallards drifting on the other side of the pond spotted them and came purposefully across, hoping for bread, and Jade wondered if the female was the one she'd rescued last year.

Above the lilies closest to them, a bright blue dragonfly hovered.

'Peace at last,' Jade said, dragging her gaze back from the rippled water towards Ursula. 'I love that so many people are keen to come and help but...'

'It can get a little too hectic,' Ursula finished. 'Yes, I get that.'

'So...' Jade began. 'Keen as I am to stop the development going ahead next door, I've come to the conclusion I don't want to sacrifice my principles, as in...' She sighed as she met Ursula's eyes. 'I can't relocate a dormouse family, or a bat family or any other live creature just to get what I want.'

'I'd guessed as much.' Ursula's face grew serious. 'That's not the way you operate, Jade, is it? I know we haven't known each other long but I knew as soon as I met you that you weren't that type of soul. You have a great deal of integrity, a quality which I much admire.'

'I was hoping there might have been some evidence of something endangered,' Jade said with a rueful smile. 'But there isn't, is there?'

'I'm afraid not.'

There was a little pause and in it, Jade heard the flutter of pigeon wings in a nearby tree and the plop of water as a mallard dived and resurfaced. She took a deep breath and smelled the clean pure air of the countryside. There was nothing like it, and she hated the thought that soon it would be replaced by the rumble of the diggers and the stink of diesel as the farmland was forever changed to accommodate lines of identical houses and new tarmac roads, no doubt called names like Meadow Row, and Foxglove Lane.

'Much as it saddens me,' Jade added, 'I don't think there's really all that much I can do to stop Rural Developments building those houses now they've bought the land.'

'It saddens me too, my dear. Conservation is part of my work, as you know, and I'm also a botanist. Too much of our beautiful countryside has been sacrificed on the altar of human need lately, but the wildlife is often forgotten. Despite all the promises the developers make. And on that note...' She paused and looked at Jade again. 'I don't know if you noticed in the course of your research, but it's not just endangered species of animals that can stop a development going ahead.'

'I had noticed,' Jade said, knowing they were on exactly the same wavelength because this thought had been going round and round in her head lately. 'It's plants too, isn't it?'

'Indeed it is.' Ursula smiled at her. 'Shall we walk around and have a chat?'

'I'd love that.'

The lily pond wasn't very big, maybe about ten metres across, so ordinarily it wouldn't have taken long to walk around the whole thing, but today it was a slow walk, because as they went, Ursula pointed out plants to Jade, naming them, sometimes in Latin, but mostly with their common names. Green leafy hornwort, marsh marigold, and greater spearwort, which looked like floating buttercups. It was an education. Ursula was very knowledgeable, as she moved from the plants in the pond itself to the plants all around them.

She bent to pick a tiny yellow flower that was growing on the path, sniffed it and handed it to Jade. 'Matricaria discoidea, more commonly known as wild pineapple. Try a bit. It tastes like pineapple too.'

Jade put it on her tongue. 'Wow, it really does.'

'You can make tea with it. It has soothing properties, a bit like chamomile.'

Ursula knew the names of everything from the tiniest mosses and grasses to the bullrushes and shrubs and even the odd fungi that grew on the trees. It seemed to Jade that they were no longer traversing a duck pond and a scrubby patch of wild land, but a whole new world of wildlife and wilderness. She knew she would never see the duck pond the same way again. It was magical.

'I can't believe you can keep all this information in your head,' Jade murmured. 'It's truly astounding.'

'Not really. It's been my life's work, and I'm sixty-six. I'll be retiring in a year, but I don't expect to ever stop learning. Plants have always fascinated me. Particularly wild plants. Quite a few have become extinct in my lifetime. A lot of that's due to us destroying their habitats. Not just in England obviously, but all over the world.'

They'd come to a pause at the other side of the duck pond, and they stood side by side, looking over at Duck Pond Cottage and the big gates of the rescue, and the land beyond, and the land beyond that – the land Jade had once hoped she might buy.

'Do you think there are any protected species of plants over there that might stop development at the eleventh hour?' Jade asked Ursula wistfully. 'And even if there were, couldn't the developers just dig them up or work round them or something?'

'They could do that, yes, although it's illegal to dig up protected species of plants. There are also mitigation measures that can be taken. Planning could be held up but not stopped.'

'So there isn't really an option to stop developers at all, then?' Jade said sadly.

'I wouldn't say that. The thing developers dislike most,' Ursula said, 'at least in my experience, are the kind of delays that impact on the overall cost of a project.'

Jade remembered what Declan had told her about the bones he'd once dug up on a development. She told Ursula this now.

'They turned out to be Roman remains so the project wasn't held up for very long. I don't suppose there's any chance of there being anything of archaeological interest over the road, is there?'

'That's always possible. But the developers wouldn't know until they'd started digging, so it might be a little late.'

Ursula's eyes had a hint of a twinkle, and Jade looked at her suspiciously.

'And I'm guessing a protected species of plant might not be enough to cause the kind of delays we'd need?' she pressed.

'You're guessing correctly. However, there are other species of plants that may cause worse delays.'

'Such as?' Jade felt a surge of hope at the merriment in Ursula's eyes. There was definitely something she wasn't telling her.

'Highly invasive species of plants, such as Japanese knotweed, and also certain types of bamboo are both terribly invasive plants.' Ursula paused for effect. 'Both of these plants, I'm sad to say' – she drew inverted commas in the air around the word 'sad' – 'are in evidence around John Lawson's erstwhile farmhouse.'

'Oh, my goodness.' Jade felt a jolt of shock. 'Did he know that when he sold the land?'

'He probably knew about the bamboo because he must have put it there, as fencing, or someone did, some time ago I'd say, as it's very well established. It already has an extensive network of underground roots which are going to be a devil to get rid of. As for the Japanese knotweed, he might not have known about that, because it's also been there a long time and it's in a different place.'

She met Jade's gaze. 'Japanese knotweed, as you may know if you've ever read horror stories online, is also very difficult to get rid of. Its roots grow really quickly and they cause significant damage to roads and buildings. It's possible to eradicate it. Anything's possible, but it's a lengthy process, which would cause significant delays. The location of it isn't good for your developers, that's for sure, and delays, as we've discussed, mean money. Suddenly, something that looks very profitable starts to have its profit margins squeezed. And, oh boy, does that hurt developers. Reputable ones anyway.'

'Wow! So it's possible that Rural Developments might have to stop the development then. Didn't they have a survey before they bought it?'

'Apparently not. They got the land cheaply enough for them to take a risk that planning permission would be granted. Your Farmer John wasn't silly.' She raised her eyebrows.

'That's brilliant news. Or at least I think it is. It's great that the development might be scuppered. But hang on – should I be worried? I mean, how long would it be before all of those terribly invasive plants started to affect my property?'

'Several years.' Ursula tapped her nose. 'It would have to be very bad to spread across to Duck Pond Cottage. There are several hectares between your properties.'

'But didn't you say it *was* very bad?'

'I said it *looked* very bad on the survey. I know who did the survey. She may have exaggerated a teeny tiny bit.' She tapped her nose.

'But Ursula,' Jade gasped as the penny dropped. 'Won't you get into trouble when they find out?'

'They can't find out. No one's going to bother doing a second survey, and frankly if they ever did, I'd be retired. They'd just put it down to me being overcautious, I expect. It's usually better to be overcautious when doing important surveys, wouldn't you say?'

'I don't know what to say.' Jade shook her head in wonderment. 'That is truly amazing.'

Ursula gave her a little smile. 'Consider it my very small contribution to the valuable work you're doing here,' she said quietly. 'And naturally if anyone was ever to question my survey, I'd deny all knowledge of any wrongdoing.'

'You haven't done anything wrong,' Jade agreed swiftly.

'I said to you earlier that I very much admire integrity,' Ursula said, 'but I do find it's one of those qualities I can admire from a distance.' She winked.

Jade nodded. Ursula reminded her of a much older version of Sarah. Rules were there to be broken – at least they were if you didn't agree with them. Jade wasn't planning on telling Sarah – or anyone else – about this conversation, but she knew if she did then Sarah would have heartily approved.

27

'I was beginning to think you'd got lost,' Sarah said as Jade strolled back into reception, having waved goodbye to Ursula, who'd said she'd promised to help with the cattery clean, and disappeared up the yard. Three cats had gone off to new homes today. It was a bumper rehoming day, and the cattery block would be deep cleaned in preparation for the next arrivals.

'Ursula was teaching me the names of all the plants that grow over at the duck pond,' Jade told Sarah. 'Not that I've got a hope in hell of remembering them all. That woman is like a walking encyclopaedia.'

'Did she know the whereabouts of any cute little tight roping dormice?' Sarah quipped. 'Or chatterbox toads ready to mate?'

'I don't know. I didn't ask. I've decided I'm not going down that route,' Jade said firmly. 'Fun as it would have been to go camping with you... although... we could still go camping and discuss wedding plans, if you like?' She laughed at Sarah's horrified expression.

'It's impossible to drag Ben away from that flaming fox,'

Sarah said quickly. 'I mean, I would have loved to go camping otherwise. Obvs.'

'Sure you would.' Jade laughed with her. She was feeling a lightness she hadn't felt for weeks. Was it really possible that she didn't have to worry about the development any more?

Ursula had said she was unlikely to hear anything very quickly. Planning applications and surveys and anything to do with planning took ages, but it certainly looked as though she could be cautiously optimistic. Ursula had told her she'd keep her posted and let her know the minute there was any news.

She hadn't said 'any news'. She'd actually said 'any developments', and they'd both laughed at this as Ursula had added a swift rider that hopefully there definitely wouldn't be any of those for a while.

Jade had decided it would be wise to keep quiet about the death knell of a survey. It wouldn't look good for Ursula if it was ever discovered that Jade had any prior knowledge.

But this was a secret Jade didn't mind keeping. It wasn't a secret that could hurt anyone she cared about.

'How do you feel about doing a protest then?' Sarah said, interrupting Jade's thoughts. 'We could get some placards and march up and down in the field. "Save our green spaces."'

'Not many people are going to spot us in that field, are they?'

'OK, the road then. Although it is a bit busy, that road. Maybe we should march up and down outside the planning office in Salisbury.'

'Or maybe we should just accept that sometimes things are going to happen, whether we like it or not.'

Sarah looked at her carefully. 'Ursula did say something, didn't she? You're far too laid back about all this. What's going on?'

Fortunately Mr Spock chose that moment to burst into

another rendition of 'Here Comes the Bride', and at the same moment, Zack came in with a sack over his shoulder.

'Evening, Jade, I just got this. Some of the kids at school did a fundraiser at the summer fete. It's bird food.'

'Not much of a fundraiser if they only got one sack of food,' Sarah called across to him. 'What was it? A sponsored silence or something?'

He laughed good naturedly. 'They raised enough money for twenty sacks of animal feed. This is just one of them. The rest are in the back of Dad's car.'

'Good grief,' Jade said. 'Thanks. That'll last us ages.'

'We didn't just get chicken food, that's good for the geese too – I checked – we got dog and cat biscuits, and some horse feed. All the usual stuff you buy. We didn't want to leave anyone out.'

'That's so brilliant, Zack. Thank you.' Jade felt a rush of warmth towards the big-hearted teenager. He was definitely one of the good guys. 'I think we'd better put the sacks straight into the feed room. I'll come and give you a hand.'

She went to help him do it, and by the time she came back, Sarah had tracked down Ben and, much to Jade's relief, seemed to have forgotten that she'd been midway through interrogating Jade.

'We'd better get off,' Sarah told Jade. 'But thank you again for having him. Ben, have you said goodbye to your dad?'

'He has,' Finn said, coming into reception. 'When are we going to see you again then, Ben?'

'Tomorrow!' Ben shouted gleefully.

'Not tomorrow,' Sarah corrected. 'We've got to get you some new school shoes, you know we have.'

'Do I have to go? Can't you get them?'

'You know I can't, love. You've got to try them on.'

Ben pouted. 'I don't. My feet haven't even growed for ages.'

'If they hadn't growed – grown,' Sarah corrected herself, 'then you wouldn't even need new shoes, would you?'

'They haven't. They're the same.' Ben's voice was getting louder. He'd got that mutinous look on his face that they all knew so well.

Finn and Jade exchanged 'who'd have kids?' glances. Then Jade said softly, 'Carmelita's going to be ready for release soon, Ben. So the next time we see you, maybe you could help with that. If you've been good and your mum agrees.'

Sarah shot her a grateful look. 'Did you hear that? Auntie Jade said, only if you're good.'

'I can be good. I can be very, very good.' Ben's expression changed from a scowl to a smile in seconds. He was so mercurial, Jade thought, not for the first time. He reminded her so much of his mother, who'd always changed her mood like the wind when she'd been younger.

'Right then, shoes tomorrow, and we'll see about Carmelita.' Sarah held out her hand to Ben, and after a quick glance over his shoulder to make sure no one important was looking, he took it.

'OK, Mum.' He beamed like an angel.

When they left, Jade saw that Finn was still smiling. 'Bless his little cotton socks. I wasn't as feisty as him when I was that age. I was way more serious and quieter.'

'Sarah wasn't. She was as anti-authority as they came. She'd kick out at anyone who told her what to do. She'd argue red was blue if a teacher said the opposite. I used to think it was because she'd started life in a children's home, but now I'm beginning to think it's genetic.'

She regretted using the word genetic as soon as she'd said it, because she saw the flash of pain in Finn's eyes.

'Still no news from Thomas then?' she asked him gently.

He hadn't mentioned Bridie lately, or anything else about his quest to track down his mother, and Jade hadn't liked to bring it up.

Finn shook his head. 'No. I never did ring him back. But it's been more than two weeks. If he was going to call back, he would have done by now, wouldn't he?'

There was no one else in reception now, and Jade went across to him and hugged him. 'The waiting must be torture, Finn. Would it not be better to just phone him and see what the score is?'

'I probably should have done that already, but the longer I've left it, the harder it's got.' He put his arms around her too, and kissed her. 'I don't know, Jade. I'm thinking it might be too late now. But it's fine. Honestly. There was always a chance she wouldn't want to know.' He paused. 'Shall I go and lock up or is it too early?'

'It's not too early.' She ached for him. It was so hard watching him go through this. 'I'll just go and check everyone is off the premises, and then we can lock up. And then maybe we should open a bottle of wine and just chill out for the evening. Thanks for doing those adoption packs.' She glanced at the pile on the table.

'My pleasure. Wine sounds wonderful.'

An hour later they'd both showered, had a quiche and some salad and new potatoes that had been left over from the day before and they were sitting in the back room with a bottle of wine, half drunk, and a contented Mickey. He loved it when both his humans were in the same place.

Jade wasn't sure whether to bring the subject of Bridie and Thomas back up. Finn looked so relaxed now; maybe she should just leave it until he mentioned it. She asked him about the art exhibition instead, which was getting closer now.

'Are you getting excited? Does it seem real yet?'

'I mostly try not to think about it, to be honest. And I think I'm doing quite well apart from the fact I have the occasional nightmare.'

'Oh? What kind of nightmare?'

He sipped his wine. 'Crazy stuff. There's the one where no one turns up, and I'm just standing there by my paintings on my own, forcing myself to smile.'

'Oh, Finn, that's definitely not going to happen.'

'It's not that likely. Because there will be other artists' work there too.' He blinked. 'Then there's the one where there's a flood and all the paintings are being washed away down the main High Street. That's nasty.' He took another sip of his wine. 'And then there's the one where I arrive at the town hall and find the place is all boarded up, even the windows, and there's this guy in a bowler hat, standing by the door, who tells me it's been like that for years. But they used to have exhibitions there once.'

'Bloody hell, they're horrible, honey. Why didn't you tell me before?'

'Because I know they're nonsense. Just a byproduct of my crazy brain. It's just nerves, isn't it? I never thought I'd be in this position. I never thought it was possible that people would want to buy my work.'

'But loads of people have bought your work.'

'I always thought they were just being nice, and it's hard to get that belief out of my head. My subconscious head anyway.' He bent forward and filled up their glasses. 'I know it sounds crazy.'

Jade leaped off the sofa where she'd been sitting and went across to the wall where the painting called *Hope* hung.

'Finn, I know I'm not any kind of expert, but this is so beautiful. It draws you into the landscape, but it doesn't just do that, it makes you feel something. It's the same thing I feel when I hear an amazing piece of music. It hits me like an ice pick in the heart.'

'That doesn't sound so good, I have to say.' He raised his eyebrows. 'It sounds bloody painful.'

'It is but in a good way. I'm not explaining this very well.' She clasped her hands together and screwed up her face in frustration. 'I'm not any kind of critic, I don't know the right words. But it's deep. It's deep and it's brilliant.'

'Deep and brilliant will do me.' He got up and came to stand beside her. 'I do love you, Jade Foster. I can't wait to marry you.'

He put his arms around her, and she turned towards him and looked into his eyes.

'I can't wait to marry you either. I can't wait to have your babies.' She clapped her hand over her mouth. 'Shit. I don't even know where that came from. It just slipped out.'

'You meant it though, didn't you?'

She could feel his eyes and she knew her face was burning. 'We've never really discussed babies, have we?'

'No, but I'd love more children. Is there something you're not telling me?' He stood back from her slightly, studying her face.

'No, I'm not pregnant.' She felt flustered. It was weird but until that moment she hadn't really thought about being pregnant either. Was that true? Sometimes when she looked at Ben, she longed for a child.

'There are lots of good reasons not to get pregnant either,' she continued. 'No maternity leave, several dozen animals to look after... Huge disruption to our lives.' She counted them off on her fingers.

'They're not good reasons, not with two of us on the case. We'd cope.' He looked much keener on the idea than she'd anticipated. Jade felt warmed.

She longed for a family and she longed for her and Finn to be a unit and to live happily ever after, even though she'd never really believed in happy ever after.

Like Finn, she'd never dared to hope that happy ever afters might be possible.

Now, standing here in his arms, she felt that they might be. What with Ursula's news and the news that Finn was as keen on the idea of extending his family as she was, all things suddenly felt possible.

28

Two days after that conversation, when Finn was finishing a big painting of Stonehenge, which he had set up on an easel in the attic room, he got a call from a Salisbury phone number.

He saw it flash up on the screen and he answered it unthinkingly. He'd opened a new account lately for painting supplies and they'd called him a couple of times to let him know things he was waiting for had arrived.

'Hi, Finn McTaggart.' He answered the call as he usually did these days, when he didn't recognise a number. Brusque and businesslike.

'Hi, Finn,' said a woman's voice. Soft and a little tentative. 'This is Bridie, your biological mother.'

Everything in the room went still, and Finn knew suddenly what people meant when they said they'd remember a moment forever because it had been freeze-framed in time. The grey stones of the henge on the canvas in front of him were suddenly outlined in sharp contrast to the white creamy sky, and he could hear the drip drip of the leaky tap as water plopped periodically into the hand washbasin on the wall. He could hear his heart too. Thundering as the blood rushed around his veins. The paintbrush he was holding felt clumsy in his fingers.

'Bridie.' The word felt like a croak in the back of his throat. Barely there, and also damningly exposing.

'I've shocked you, Finn. I'm sorry. But it's so good to hear your voice.' Her voice was husky too. 'You can't imagine how long I have prayed for this day.'

He could hear her Irish accent suddenly. So living in England all these years hadn't changed that then.

'Finn, say something, please.'

He gathered himself and his shock, worried she might hang up. 'Thank you for calling.' That sounded so inane in the circumstances. 'Was it Thomas who told you I was looking for you?'

'Aye, it was Thomas. A week or so ago. I've been trying to pluck up the courage to call you. How are you? How's Ray? Does he know you've been trying to contact me?'

'I'm OK. And he does, yeah. He kind of suggested it... Could we – um – could we maybe... meet?' He'd dropped the paintbrush, he realised. It lay on the threadbare carpet. He'd promised to recarpet this room if he made too much mess up here. Jade had told him not to be daft. The carpet was long past its sell-by date, and she'd never much liked it anyway.

Why on earth was he thinking about carpets?

'Yes, we could meet. Are you in Arleston, Finn?'

'Yes, I am.' Thomas must have told her. 'Where are you, M...?' He'd wanted to say Mum, but the word wouldn't come out. It was too unfamiliar, too old, too much a part of his childhood. Not for now.

'I'm living on the outskirts of Salisbury.'

Not Southampton then. That was even more of a shock. She

was even closer than he'd thought. The word bounced around in his head and each time it landed it shocked him more.

'What do you mean, you're in Salisbury?' he managed finally. 'How long? I mean, have you always lived there?'

'No, no. We were in Southampton for a while, but we moved for my husband's business about ten years back. We're in Barford St Martin. Just on the other side of Wilton.'

Less than half an hour away, Finn thought, bending to pick up the paintbrush, squeezing it tight between his fingers as he put it back on the table of paints beside him. All this time and she'd lived less than half an hour away from him, from his grandparents' cottage. It didn't compute. He couldn't take it in.

'Are you still there, Finn?'

'I'm here. Sorry. It's a lot to get my head around.'

'It is.' She left the words hanging and he knew it was up to him to push it – to see if they could arrange a time and place.

'When can we meet?' He tried to get his voice back on to an even keel – act like this was some unimportant business meeting. 'Are you free in the day? Do you work?'

'I work for my husband – but he'd probably let me out of an afternoon.'

'Have you... have you told him about me?'

'Yes. He knows. It was a long time ago that I told him. Back when I thought – hoped – there was a chance we may get to have regular contact.' She paused again. 'I haven't said you've been in touch since Thomas spoke to me. I'd been trying to get used to the idea. Before I said anything, you know?'

Finn knew. Hadn't he done the same thing?

'So how about tomorrow morning?' Afraid that sounded too needy, he added, 'Or afternoon?'

'Wednesday afternoon – that could work? Do you know the pub called The Wilton Hare? I think that one's open all day.'

'I can find it. What time?'

'Three would work for me – if that's OK with you, Finn?'

'I'll see you at three.'

'I'll be in the lounge bar. Until tomorrow then.'

'Until tomorrow.' It was only when he'd disconnected that he wondered whether he should have asked how he'd recognise her. Would she have changed very much? It had been twenty-six years since he'd seen her and even though her image was burned in his brain, she might not look like that any more.

It was too late now. He wasn't going to phone her back. He stayed where he was, sitting upright in his chair, trying to process what had just happened. He was going to meet his mother. In less than twenty-four hours. He was galvanised into movement. He had to tell Jade.

In his haste, he missed the last step of the stairs and jolted his back. He cursed softly and headed for the lounge door.

'You OK?' Jade glanced up at him, looking concerned. 'It's not your wrist playing up, is it?'

'No, I just missed my footing. I was in too much of a hurry.' He halted in the doorway. 'She just called me,' he explained. 'Bridie just phoned. We're going to meet.'

'Oh my God, Finn. That's, wow... that's amazing. How do you feel? What was it like?'

'It was surreal. And I don't know how I feel. Weird, I think. Excited. Pretty scared. You're never going to believe where she lives.'

* * *

The surreal feeling hadn't properly worn off, Finn thought as he got ready to go out and meet Bridie the next afternoon.

He'd been pulling out stalks of yellow ragwort from the hen

field that morning – there wasn't much but they'd been worried it might seed and spread into the horse paddock. It was poisonous to horses. Then he'd repaired one of the hen coops, but the jobs had taken much longer than usual because he'd been so distracted.

He'd come into the cottage to shower and shave and now he was tugging on his best jeans and one of his few shirts. There wasn't a lot of call for shirts at Duck Pond Rescue, although he'd resolved to get a new one for the art fair, which was in less than three weeks' time.

An exhibition of his work and a meeting with his mother in the same month. Must be something in the stars – not that he was superstitious. He hadn't told Ray yet. He'd decided he would tell him afterwards. He didn't want to jinx anything. Bridie might get cold feet and not show. He didn't think he could bear it if that happened.

'Are you sure you don't want me to come with you?' Jade's voice interrupted his thoughts, and he realised she'd just come into the bedroom. 'To sit in the car outside and give you moral support, I mean – not to come in.'

'It's OK, darling. I'll be fine.' If Bridie wasn't there, he'd be heartbroken. He'd always been good at putting on armour, putting up walls – the metaphorical kind anyway – but he'd dropped his defences since he'd met Jade. He'd had to drop them – love did that to you – but now it felt like he couldn't get his armour back on. He felt as if he had no skin, as though all his nerve endings were exposed.

'I'll call you after we've met and let you know how it went. I shouldn't think we'd be too long chatting.'

'Finn, what are you like? You've got years of catching up to do. You can tell me about it when you get back. There's no rush.' She gave him an appraising look. 'That shirt suits you.'

'Are you sure? I thought maybe the grey.'

'The blue's fine.'

She came to him and put her hands on his shoulders. 'She'll love you, and if she doesn't, tell her she'll have me to answer to.' Her voice was fierce – fiercer even than when she was arguing the case for an animal. High praise indeed. Finn smiled at her.

He had never loved her more. 'I'd better get going,' he said, glancing at his watch. 'Or she might think I'm not coming.'

'She'll wait,' Jade said. 'You've waited for her long enough.'

* * *

The Wilton Hare looked like one of those places that catered for the London crowd, Finn thought as he drew into its car park. Recently refurbished, it was too neat for a locals' country pub, and this impression was heightened as he walked across its pea-gravel car park and opened the black-handled door to reveal a spacious, minimalistic bar with a light faux-wood floor and drop-down grey pendant lights over tall tables with bar stools. Straight lines and tidiness.

There were very few people in it as far as he could see. A lone man with a briefcase on the stool next to him was scrolling on his phone. A couple were sitting at the bar looking through giant plastic menus.

Finn scanned the surroundings.

Crap, he'd been joking about Bridie not turning up, but now it seemed as though the joke was on him. For a few seconds all he could feel was a crushing disappointment. She wasn't here. And he was ten minutes late.

And then a door marked 'ladies' opened on the far side of the room and a woman came through it and looked around her.

She was smaller than he recalled. Five foot six or seven.

Compared to his six foot one, she was petite. Her hair was still fair like he remembered, and she was slim. Well dressed, she reminded him of some of the posh mothers who brought their kids into Duck Pond Rescue during the summer holidays.

He couldn't take his eyes off her as she walked across the expanse of tiled floor between them, and he could see that she felt the same. Both of them were searching each other's faces. Searching for something they recognised.

Then, there she was in front of him. Her eyes weren't grey, like his and Dad's and Ben's. They were more of a light hazel colour. He recognised her eyes. They were painfully familiar, even though in his memories of her he'd often had trouble recalling them.

'Will I shake your hand or hug you, Finn...?'

He wasn't ready for hugs. Maybe he shrank back a little, because she didn't move another step towards him, but instead held out her hand politely.

Finn shook it. 'Hello.'

'Hey.' It was her voice he recognised the most. A voice made up of teddy bears and bedtime stories. It hooked his memories down the years. Rolled him back to the six-year-old he'd been the last time he'd seen her. Made him ache for a mother he'd prayed and hoped would come back as he'd lain in bed, night after night, cuddling his pillow, imagining that every soft step on the stairs was hers.

'Will we grab a seat?' She looked around her. 'Not that there's a shortage. We've missed the lunchtime rush.'

She took charge, walking across towards the window, and Finn saw for the first time there were lower coffee tables with couches on either side of them, and this was where Bridie was headed.

A few moments later, they were facing each other across a

coffee table. They had a couch each. She scanned what he'd assumed was a wine list in a plastic stand but turned out to be a coffee menu.

'They do good cake here, Finn. Or would you like something more substantial? They do food all day.'

'I've had my lunch.'

'Me too, cake then?'

'Just an Americano, I think. Do you have to go to the bar to order it?'

'That's right.' She started to rise.

'I'll get it,' he said. 'What would you like to drink? Shall I get you cake?'

'No, no, it's fine. An Americano for me too, please, Finn. Maybe we should get a cafetière. Do you need some money?'

'I have money,' he said stiffly. How did she think he'd survived all these years? It was weird; if anyone had asked, he'd have said he bore his mother no resentment. But it was in there. Niggling away. Perhaps resentment was too strong a word, but there was definitely a hint of 'I've managed fine all this time without you, and I don't need you now either.'

He paid for the drinks and the barmaid said she'd bring them over. No need to wait. So Finn went back. Bridie's phone was on the table, but she wasn't looking at it, she was staring out of the window. As he sat down, she glanced at him, and he saw that her eyes were glittery. She wasn't as composed as she seemed then.

'Finn, I'm so sorry.'

He nodded. He didn't know what to say so he waited and after a few moments she went on.

'I was young and stupid, and I didn't know what to do.'

'You didn't consider taking me with you,' he said, trying not to let his emotions show. There was a tight hard knot in his heart. 'You didn't stop and think I might be devastated, not knowing where you'd gone. Wondering every day if you were ever coming back.'

'I wanted to take you. Of course I did, but I couldn't have done it to your daddy. He adored you. I knew it would break him enough that I was leaving. It wasn't his fault, Finn. He'd done nothing wrong. He was a good man. How is he now? Is he OK?'

'He's fine.'

Bridie had got a handkerchief out of her bag. She sniffed, dabbed at her face, then twirled it in her hands. 'And you, yourself? You look grand. Just as I imagined you'd look. You've grown into a fine man.'

It was hard to know how to answer that. He hadn't expected it to be like this. The two of them sitting here like strangers and him with the biggest ache in his throat. A mass of unshed emotion. He hadn't expected it to be as though nothing had changed though either. Not when so many years had gone by. Not when so much water had gone under the bridge. God, that was such an awful expression, because water meant time, stuff happening that could never be altered. Regrets.

He cleared his throat. 'Dad said you were pregnant when you left him.'

She nodded, met his eyes fleetingly, then lowered her gaze. 'That's right. I was pregnant with your brother.'

'So you were having an affair.'

'Yes, and no. I was seeing Christopher again. We were childhood sweethearts in Ireland, but we'd lost touch.' She broke off. 'It's a long story. You don't want to hear all that.'

'I do,' he contradicted her. 'I want to hear it all.'

29

Bridie paused because the barmaid had just arrived with a tray, and they waited while she transferred everything to the table. A cafetière, two white mugs, two napkins, a tiny china milk churn and a bowl of brown and white sugar lumps.

The rich scent of good coffee hit Finn as Bridie thanked her.

'You're welcome. Have a great day.'

Finn wondered what she would think if she knew this was a long-lost mother and son reunion. Better than TV, although maybe not as volatile as Jeremy Kyle. Was Jeremy Kyle still going? Finn had a vague memory of a scandal.

Actually, it was nothing like Jeremy Kyle. They were both way too controlled – edging their way around the emotional minefield that led from the past to today to this sanitised bar made up of straight lines and wooden floors and grey pendulum lights.

He wanted to run away. It was on the tip of his tongue to say, *I can't do this. It was a mistake finding you. Let's just leave the whole thing, let's just forget it*, but he was frozen on the hard cushioned couch that had hardly given at all when he'd sat down on it.

He watched as Bridie pushed a mug and the sugar bowl towards him. 'Will you have sugar? I'm not sure how you take it.' Her voice was apologetic.

A few minutes later, when she'd pressed down the plunger on the cafetière, he saw they took it the same way. Not much milk and two lumps of brown sugar.

'Are you in a hurry, Finn?' She broke the silence.

'No,' Finn said as he stirred his drink. 'Why? Are you rushing back?' He resisted the temptation to add 'to your other family' but the words were there, swinging in the air.

'No. I've nowhere to be. And you've every right to know what happened. I owe you that.' She sipped her coffee and straightened her back and took a deep breath. 'OK, well, Christopher and I met at school in the seventies in Belfast. We were eleven when we met. He was the only English boy at our school and he was bullied because he was English, he was different. You know how kids are. And we were also in the midst of the Troubles. I was one of the few kids who'd share a civil word with him. That was how it began. We got talking. We realised we had masses in common and later on I fell for him.'

'At the age of eleven?'

'That's right.' She shrugged. 'I think when you meet your *anamchara*, your soulmate, you know it. However young you are, and that's what happened to us. He said he would marry me as soon as we were old enough. And I wanted that too. I adored him.'

'So what happened?'

'When he was fourteen, his family moved back to England, and he had to go with them. I wanted to go, but I was too young, of course. My mammy and daddy wouldn't hear of such a thing. They said it was a crush, they said I'd forget him once I found a nice Irish boy. I knew they were wrong. Christopher and I promised we'd keep in touch, and we did.

'For the next eighteen months we wrote letters. There was no internet in those days, no mobile phones. We did have the land-lines, but phone calls to foreign countries were expensive. Our folks weren't happy about us running up expensive bills.'

Her eyes shadowed. 'Then the letters from him stopped coming. I was frantic. I thought he might be dead. I waited and waited. After a while I realised he must have moved house. I tried to trace him. I managed to get in touch with the people who were now at his address, and they said the previous family had left no forwarding details. I was heartbroken.'

Her voice was steady as she met his eyes, and for the first time, Finn felt a stab of empathy for her. As he'd have felt for anyone, he realised, who'd been recounting the same experience to him.

'So you forgot about him?' he asked.

'I didn't forget about him, no. When I was seventeen, I packed a bag and I got the ferry from Belfast to Liverpool and I went to England to look for him. I went to the address where he'd been living and there was another new family, who told me the last family had gone, and they'd left no forwarding details either. So the trail went dead. After that I did stop looking for him, yes. I fell out with my family too. I was sure they'd conspired somehow with Christopher's parents to keep us apart, although they always swore they hadn't.' She took another quick sip of her coffee. 'I never went back home. I stayed in England. I felt closer to Christopher in England. There was always the hope that I'd bump into him. So in time I moved on. I had to. I'd got work with the only one of my family I hadn't fallen out with. My uncle Paddy, who's a showman. He did the fairs and I went with him. I helped with the rides. There was a lot of travelling.

We were at the goose fair in Nottingham when I met your father.
I expect he's told you.'

She looked up into Finn's eyes. 'He was different from the
usual lads I met. He was kind, romantic. He swept me off my
feet. And then I got pregnant with you and he wanted us to
settle down. I thought I wanted that too.'

'Did you ever love him?' Finn's voice was harsher than he'd
intended, and she jumped, swallowed and nodded slowly. 'I
think I did, Finn. Yes.' She paused and he could see that she was
back in the past, reliving it all, her face sad.

'Then in 1997 I met Christopher again. I found out he'd been
looking for me too. He knew I had connections with the fair
through my uncle and he'd been going every year, thinking I
might be there. He never forgot me either.'

'So you got back together.'

'I'm not proud of myself, Finn. I was with your father. You
were a wee child, and I loved every hair on your head. But yes, I
got back with Christopher.' Her eyes filled with tears. 'And then I
got pregnant again. And I didn't know what to do.'

'You could have told my dad.'

'He'd never have been able to forgive me.' A tear rolled down
her face. 'I suppose if I'm truly honest, I didn't want his forgive-
ness. The feelings for Christopher were the same, you see. The
same as they'd always been.' More tears were running down her
face and she wiped them from her cheeks with her hanky, and
met his eyes. 'He was still my *anamchara*.'

It was Finn who dropped his gaze first.

He wanted to cry too but he couldn't. He also wanted to hug
her and tell her it was OK. It would all be fine. But it wasn't OK
and he didn't know if it would ever be fine. He felt so terribly
conflicted about the fact she had chosen another family over

him and his dad, and the space between them felt as unbreachable as it had when they'd first arrived.

A few more people had come into the pub. A pair of women who were obviously good friends sat at another of the low coffee tables, further down the window. They were talking in low voices and occasionally a burst of laughter came from their table. An older couple had just sat at one of the tall tables with stools and were discussing cake.

Bridie broke the deadlock. 'I'm not proud of myself. I'm deeply ashamed, Finn, you have to believe me. Especially about leaving you. I didn't think I was the kind of woman who'd abandon her own wee child. How have you been?' She looked at him imploringly. 'Have you been OK? Are you married? Do you have a family?'

'Yeah. I've been OK. Not married.' He didn't want to tell her about Jade or Ben just yet. He wasn't sure why. Maybe he wasn't ready to let her into his life so soon.

There was another gap, shorter this time, and then Bridie said tentatively, 'Ask me anything you want to know. Anything. I want to make it right. I want to make it up to you. Will I get us some more coffee?'

She signalled to the barmaid who'd just walked past.

'Same again?' the barmaid asked, and Bridie glanced at Finn.

He nodded. He was torn. He didn't want to stay but he didn't want to go either. He hadn't expected it to be like this. This pain. It was so obvious she felt as devastated now as he had when she'd left. And in another world – a world where Bridie wasn't his mother – he might have liked her. She was direct and he was pretty sure she'd been honest too. Everything she'd told him matched with what Ray had said.

He gathered himself. 'So you're married to Christopher still?'

'I am.'

'And you have other children?'

'We do. We have three. There's your brother Declan, he's twenty-seven, and there's your sister, Alice, she's twenty-two, and there's wee Molly, she's the baby of the family. She's nineteen.'

Three siblings who'd grown up without him. Good God. He bit the inside of his cheek, trying not to react.

'Do they all live in Salisbury too?'

'Molly's on her gap year – she's in Spain right now. Alice and Declan both work for the family business, same as myself.'

'What is the family business?'

'We're builders, it's the same company Christopher's father, Nick, started, back in the seventies. But we've expanded since then, gone more into the property development side. We're not that big but it's local. You may have heard of the company...'

She broke off while the barmaid replenished their cafetière and mugs and milk and sugar.

'Thanks, love. Sorry...' She turned back to Finn. 'Where was I? Ah, yes, our wee company. We're called Rural Developments.'

Finn felt his head spin a little. He'd been alerted by the name Declan, but not massively because it was an Irish name – there must be thousands of Declans in Ireland. But there couldn't be that many companies called Rural Developments. Not in Wiltshire. Oh my God. Surely not...

'What is it, Finn? You've gone awful pale.' She was looking at him in alarm.

'Your son is Declan Stone.' He held her gaze, and it was Bridie's turn to go pale.

'That's right. Declan's my boy. Why? Do you know him?'

Finn didn't know whether he should tell her that just over a month ago he'd bloodied Declan's nose and that his wrist still ached from the punch. And maybe it was the shock of the revelation or the way Bridie was looking at him or simply the total ludicrousness of the whole situation, but he started to laugh. And he couldn't stop.

And the more she sat there looking at him with a slightly bemused expression on her face, the funnier the whole thing seemed.

* * *

At Duck Pond Rescue, Jade had just finished doing the final dog walks of the day and she was about to help Dawn with the feeding round.

She hadn't heard anything from Finn, other than to say he'd arrived at the pub. She hoped that meant things were going well, and not that they weren't and he was walking around Salisbury trying to get his head around it all.

Jade couldn't imagine how he must feel. She had never known her own dad, because he'd gone before she'd been old enough to ever meet him, so when she looked back at the past, or at the mental image she had of her family tree, there had only ever been her mother.

In the space on her family tree marked 'father', there was just a blank outline in her mind. Like a profile picture online when someone hasn't uploaded a photo. She knew his name because it was on her birth certificate. But that was it. Nothing more.

For Finn it was different. He'd known his mum right up until the age of six. Bridie had been there in his formative years. He'd known what it was like to feel her love, and then she'd left him. That must feel so much worse. All of the recent revelations from Ray about Bridie leaving because she was pregnant couldn't have helped either.

Jade couldn't imagine what it must feel like to find out your mother had chosen a new life with new children over you. The ultimate rejection.

She stopped to chat with Ursula, who'd taken to popping by regularly to help, although there were no official updates yet on the planning application that was going on next door.

'I'll have to start paying you if you come here any more often,' she told the older woman as she emerged from the hospital block with a half-empty container of water.

'You definitely won't have to do that. I'm paid perfectly well, and when I retire I might come in even more – if you'll have me?'

'You will always be very welcome here,' Jade said. 'You never need to ask.'

Ursula flashed her a smile, her teeth very white in the early evening sunlight. 'Carmelita's leg looks good. I've just topped up her water. She must be ready to go back to the wild soon.'

'She is, but I promised Ben he could help with the release. We're doing it tomorrow night.'

'Where will you take her?'

'That's trickier. With wildlife I'd usually release somewhere close to where I find them. But we actually found her in Ben's garden, so that's not going to work. I don't want to release her too close to here either, or she might decide she fancies a chicken supper, and although my lot go in at night, Carmelita might be brave enough to try a daytime strike. She's not exactly scared of people.'

'No, I guess that's always difficult with wild things. You don't want them to be terrified of us, but you definitely don't want them too tame either.'

'Precisely. It's a tricky balance.'

The sound of a car coming in through the main gates interrupted their chat and both women glanced towards reception.

'Ah, Finn's back. I'm just going to check in with him.'

'Is there anything I can do?'

'I was just on my way to help Dawn with the feeds. Would you have time to take over that?'

'Consider it done.' Ursula headed towards the feed store, and Jade hurried towards reception.

Finn looked serene, although it could be difficult to read him. She kept her fingers crossed as she went to greet him.

30

Finn told Jade about the afternoon's events over a bottle of red wine in their back room, with Mickey lying full length across both their laps on the sofa.

She looked vulnerable. Almost as vulnerable as he'd felt earlier, and for the first time he realised this must be almost as difficult for her as it was for him. Digging up the past wasn't something that would ever be easy for either of them.

'It was awkward at first, Jade. There was a point where I thought I might not even see Bridie again. We had so much in common, but also so little. If that doesn't sound completely daft.'

'It doesn't sound daft at all. It sounds real.' She paused. 'But then it changed? You managed to find some common ground?'

'We did. And I don't quite know how to tell you this.' He took a gulp of wine and met her eyes. 'I found out that my half-brother's name is Declan Stone.'

Jade's eyes widened in shock. 'Not the Declan Stone that we know...'

'Yep. Rural Developments is Bridie's company. To be strictly accurate it's her husband's company. His name's Christopher

Stone. He inherited the company from his father who set it up way back in the eighties in Ireland. Apparently they started off rebuilding bomb sites in Ireland during the Troubles. Christopher's the man Bridie left my dad for – the man who was her childhood sweetheart. I'm not making much sense, am I?'

'Um, I'm kind of following. Are you saying that Bridie, your mother, was pregnant with Declan and that's the reason she left you and your dad?'

'I am. Honestly, darling. You couldn't make it up.'

Jade shook her head in astonishment. 'So did you tell Bridie you'd already met him?'

'I did. And that I'd given him a well-deserved punch for coming on to my fiancée. She already knew. Well, she didn't know the reason but she knew he'd been punched because he'd turned up at work one morning with a black eye.'

Despite everything, he was still pleased about that, Finn realised with a little shock of awareness. It was probably best he didn't analyse that one too deeply.

'Oh my God. What on earth did she say?'

'She said Declan was always getting into trouble over women and she'd thought at the time that he'd probably deserved his black eye.'

'Blimey. Although I didn't really mean that. I meant about the fact you'd already met. Was she surprised?'

'She was flabbergasted. We both were. So it was a huge ice breaker of sorts. When she told me Declan was my half-brother I couldn't stop laughing. I think it was as much shock as anything else.'

'So after that, how did it go? Did you like her? Will you see her again and meet the rest of the family?'

'I think I'll see her again. I'm not sure about meeting the rest of the family. My head's still spinning.'

'Baby steps. It's a lot to take in.'

'Understatement.' He downed the rest of his glass in one. 'I think we might need more than one bottle of this.'

'Lucky there's another one in the kitchen then.'

* * *

The next day, Finn's hangover wasn't as bad as he'd expected. He rarely drank much red wine and Jade, mindful of their early start, had hardly drunk any at all. She'd just listened while he poured the whole lot out. His emotions of years – not that they were very coherent. Everything still felt mixed up in his head and he had a feeling it would for a while. You couldn't rewrite your history so radically without it being messy.

When they'd finally gone to bed, they'd made love. It had felt like a life-affirming, love-affirming thing to do. A beautiful constant in his life, despite all the changes. Jade had fallen asleep in his arms.

Unsurprisingly, Finn had dreamed about Declan. They'd been having dinner together at the Red Lion and had sorted out their differences. They'd both apologised and had agreed to move on. The dream was so real that when he woke up he felt as if it had already happened.

Which of course it hadn't. He tried to imagine it happening at some point in the future – him and Declan laughing about the fact they'd had a punch-up before they'd known they were brothers. Maybe that was as crazy as him thinking he and Bridie would find the years melting away when they met as adults.

It hadn't been like that, even when they'd really got talking. He had told her about Ben in the end. After the Declan shock, he had finally opened up to her about his own family.

Bridie had been delighted he was happily settled with a

good woman, as she called Jade. And she'd been over the moon to discover she had a grandson. He had seen the light go on in her eyes and when he'd shown her photos of Ben on his phone, she had cried.

'Oh, sweet Jesus, Finn, he's the spit of you when you were his age. He's gorgeous.'

She couldn't stop scrolling through the dozens of pictures Finn had taken of Ben since he'd known him. And although there was a part of Finn that had known she was so enamoured because meeting Ben must feel like a second chance for Bridie, it had no longer really mattered.

They'd agreed when they'd finally parted that they would take things slowly. But that they did want a relationship. It wasn't going to stop here. This was just the first of many meetings. Bridie had also told him she planned to contact her sister, Caitlin, once more, so something very positive had come of him stirring up the past, Finn thought with relief.

But all of that was in the future. There were other more pressing things on Finn's horizon first. The art exhibition was just one week away. He hadn't mentioned that to Bridie. He hadn't made a conscious decision not to, it just hadn't come up. He didn't talk about it much to anyone, but it took up a hell of a lot of head space.

After the exhibition, he would know for sure whether he had a chance of making it as an artist. Whether it was really going to be a career or a just a glorified hobby. Worst-case scenario, he had no sales and Eleanor dropped him.

If that happened, he'd get another engineering job so he could properly pay his way and he'd carry on painting as a hobby. He couldn't imagine stopping painting completely but he was a realist. Not many people made any proper money out of art.

More immediately he had a list of jobs for today. First up was changing a washer on the drippy tap in the spare room and there were some bills that needed paying too, the mundanity of life. Then there was some fencing that Jade had said needed attention. Then later after they'd closed up he and Jade were picking up Ben.

It was the day Carmelita was going back to the wild. They'd agreed with Sarah that they'd collect him just before dusk on their way to take Carmelita to the release spot. Jade had chosen some heathland about half a mile as the crow flies from where Sarah and Ben lived.

'I think that's probably where she came from in the first place,' Jade had told them all. 'It's the best we're going to get anyway.'

Finn gave himself a little shake. Changing tap washers, fixing fences, releasing foxes back to the wild – these were all in a day's work at Duck Pond Cottage. Seeing his son was a massive bonus. Seeing Ben was always a bonus.

Sometimes he couldn't believe how much his life had changed in the last year.

He'd gone from being a single guy, living in the city of Nottingham, to reconnecting with his one-night stand and realising he had a son. It had been amazing discovering he was a father, and getting to know his son was an ongoing miracle of a journey.

He'd also met his soulmate and moved to an idyllic small-holding in the Wiltshire countryside – meeting your soulmate was something else he'd identified with when Bridie had been relating her story. When you knew someone was right for you, you just knew.

Going from being an only child to finding out he had three

siblings, not to mention a mother and a myriad of uncles, aunts and cousins, was pretty amazing too.

Finn had to confess it was all a bit mind blowing. It was all good stuff too, although that didn't make it any less of an emotional rollercoaster – sometimes in his darker moments a small voice in his head said it was all too good to be true. That the winds of change didn't just bring good stuff. They were always counterbalanced by disaster.

Finn was trying very hard to ignore that small voice. Nothing was going to go wrong. Good things didn't have to be counterbalanced by disaster. There didn't have to be a fly in the ointment, did there?

31

Finn had finished the indoor jobs and had started on a fence repair that needed doing in the horses' paddock when he saw Aiden's yellow jeep draw into the yard.

He'd planned to stop work and grab a sandwich soon anyway, so he went up to meet the vet. When he got there, he saw Jade had beaten him to it.

She was talking to someone through the driver's window, who wasn't Aiden, Finn realised. He recognised Kate's coppery-red hair and remembered Aiden had mentioned he planned to propose to her in Venice. That must have gone well then. They were still together anyway.

Kate opened the driver's door and got out. 'Hi, Finn,' she said, spotting him. 'I was just saying to Jade here that we had a bit of a disaster when we were away. But you must promise me you won't laugh.'

'Why would we laugh at your disaster?' Finn said, glancing at Jade, who just shrugged slightly, clearly as mystified as he was.

'Because it's kind of funny too,' Kate said. 'Right then. Are you ready? Prepare yourselves.'

The passenger door of the jeep opened and someone got out. At first it was hard to see who it was because the figure had a wide white bandage obscuring the top half of his face. He also had his left arm in plaster and he was leaning on a stick.

'Aiden,' Jade gasped in alarm. 'What on earth happened to you?'

'Broken dose, fractured elbow and a cracked big toe.'

'Blimey,' Jade said, at the same moment as Finn swore under his breath. 'How on earth did all that happen? You didn't have another run-in with a goat, did you?'

'Not a goat,' Kate said.

'More of a boat,' Aiden finished with a wince.

'A boat?' Jade shook her head in disbelief. 'What boat?'

'It's a long story. If you want the unedited version, I may need to sit down.'

'Sure. Come into reception,' Jade said. 'I'll make you both a cuppa.'

A few moments later, they were all in reception, Aiden was installed in the visitor's chair and Finn and Kate were both standing up.

Mickey had started barking as soon as he'd set eyes on Aiden so Jade had been forced to evict him. As she came back into the reception, she heard Mr Spock say something that sounded suspiciously like 'Day of the mummy'. Luckily no one else seemed to have noticed and the parrot was quiet now, although he was gazing at Aiden with his head on one side, as though in deep thought. Jade hoped that whatever he was deep in thought about would stay locked in his little parrot head.

'You might remember I said I was planning to take Kate to Venice and propose?' Aiden began.

'That's right,' Jade said. 'We do.'

'Did I also tell you I planned to do it on a gondola?'

'I think you might have mentioned that.'

'It was all going according to plan. I'd got the ring, I'd warned the skipper chappie what I was going to do and he was good with it. He told me the best place to kneel – you know, so I wouldn't unbalance the gondola. So there I was clutching the ring box in my hand, on my knees...'

He paused for dramatic effect.

Finn and Jade leaned forwards in expectation.

'The mummy returns,' Mr Spock said, a little louder this time.

Aiden shot him an exasperated glance before carrying on with his story. 'I got out the ring and popped the question – Kate said yes – as you can imagine I was over the moon and I, er, jumped up too quickly, overbalanced and fell out of the gondola.'

'One minute he was there and the next he wasn't.' Kate took up the story. 'He went right into the canal. I screamed. The gondolier was yelling. We were both looking around frantically for him.'

'And that's how you broke your nose?' Jade murmured, shocked. 'You poor love.'

'No, it's how I broke my arm. I landed on a pizza delivery bike in the canal.'

'In the canal,' Finn echoed in amazement.

'Yes, in the canal. Complete with a soggy pizza in the basket. That's how we knew it was a delivery bike. Presumably vandals had thrown it in fairly recently; the top half was still sticking up. Anyway...' Aiden winced at the memory. '...I thought I was going to drown. That water's deeper than it looks. And darker. I surfaced quite quickly luckily. Unfortunately I came up too near the boat.'

'It was very unfortunate because we ran him over,' Kate said. Jade could see she was desperately trying to suppress a smile.

'Blimey O Riley.' Finn shook his head. 'That's unbelievable. So is that how you broke your nose too?'

'No.' Aiden's face was deadpan. 'I did that the second time I fell out of the boat.'

Finn snorted. Jade dared not meet his eyes for fear of joining in.

'You fell out of the boat again?' Finn's voice was even more incredulous.

'Twice more,' Aiden said. 'I was kind of in the swing of things by then.'

'The mummy returns. The mummy returns,' Mr Spock yelled, clearly in the swing of things now too.

Aiden glared at him and touched the bandage on his head. 'Enough of the mummy wisecracks, parrot.'

'It wasn't strictly Aiden's fault,' Kate put in. 'The gondolier guy was a bit panicked. And I don't think he'd been in the job that long. Those things aren't that steady.'

A small chuckle was playing around her lips now, and Jade could see Finn biting his lip hard in an effort not to laugh.

'That's awful,' Jade said. The effort of keeping a straight face was hurting her. 'What about your toe? How did that happen?'

'That was a bit later. We got back to the gondola station finally and I'd just stepped up onto the wooden platform and I thought I was home and dry, metaphorically anyway – as you can imagine I was soaked through and I'd lost a shoe, and somehow I slipped and... well, you can probably guess the rest.'

'He fell in again,' Kate finished.

'Although I think I broke my toe when I was trying to get back onto the platform,' Aiden added.

Finn exploded with mirth. 'I'm sorry, I'm sorry.' His shoulders were heaving with the effort of trying to stop. 'It's just…'

'A bit of an epic tale,' Kate said, smiling broadly. 'We are starting to see the funny side, aren't we, Aiden?'

'I guess.' His lips quirked. 'The main thing is that she said yes.'

He looked at Kate tenderly.

'It's a great story to tell the grandchildren,' Finn said when he'd got himself back in control. 'It sounds like the title of an epic film. But instead of *Planes, Trains and Automobiles*, it would be *Moats, Boats and Broken Doses*.'

Everyone except Aiden snorted with laughter.

'Sorry. Too soon,' Finn apologised.

'No, it's OK, mate. I suppose the story does actually sound quite funny when you say it out loud.'

'But it has a happy ending because as you know I did actually say yes,' Kate added, flashing her sparkly diamond ring at them both. 'And I haven't retracted it since – despite the fact I've found out how accident prone my fiancé actually is. Lucky I'm a nurse, huh!'

She went across the room and kissed Aiden on a bit of his cheek that was actually uncovered.

Aiden's eyes softened. 'I'm the lucky one. I'm the luckiest bloke alive.'

'I think I might dispute that one if I was a bookie,' Finn murmured, and they all laughed again. This time even Aiden joined in.

'My insurance claim made interesting reading,' he confessed. 'I had to phone up the company and the guy on the phone kept putting me on hold because he couldn't seem to speak. He said he had a frog in his throat or something. It took flaming ages, that call.'

'Have you been in the Red Lion yet?' Jade asked him. 'I'm sure Mike would give you drinks on the house all night if you told him that story.'

'Hmmm, I'm not sure free drinks for a night would be worth Mike ribbing me every time I show my face in the pub for the next five years.'

'Ten at least,' Kate said, and they all started to laugh again.

'Congratulations to you both,' Jade said. 'Drinks are on us next time we're at the Red Lion. In the meantime, can I offer you both a cup of coffee and a celebration chocolate or two?' She glanced at Mr Spock and he burst into song at his favourite cue word.

* * *

'Poor Aiden,' Jade said as they locked up later that day. 'He does get himself into some scrapes, doesn't he?'

Finn smiled. 'He does, and I know we didn't see eye to eye when we first met, but I've come to quite like the guy since then.'

'His heart's in the right place. And I'm really glad he found Kate. They seem happy, don't they?'

'Yes, they do.' Finn touched her arm. 'You're happy too, aren't you?' He sounded slightly anxious, and she looked at him, concerned.

'Of course I am. Do you even need to ask? Why? Aren't you?'

'I'm happier than I've ever been in my life. And I know this probably sounds daft, but I think that's why I'm asking. My life has changed beyond belief in the last couple of years. And all of it is good: falling in love with you; finding out I had a son; finding out I've got new family everywhere in fact...' He opened his hands to encompass the enormity of it all. 'Not to mention realising I could maybe make a career out of my dream job. I feel like my cup runneth over – if that doesn't sound too biblical and corny. But I really do, then I look at you and I wonder how it is for you.'

'Oh, Finn, I love that you've found a new family. I love all of that too.'

'Really?'

'Of course I do.'

'Phew. When Aiden told us about his epic tale of a proposal gone wrong, I felt a little bit guilty that for us it had all been so easy.'

'Was that before or after you laughed your socks off?' she asked him, putting her tongue firmly in her cheek.

He looked startled. 'I know. That wasn't very nice. I did apologise.'

'Finn, I'm teasing you. It was funny. Anyway, it wasn't so easy for us in the beginning, was it?'

'I suppose it wasn't all plain sailing.'

'Is that another reference to Aiden?'

'No, it was a Freudian slip, I swear.'

She burst out laughing and caught hold of his hands. 'Stop beating yourself up. It's all good. We'd better go and get Carmelita ready for her big release, hadn't we?'

'Yes, what does that involve?'

'Mainly it involves putting the animal transporter in the Land Rover and then getting her in it. I've already checked she's ready to go – she can walk fine on all four legs. The injury to her side has healed nicely.'

'I'll get the transporter.'

She watched him walk down the yard to get it, loping in that easy way he had. Animal releases could be hard, and she was glad they were doing it as a family. She thought of Ben as half hers, even though he wasn't and had a perfectly good mother already. Families were strange and complex things. She was thrilled that Finn had found so many of his.

His experiences in finding his own family had stirred a deeply buried curiosity in her that had become difficult to ignore lately. For a while now she'd wondered if maybe she should look for her own father, after all. Just in case there was an outside chance her mother had been wrong and that the man Jade had always thought of as little more than a sperm donor might want to know his daughter.

The idea, which at first hadn't been more than a tiny kernel of curiosity, had grown until it was impossible to ignore. It would be great to get closure, if nothing else. After all, it had worked out for Finn. And although it had been a bit of a roller-coaster ride, there had also been a happy ending of sorts.

Also, unlike Finn, Jade had an advantage. She had always known her father's name because it was on her birth certificate, and it was an unusual name too. There weren't many men about called Hector Ajax Foster.

Last night, when Finn had fallen asleep, exhausted with the events of the day, Jade had reached for her phone and under the duvet she'd typed Hector Ajax Foster into a search engine. She'd only found one result.

He lived in Devon. Another slightly lengthier search had thrown up an address and this afternoon when Finn had been fixing fences, and before she could talk herself out of it, Jade had slipped out for five minutes and posted a letter to The Rookery, Ashton Point, Devon. She hadn't been as tentative as Finn; she'd put one piece of paper in the envelope, which had said simply:

My name is Jade Foster, I'm the daughter of Elizabeth Foster, and I'm hoping to trace my father. Please can you help.

Like Finn, Jade had decided she wouldn't tell anyone what she'd done until she'd had some kind of answer. Nothing might ever come of it, and Finn had enough upheaval going on in his life at the moment.

32

The heathland where they'd decided to release Carmelita was about a mile square. It was a pocket of scrappy common land dotted with trees and bushes, crisscrossed with narrow tracks, and squashed between two newish red-brick housing estates. It hadn't been developed for housing so far, according to local knowledge anyway, because it was home to a population of sand lizards, a protected species.

They'd been chatting about building houses on the way over, along with the revelation that the survey for the planning application for Farmer John's land had thrown up some invasive plant species. At least it had been a revelation to Finn and Ben.

'What are invasive plants, Dad?' Ben asked from the back of the Land Rover, where he was keeping an eye on Carmelita, who was securely in the transporter, her russet-gold coat visible through the bars.

'They're plants that can grow through the floor of your house and wreck it,' Finn told him. 'So they'd all need to be dug up and moved before any building can be done.'

'But weren't the plants there first?' Ben asked with a frown.

'Can't we just leave the plants alone and build the houses in another place?'

'We haven't got that many places we can build on. And we need lots of houses.'

'OK.' It was clear from Ben's voice that he'd lost interest. 'Will we see the sand lizards today, Auntie Jade?'

'I don't think so, love. They'll probably all have gone to bed.'

'Maybe one of them will be having a late night,' Ben said hopefully.

'You never know.' Jade suppressed a smile and thought that any self-respecting sand lizard would be long gone as soon as the Land Rover drew up, even if it did happen to be having a late night!

They'd just arrived, and she parked on a patch of ochre sandy ground that served as a car park for the locals who came here. According to Sarah, it was mostly dog walkers who used the heath, but luckily they had the place to themselves tonight. The sun had set a few minutes ago and the sky was already a deep lilac, deepening in places into navy blue. High above their heads, a sliver of silver moon hung like a night light waiting to greet the first few stars.

Finn and Ben hopped out and they went round to open the back of the Land Rover. Jade had backed up close to the tangle of olive and brown undergrowth and they'd positioned the transporter so when they opened its doors, it would be possible for Carmelita to go straight out into the heathland. A ramp led from the back of the Land Rover down to the ground – not that the little vixen couldn't jump, but Jade wanted to make it as easy as possible for her.

Just in case she was wary, Jade had brought along a bribe. Some small pieces of meat, which she now used to lay a trail down the ramp and into the undergrowth.

'Right then, are you ready?' she said to Ben. 'We'll need to give her plenty of space, so you and your dad can stand well clear. Then I'm going to open the transporter and let her out.'

Ben nodded, and Finn made sure the boy was close to him as Jade leaned in and unlatched the transporter. For a few seconds, the vixen stared out at her freedom without moving. Her brown eyes were round with curiosity and her russet black-tipped ears pricked on full alert.

'I don't think she wants to go,' Ben said in a stage whisper.

But as he spoke, Carmelita raised her auburn snout and scented the air.

'She can smell home,' Jade murmured, wondering if she should throw a piece of meat down onto the ground. There were already some bits on the ramp. She decided to give it a minute.

They all waited. Except for a few nocturnal rustlings, it was quiet in the dusk. There was a very slight breeze that shivered through the trees and sent a handful of yellow and gold leaves swirling down from on high, a reminder that autumn was well and truly on its way.

The sky had grown a little darker and the slice of moon was brighter and more lemony now. Several more stars had come out, pricking the dark like tiny diamonds.

Then, all at once, Carmelita seemed to make up her mind. She took a few tentative steps, putting all four pads firmly onto the ramp, delicately took the first bribe, then ignored the second and leapt suddenly into the undergrowth and was gone with a flick of her bushy black-tipped tail.

'She didn't hang around long,' Ben said, and his voice wobbled a bit.

'I expect she's pleased to be home,' Finn told him. 'She's probably got friends round here.'

'So she won't be too lonely without us?' There was a note of wistfulness in Ben's voice as he looked from his father back to Jade. His long-lashed eyes were bright with tears.

'She won't be lonely, love. She'll be with all of her fox friends.'

'Do you think she'll ever come back to the garden to see me and Mum? Will she remember that we made her better?'

'You never know,' Jade said. 'You might see her again. But the main thing is that she's with her own kind, which is where she should be.'

Ben digested this for a moment before wiping his eyes with his coat sleeve. 'One of the kids at school said some people keep foxes as pets. Is that true, Auntie Jade?'

'It might be true, but that doesn't mean it's the right thing to do, love. Foxes are wild creatures and they need to be in the wild, looking after themselves.'

'That's what I told him.' Ben sounded half relieved and half upset.

Finn put an arm around his son's shoulders and for a few seconds Ben leaned against him before standing tall again and putting his hands in his coat pockets. Jade found she was blinking back a few tears herself. Letting go was such a hard lesson to learn.

The only thing that had ever made it better for her was being surrounded with love. Like Ben was now. She moved across to where man and boy stood, and for a little while they all stayed where they were, wrapped in darkness and listening to the nighttime rustlings of the heathland beneath the quiet beauty of the stars.

33

Three days before the art exhibition, Jade had a phone call from Phoebe Dashwood at Puddleduck Farm.

'Hey, it's lovely to hear from you,' Jade said, recognising the other woman's voice immediately. 'How are you? How's everything at Puddleduck Farm?'

'Busy as always.' Phoebe hesitated. 'This is terribly cheeky, Jade, but I was wondering if you could help me out with something. Please say no if you can't.' She swallowed and Jade could hear the strain in her voice when she went on.

'We've just been landed with a litter of two-week-old puppies. The mother died unfortunately, so they need hand-feeding every four hours and I'm not able to do it at the moment.'

There was a thin reedy cry in the background and Jade pricked up her ears. 'Don't worry. We should be able to take them. We can have them in the cottage for a bit. Was that a baby I just heard?'

'Um, yes. That's Lily. She was born six weeks ago. She's keeping us very busy at the moment.'

'Oh, that's amazing. Congratulations. I didn't even know you were pregnant.'

'It wasn't exactly planned. But we're delighted. She's an utter sweetheart. Sam's besotted. He's a very hands-on daddy.'

Jade could hear the love in her voice as she went on. 'Sam does a lot of the night feeds because I'm with Lily all day. I don't think she ever sleeps. But I can't ask him to look after puppies as well. Although he'd probably say yes.'

'We're fine to have them. What kind of pups?'

'It's hard to say. There's two brindle and white and one brown. Mum was a brown spaniel-type cross. Not sure about Dad.'

'We'll come and pick them up,' Jade said. 'It's no problem at all.' She looked at the clock in reception. It was just before three thirty. 'We can come about five if you like. I'll lock up early.'

'Thanks so much, Jade. I owe you one, big time.'

'Of course you don't. You've helped me out loads in the past.' Last year she and Finn had taken a donkey from Skegness to Puddleduck because they already had three. All sanctuaries helped each other out if they could.

* * *

Jade went to tell Finn what she was planning and as she'd expected, he nodded and smiled, but didn't object.

Before they went to collect the pups, Jade prepared a crate in the back room with a box and some fleece puppy bedding while Mickey sniffed about curiously, knowing something was afoot.

'We're getting some babies,' Jade told the little dog. 'You'll practically be a daddy.'

Finn gave her a quick smile. 'You're bonkers.'

'So are you if you've only just realised that.'

'Touche.'

Puddleduck Pets was an hour away from them in the heart of the beautiful New Forest, but it was a gorgeous drive. September had got out her paint palette. The ferns were the colour of burnished gold and a scattering of red and yellow leaves littered the landscape.

Ancient trees and a mixture of evergreen and browning heathland contrasted against the backdrop of a milky-white sky.

Every so often they saw small herds of brown ponies strolling through the red and gold leaves and occasionally wandering across the unfenced roads.

'They've got no road sense, have they?' Finn remarked, slowing the Land Rover as he approached a little group near to the roadside. 'It's a good job most drivers are respectful enough to stick to the 40 miles per hour speed limit.'

'Definitely.'

They talked about Declan for a bit and the fact he was Finn's brother and how surprising it was that they'd never heard anything else from him after Finn had knocked him over in reception.

'That'll be interesting next time we meet,' Finn said. 'I'm going to have to apologise to him, aren't I? Although Dad still reckons he deserved it.'

'He did,' Jade said, leaning across and touching Finn's wrist. 'I'm just glad you didn't damage yourself too much in the process.'

'Dad said that too.'

'I'm so glad he's OK with everything,' she murmured.

A couple of days after he'd met Bridie, Finn had spent over an hour updating Ray and Dorrie on everything that had happened. They'd chatted on Zoom, which was Ray's latest venture into the twenty-first century, and Ray and Dorrie had listened quietly when Finn had told them about his meeting with Bridie.

When he'd said he was going to meet her again, and that hopefully he would meet his half-brother and sisters too, Ray had nodded.

'I'm pleased for you, son, and I'm glad she's OK.'

'Me too,' Dorrie had added. Then she'd confided she'd had a sister who'd died in a car accident during a three-month period when they weren't speaking to each other and she'd felt terribly guilty about that. It was one of the reasons she'd wanted Ray to encourage Finn to find his mother. Just in case he ever tried in the future and found out he'd left it too late.

That had been a very emotional conversation. Both Jade and Finn had blinked away tears as Dorrie had told them what had happened.

'The more I get to know Dorrie, the more I like her,' Finn had said to Jade afterwards. 'She was right to encourage me to find Bridie. And I think it gave Dad some closure too.'

Closure was definitely the word of the moment, Jade thought now as they drove along the long wall that bordered the posh estate next door to Puddleduck Pets with the full-size statue of the stag standing on sentry duty over its gates.

It would be good to get some of that for herself. She'd heard nothing since she'd sent her letter to The Rookery. But it was still early days. She sighed.

'What?' Finn asked.

Jade bit her lip. She still hadn't told him about that. 'I was just, um, thinking it's a pity I didn't buy a plot of land next door to the landed gentry. And then no one would be building on it.'

'Ah, well. Who knows what the future holds.' They had talked a lot about the implications of Rural Developments being owned by Finn's family, but they'd decided in the end that unfortunately it probably wouldn't make too much difference. It would still be built on eventually.

They arrived just after five as they'd promised and a few moments later were walking through a side gate to Puddleduck Pets. Phoebe was a vet and her practice, Puddleduck Vets, was based in a converted barn on site.

The vet practice was still open and as Jade and Finn approached the glass doors, Phoebe came out to meet them. She had a baby in a papoose across her chest, and they both stopped to coo over Lily.

'She's gorgeous,' Jade said truthfully as the blue-eyed baby blew bubbles at her. 'You're not working, surely?'

'No, I'm on maternity leave. But I pop in now and then. Sam and I live in the house on site anyway. I just saw your Land Rover pulling in so I thought I'd come and say hi.'

Phoebe looked the picture of happiness, although she was clearly tired too. Dark circles smudged her eyes. 'Thanks so much for this, Jade. Sam and I could just about manage puppy feeds as well but it'd be a struggle, and I didn't want to ask my gran. Maggie thinks she's still a spring chicken but she's the wrong side of seventy-five and she's supposed to be stepping back from the animal side since we moved into Puddleduck Farm.' She grinned. 'The puppies are in the house. Follow me.'

A few moments later, Jade and Finn were looking down at the tangle of brown and brindle pups who'd been asleep when they arrived but had become aware of the humans and were now waking up and mewling blindly.

Jade felt her heart turn over as she always did when confronted with such helpless vulnerability.

'Gorgeous little ones. Why did their mum die?'

'Lack of nutrition from what I could see, and she wasn't that young, bless her. The woman who brought them in didn't hang around very long. Said they weren't hers. We didn't ask too many questions. What's the point? People lie anyway, don't they? But it was nothing infectious, I did check that.'

She and Jade exchanged glances. 'At least she brought them in,' Phoebe added. 'Even though it was a bit late.'

Jade nodded. She knew she'd have been less forgiving, but Phoebe was right, it was pointless getting into altercations with people. When you ran an animal sanctuary you came across the best and the worst in people. It was just a fact of life.

Finn carried the box of pups out to the Land Rover and placed them gently in the animal transporter. Jade brought the rest of the bits and pieces Phoebe insisted on giving them. 'There's enough formula milk to last them until they're weaned. If you bring them back when they're old enough I'll do the worming and inoculations too. I don't want this to cost you anything. Apart from sleep,' she murmured, suppressing a yawn. 'Thanks so much again.'

'It's our pleasure,' Jade said and gave Phoebe an impulsive hug. 'You look after yourself and this little one. Don't go back to work too early.'

'Oh, I shan't,' Phoebe said. 'I can't risk falling asleep halfway through a consultation. You will keep me posted on their progress, won't you?' She blew a kiss in the direction of the puppies. 'They haven't had the best start.'

'They'll be absolutely fine,' Jade promised as she and Finn climbed back into the Land Rover. 'We'll take very good care of them.'

'I wish we lived closer,' she murmured as they set off for home. 'I think Phoebe and I would be really good friends.'

'You won't be saying that when you're doing the 4 a.m. feeds for those puppies,' Finn quipped.

'Oh, but I assumed you'd be doing the 4 a.m. ones,' she shot back.

'I've got an exhibition to prepare for – I can't look like a haggard old man, can I?'

'I thought artists were supposed to be gaunt and haggard. It's traditional. It adds that enigmatic touch of authenticity – proof that you suffer for your art. Aren't you supposed to be starving in a garret too?'

'Definitely not, these days.' Finn slanted her a glance. 'I've got an idea though. We can rope Dad and Dorrie in. They're coming down for the exhibition and they love puppies.'

'I bet they won't love them so much at 4 a.m. Anyway, I thought they weren't coming down until the day before. What about tonight and tomorrow?'

The banter went back and forth all the way home, but Jade knew as well as Finn did that they would both look after the pups together. Like they did everything else together. They were a team.

She felt another twinge of guilt that she hadn't told him about the letter she'd sent to Hector Ajax Foster, but as yet she'd heard absolutely nothing. So maybe it was a wild goose chase anyway.

It was perfectly possible to hand feed puppies in your sleep, Jade decided after that first night. If you didn't open your eyes fully and you had everything prepared and ready – the pups' crate had been moved into their bedroom – you hardly knew you'd woken up.

Finn had agreed with her when he'd taken his turn on the second night. 'It's good preparation for when we have babies,' he'd murmured as he'd climbed back into bed after a feeding session and warmed his cold toes up on her legs.

'Gerroff,' Jade had muttered, pretending to be half asleep, but she'd heard him loud and clear and it had left a warmth in her heart. They'd have babies one day. Their babies would be brought up surrounded by unconditional love. They would get their happy ending. Despite all the churning up of the past that had been done lately, the future was looking pretty rosy.

34

The morning before the art exhibition, Ray and Dorrie arrived, laden with gifts. There was a bottle of Moët for Finn to celebrate his first exhibition, there was a huge gold box of Belgian chocolates for Jade and even a squeaky toy for Mickey, who wasn't interested in toys unless he'd stolen them. There were toys for the new puppies too, although Jade had explained they were a bit young for toys at the moment. That had got lost in translation.

They both insisted on helping out around the sanctuary and Ray laughed his head off at Mr Spock's bad language, which no one had yet managed to curb. Dorrie took over the puppy feeding for the day. She was enamoured with the little ones.

'Maybe Ray and I could have one when they're old enough,' she said to Jade when everyone else was out of earshot. 'I know he'd love it. I'll speak to him.'

That night, they all went to the Red Lion for supper where they were greeted by a jubilant Mike.

'Have you heard the news? The plans for the new housing estate have been put on indefinite hold!' His voice was triumphant as he pulled a pint of Guinness for Ray and clunked it onto the long wooden bar. Jade and Dorrie were sharing a bottle of white wine and Finn had said he wouldn't have any because he wanted to keep a clear head for the following day.

'What does indefinite hold mean?' Jade asked Mike, looking at him with interest, even though she'd had a phone call from Ursula, so she and Finn already knew the plans were on hold.

'They withdrew them completely when they saw the survey. Too costly to proceed. I suppose they can resubmit them again at some point in the future. But they won't be wanting to sit on a big plot like that for too long without doing anything. That'd cost money.'

Jade nodded politely. She and Finn might have inside information but they were also both painfully aware that Rural Developments would need to build houses at some point to get their investment back. Or they'd have to sell it on again to some other developer who'd do the same thing. At the moment, all they had was a stay of execution.

The four of them were just heading to their table with their drinks when Mike shouted after them. 'Have you seen Aiden lately? That daft vet got himself into a spot of bother in Venice, did you hear about that?'

Jade shook her head when Ray nudged her arm. 'What's all that about then?'

'We'll leave it to Mike to fill you in later,' Finn said. 'It's quite a long story!'

* * *

The next day, everyone was going to the exhibition in separate vehicles.

Jade, Ray and Dorrie were going from Duck Pond Cottage. Sarah, Callum and Ben were meeting them there.

Finn was going early to meet Eleanor as he'd have to be there for the duration. The others would be there for the official opening time which was 11 a.m.

Aiden and Kate had said they would pop along too. 'It will be a good distraction,' Aiden had said. 'And it's not as though I can work at the moment. I'm still signed off.'

Ray had asked if Bridie would be at the exhibition, and Finn had said no because she didn't know about it. 'I told her I worked as a handyman. I didn't mention I was an artist.'

'Why on earth not?'

'Because until I've sold some more of my work, Dad, I still don't feel as though I really am.'

On the morning itself, Finn couldn't decide whether he felt more or less nervous than the day he'd gone to meet Bridie.

'I think it might be more,' he said to Jade as, suited and booted, he finally got into the Toyota.

'At least this time you'll have rent-a-crowd to support you,' Jade said, bending to kiss him. 'You never know. This time this evening you might be rich. Richer, anyway,' she added swiftly when she saw his frown.

'Yes, don't jinx it. Anyway, I don't really mind if I don't sell anything. It's the kudos of being there that's the main thing.'

'Finn McTaggart, you're a hopeless liar.'

'You're right. I am. Of course I want someone to buy something. I just can't imagine anyone actually will.'

Jade rolled her eyes. 'Let's hope you're feeling a bit more confident by the end of the day. See you very soon.'

She waved him off. It would be another hour or so before she'd leave to join him. She'd already made breakfast for Ray and Dorrie and Dorrie had helped with the early puppy feeds, which they'd also had to time around the art exhibition. Now, feeling at a loose end, she strolled down the yard to talk to Dawn.

* * *

The exhibition was being held at The Guildhall in Salisbury, an imposing municipal building dating back to 1795, and the city's equivalent of a town hall. It was a place that was hard to miss if you visited Salisbury because it was set bang in the middle of the city next to the marketplace and was often used for exhibitions and fairs.

Today, Finn found himself looking up at the impressive grey building with its tall stone pillars and huge oval windows with new eyes. He felt nervous as hell and it was a major effort to walk up the steps through the pillars and go through the main entrance into the foyer.

The exhibition was signposted and when he got to the room itself, he found a hive of activity.

The venue, a large room with hugely high ceilings, oval windows, sparkling lead crystal chandeliers and mustard-yellow walls, had been divided up into alcoves with the clever use of room dividers, so that it was both one big space but also several individual spaces too.

This way each artist had their own unique section of hall. There were only three artists, Eleanor had told Finn, and this was fairly standard for a multi-artist event. The other two were well established – Finn had seen and admired both of their work – and this made him feel even more nervous, but also very privileged and pleased too, to be there alongside them.

The paintings were already up, but there were white-shirted waiters and waitresses scurrying around setting up tables and cups and saucers in one of the spaces. Coffee, tea and tiny dainty cakes would be served when the event opened.

Finn saw that Eleanor was deep in conversation with a middle-aged man in purple checked trousers and a sky-blue jacket, sporting a short beard and a grey ponytail. They were chatting beside a window, adorned with red and gold velvet drapes, held back with gold tasselled cords.

Finn assumed the guy must be another artist until Eleanor spotted him and beckoned him over. 'Finn, this is Henry Barton, my favourite art dealer. Henry, this is Finn McTaggart, one of my artists.'

Henry turned towards him and held out his hand. He had hard blue eyes and a wide smile. 'Finn, what a pleasure to meet you.'

'It's great to meet you too, sir.' Finn knew Henry Barton by reputation if not by sight. Everyone knew who Henry Barton was.

'You can drop the sir.' The art dealer looked amused. 'I didn't have a knighthood last time I looked.' He exchanged a smile with Eleanor, who smiled ingratiatingly back.

'This is Finn's first fair, Henry.'

Finn flushed, feeling as though he had already committed a faux pas and they were still an hour off opening the doors.

To his huge relief, the situation improved a hundredfold with Henry's next words. 'You're doing OK, son. I see you have some "reserved" stickers already.'

'Do I?' Finn glanced at Eleanor, doing his best to keep his voice ultra casual, while at the same time resisting the urge to jump up and down and shout 'Yay!' at the top of his voice.

'Indeed you do,' she said, gesturing towards the alcove at the back of the room. 'Go and see.'

Finn went to see, and he was amazed to find that the big

canvas of Stonehenge, which was one of the most expensive pictures he had on display, had a reserved sticker on it. He stood there looking at it with his heart pounding. Wow. Someone had liked his painting enough to reserve it. Eleanor had told him about presales, which happened when galleries sent digital images of pictures to a select handful of their most valued clients.

But Finn hadn't expected for a second he would get any presales. He glanced around at his other paintings and saw reserved stickers on a couple of the other small pictures too.

Reserved didn't necessarily mean that the picture was definitely sold. The collector usually wanted to see a painting in person before clinching the deal and handing over any actual money, but it was a very good sign. And it was an excellent start to the day. Finn felt his confidence ratchet up a few notches.

The sales of these three paintings alone would pay for their wedding. If things continued to go as well as this, he could splash out on a honeymoon.

35

'I think I'm almost as nervous as Finn is,' Jade said to Dorrie and Ray as the three of them strolled towards the marketplace in the morning sunshine.

'It's a big day,' Dorrie said. 'I bet you're really proud.'

'I am.' Jade glanced at Ray. 'You must be very proud too.'

The old man, who in Finn's words had never been big on emotion, grunted noncommittally. 'Course I am. It's what he wants.'

Dorrie gave him a playful slap on the arm. 'He's immensely proud, aren't you, pumpkin. Your boy having his paintings on sale to the public in a big exhibition. It's amazing.'

'Beats being a miner. I'll give you that.' Ray cleared his throat and winked.

'He's jumping up and down with joy on the inside,' Dorrie teased. 'It's just not all on show, is it, love?'

Ray flushed a little and Jade suppressed a smile. Dorrie and Ray were such opposites. Dorrie was so bouncy and extrovert and Ray was so dour and taciturn, but the love between them was very clear.

She and Finn were much more similar in personality. Both of them were natural introverts. Finn preferred the solitude of his own company – he'd have been happy painting pictures full time and never seeing anyone but her and Ben, and Jade was most relaxed when she was around people she loved like Sarah, Finn and Ben, or her animals.

She wondered if Ray was worried about Finn and Bridie's reconciliation and all of the past resurfacing. He'd said he was happy to know she was still settled with Christopher. But it must still be difficult for him. Jade hoped Finn was right and Bridie wouldn't by some coincidence appear. She didn't want any awkwardness to spoil Finn's day. He was nervous enough already.

They went up the stone steps and through the pillars into the Guildhall, and as they were directed to the exhibition by a helpful member of staff, Jade made a conscious decision to relax. This was Finn's day and she was determined to make it as enjoyable as possible for him. She was pleased to see that even though they were ten minutes early there was already a small crowd gathered outside the door. Expensively dressed arty types mingled with locals and she could hear the odd posh-voiced yahs and oh my goshes floating around on the air.

She spotted Sarah, Callum and Ben. They had joined them, and the little group were all exchanging pleasantries when the doors were opened bang on eleven and a smiling, beautifully dressed woman invited them in.

Coffee and cake was being served on their left and they were greeted by more smiles before a man who introduced himself as their host but whose name Jade didn't catch told them a bit about each artist before inviting them all to have a wander around to look at the fabulous art.

Jade watched Ray as their host did the introductions. Dorrie was right. He was lit up on the inside. Pride was written all over his face. Then they were finally let loose inside the exhibition hall. Jade spotted Finn standing beside a man with a sky-blue jacket and purple trousers. She waved to him, and he smiled back at her and lifted a hand in acknowledgement. She swallowed a lump in her throat. This was such a big day for him.

Sarah and Callum seemed almost as overawed as Ray had been outside, but Ben soon broke the ice with his cries of, 'Daddy, Daddy, your pictures are definitely the best.'

'You haven't even seen them yet,' Finn said, striding across and sweeping his son off his feet for a hug.

'I've seen all of them at home,' Ben said, pursing his lips and casting a disparaging look at a bronze head that was displayed on a plinth nearby. 'That one's got a wonky nose,' he pointed out loudly. 'Dad doesn't do wonky noses, do you, Dad?'

'Maybe the model had a wonky nose,' Sarah said, looking around nervously as several people glanced their way.

'He did,' commented a woman who'd overheard them. 'I'm the sculptor. Thank you for coming.' She winked at Ben and he looked delighted and winked back.

Ray looked too overawed to speak, but as they walked along to Finn's section of the room he stood with his hands clasped behind his back and studied each painting in turn.

'My son's an artist,' he said to no one in particular. 'My son's a really talented artist. I've no idea where he gets it from.'

He hurried across to Finn and touched his arm. 'I'm so proud of you, son.'

* * *

They were an hour into the exhibition and Finn had just started to relax and get used to the bizarre experience of talking to strangers about his work when he thought he saw a familiar face.

Across the room, talking to a woman in a navy dress, was a man he recognised. It was Declan Stone, he realised, remembering Ben's comment about wonky noses. Or if it wasn't him, it was someone who looked very much like him. He felt his heart dive towards his polished shoes and sent up a silent prayer to the universe that it wasn't Declan, just someone who just looked like him.

Then, almost as if the man sensed he was being observed, he turned slightly and met Finn's eyes.

Shit, it was definitely Declan. To Finn's relief, his nose looked quite straight. He hadn't done any permanent damage then. But he didn't look particularly happy. Could it be coincidence he was visiting the fair, or had he known Finn would be here? Finn suspected he was about to find out because Declan had broken off his conversation with his companion and was heading across.

Jade had spotted Declan too. She'd seen him about ten seconds after Finn had done and now, instinctively, she moved closer to Finn. 'I take it you didn't invite him?'

'No, I didn't.'

'Do you think he knows who you are? Has Bridie told him?'

'Your guess is as good as mine.' Finn fixed a pleasant smile on his face as Declan reached them.

'Good morning, Jade.' He addressed her first and gave her a charming smile before turning towards Finn.

'Good morning, Finn – or should I be saying big bruv?'

'Morning.' Finn's voice was even. Jade registered that he was very still. He always went still when he was in a state of high emotion. He was one of the most contained and self-controlled people she'd ever met, which made it all the more surprising he had given Declan a right hook the first time the two men had met. Although Declan had been pretty provocative on that occasion.

'I should probably knock you over,' Declan said conversationally. 'I owe you one.' He paused, his eyes glittering slightly, his fists clenched at his sides, and for a moment or so the two men squared up to each other like fighting tomcats about to go to war. The tension was palpable.

'Please don't cause a scene.' Jade took a step forward. 'Not here.'

'He's not going to, are you?' Finn said, holding Declan's gaze.

There was an awfully long moment when Jade wasn't sure which way Declan would go, but then his face broke into a grin.

'He's right. I'm not.' He laughed. 'We don't want to get blood on their nice floor, do we? And who am I to scare off the punters.' He broke the gaze and looked around. 'I didn't realise painting was your thing. Mind you' – he shot Finn a glance – 'there's a few things I didn't know about you. You're quite the dark horse, aren't you?'

'I'm not sure this is the best place to talk about our shared history,' Finn said quietly. 'But I would like to talk about it with you.'

'I'm sure you would. Must be handy finding out you've got a wealthy old dear in the wings who can't wait to cook the prodigal son a fatted calf.'

Finn did the hint of a double take and his grey eyes went a shade darker. 'I didn't leave the family,' he said icily. 'If that's what you're implying.'

Declan had the grace to drop his gaze. He'd put both his hands in his pockets and he shuffled his feet on the wooden floor.

Ray, who must have picked up on the tense body language

from a distance, was heading over to see what was going on. Fortunately, no one else in the crowd seemed to have noticed anything awry.

Jade, who was beginning to think this wasn't going to end well, tried the voice of reason.

'This definitely isn't the time or place for a row. I'm sure we can talk everything through like adults though, can't we? Another time. For your mother's sake.' She glanced from Declan back to Finn and she sent him a silent plea with her eyes.

I know you're angry but please back off.

Finn shifted slightly, relaxing his stance. But it was Declan who finally took a step back. He might not have had as much to lose as Finn today but maybe there was a bit of him that was responding to the quiet logic in Jade's voice.

Ray arrived beside them, just as Declan turned away. 'See you again, Finn,' was his parting shot over his shoulder.

'I can't wait,' Finn called with only a trace of irony.

'Who was that bloke?' Ray asked, looking at Jade and Finn anxiously.

Finn told him and he saw his father's face blanch a little. Declan was the living embodiment of his erstwhile partner's infidelity. Of course he was. That was never going to be easy.

'He didn't look like he was congratulating you,' Ray said, wiping his palms on his trouser legs. 'Was he trying to cause trouble?'

'Aye, Dad. I think you could say he was.' Finn let out a small sigh of relief as he watched Declan disappear into the crowd of milling people.

'So did he turn up by coincidence or did he know you'd be here?' Dorrie asked, who'd clearly overheard enough to pick up what was going on.

'I haven't told anyone I'd be here. But clearly Bridie has told

Declan who I am and somehow he's put two and two together and worked it out. I don't know.'

Finn noticed Eleanor was heading towards them. 'You may need to excuse me for a moment. I think my agent wants a word.' He smiled at them as he spoke and added quietly, 'My agent. I don't think those two words are ever going to get old.'

Both Dorrie and Ray looked relieved, which had been his intention. Jade looked slightly less reassured, and Finn wasn't surprised.

Declan had caused trouble from the moment he'd come into their lives and it didn't look as though the fact they were brothers was going to change that any time soon.

Maybe the fly in the ointment he'd been worried about was Declan.

* * *

It wasn't until much later that day that Finn discovered it was Bridie who had bought his Stonehenge painting.

An oblivious Eleanor told him that the Stones were big art collectors and as such would have seen a presale catalogue of the works on display in case they wanted to buy early.

'It's good news that the Stones like your work, Finn. They're influential people in the art world. They wouldn't normally buy more than one item from a new artist – they like to hedge their bets – and they've reserved three of your paintings so they must be confident.'

Finn tried to look pleased and not dismayed, because Eleanor was practically rubbing her hands together with glee.

'Don't the Stones own a property company?' he said instead. 'I didn't know they were art dealers.'

She gave him a shrewd look. 'That's right. But old man Stone collects art as a hobby. Has done for years. He's always had a good eye; in fact, rumour has it that he's made more money from buying and selling art than he has from property deals, so give yourself a big pat on the back, Finn.'

He wondered whether he should say anything about the family connection, but before he got the chance, Eleanor said, 'I owe you a celebratory lunch. Call me next week and we'll compare diaries. Yah?'

36

Finn relayed this conversation to Jade, Ray and Dorrie as they sat in the Red Lion later that evening. Sarah, Ben and Callum had called in for a quick drink earlier in order to raise a glass to what had turned out to be a very successful day, but Sarah had since taken Ben off home to bed, having declared he was totally worn out.

'I had no idea Bridie was interested in art,' Finn told them quietly now. 'Although from what Eleanor was saying it's more her father-in-law who's interested.'

Jade could see he looked pained and she touched his arm. 'You seem troubled. Is that because you think they haven't bought your paintings on merit?'

He met her eyes and gave a hint of a nod. 'I must admit it did cross my mind.'

'But you sold other paintings too, didn't you?'

'Only a couple of small ones.'

'You're beating yourself up unnecessarily, lad,' Ray said fiercely. 'No one pays out that kind of money for art unless they think it's good. Even the price tags on the small ones made my eyes water.'

'I guess only time will tell on that score, Dad. We'll have to wait and see.' Finn sipped his Guinness. 'As far as my art career goes, this is just the beginning. All I can do is paint the best pictures I can and cross my fingers. Even Eleanor said there's loads of luck involved. I am going to have to sort things out with Declan though. He may not be the only one of the family who's none too happy to have a brother turn up. My half-sisters might feel the same.'

'Or they might not,' Dorrie put in brightly from across the table. 'They might be thrilled. You must think positive, Finn.'

'I agree,' Jade said. 'Declan's probably still sore about you flattening him the first time you met. Not that he didn't ask for it,' she added quickly when she saw Finn's face.

'Even so, I should probably apologise to him.'

'It might be an idea, love,' Dorrie said softly.

Finn turned towards his father. 'What do you think?'

'Up to you, lad. From what I've heard, he's the one who should be apologising. Not you.'

'But in the interests of keeping the peace, it might be the diplomatic thing to do,' Dorrie said. 'Be the bigger man.'

'Yeah, you're probably right.'

Finn looked so weary and worn that Jade ached for him. 'Why don't you sleep on it and see how you feel in the morning,' she suggested. 'A good night's sleep always makes things better. I can do the puppies.'

'Ray and I will feed the puppies,' Dorrie said firmly. 'You two need your beauty sleep and it's too late for us.'

'Speak for yourself!' Ray said, but he was grinning, and a lightness returned to the table.

Finn squeezed Jade's fingers and Jade squeezed his back. A

letter had arrived for her this morning. A letter she hadn't yet told anyone about. Her heart had leapt with optimism when she'd seen the unfamiliar handwriting on the envelope, and she'd sneaked into the bathroom to look at the contents in private.

She'd been glad she had because when she'd opened it she'd found that inside was her own letter, which had been opened, but then stuffed back into its envelope and the words 'RETURN TO SENDER' written in block capitals in red ink on the outside.

Her heart had crash dived. So that was that then. Either the occupier of The Rookery, Ashton Point, Devon wasn't her father, or he was and he wanted nothing to do with her. Red capital letters were pretty categoric. The more she'd looked at the writing, the more she'd felt the anger vibrating off the page.

Maybe a good night's sleep would make that feel better too. After all, it wasn't as though she'd lost anything. You couldn't lose what you'd never had, could you?

* * *

The next day, Jade got up just before six as she always did, leaving a sleeping Finn in bed, and slipped out of the back door of Duck Pond Cottage. It was still dark as she made her way up the yard, tiptoeing past the kennel dogs so as not to set them off barking, and on past the equine shadows in the paddock.

As September drew closer to October, the mornings had grown a lot cooler. Dew quite often sparkled across the grass and the fresh country smells filled her nostrils. Autumn was well and truly here.

It would be harvest festival next – Ben always took in fresh eggs to school for harvest festival. Then it would be Halloween with pumpkin pie and trick or treat – that was another day

Jade loved. Guy Fawkes night wasn't good for the animals but luckily they were too far away from the organised displays for them to be a problem, and not long after that it would be Christmas.

Jade couldn't wait for Christmas. As a child, she had hated Christmas because her mother had always worked. The hotels were open at Christmas and Elizabeth had always gone along to show her face.

In the whole of her childhood, Jade couldn't remember a time when she and Elizabeth had done what other families did. They'd never had a normal Christmas. They'd never been able to decorate the tree with tinsel and decorations that were family heirlooms or watch the night skies on Christmas Eve for the chance of spotting Father Christmas's sleigh. They'd never been able to eat a roast dinner on the day itself and open presents around the tree afterwards. They'd never been able to go to a pantomime in January and shout, 'He's behind you,' at the tops of their voices.

All of these things were reserved for the paying guests away for their Christmas breaks and Elizabeth would be at one or another of her hotels, making sure the punters got their magical Christmas. Making sure they knew their hostess really cared.

The family Christmas came second and would be held sometime after Twelfth Night when everyone else had taken their decorations down and gone back to work. The time when everyone else was sick and tired of Christmas was the time that Jade and her mother would sit down to celebrate it. They'd pull crackers and pretend the atmosphere was the same as it was on 25 December.

Jade had always told herself she didn't mind because she quite often snuck off to Sarah's for Christmastime anyway. Sarah's adoptive parents were deeply traditional and they did all of the classic stuff, and they always made Jade feel very welcome. But it wasn't the same.

Somewhere in Duck Pond Rescue, a cockerel crowed a welcome to the new day and Jade gave herself a little shake. It wasn't quite October. Why on earth was she thinking about Christmas? She had a good idea she knew exactly why it was.

Her mind flicked back to the letter that had come yesterday. It had stirred everything up, and memories of long ago, which she usually managed to keep locked away in tight little boxes, were swirling about in her head.

Maybe it was never a good idea to take a long pointy stick and dig around in the murky puddles of the past. After all, while Finn had discovered his mother had been pleased to see him, Declan certainly hadn't been happy. And the rest of Finn's extensive family were still an unknown quantity.

What if they all felt the same way that Declan did? That Finn was simply some unwanted interloper who'd gatecrashed into their lives in order to steal their mother/inheritance/peace of mind – delete as appropriate.

Jade's head swirled with 'what ifs'.

That letter that had carried with it the hot sting of rejection had been bad enough. Maybe it was a blessing that Jade's father hadn't replied to her. It would have been so much worse if they'd met and discovered they didn't like each other. Or if they'd met and Jade had discovered that she, too, had a pile of relatives out there who wouldn't welcome her.

She tried to push these thoughts away as she began the routines of the day, starting with the geese and the hens, letting them out, feeding them, collecting the eggs, but it was difficult, and by the time it was fully daylight she already felt as though she'd been through an emotional wringer.

At seven fifteen, she saw Finn heading across the yard to the kennels where she'd just finished feeding the dogs and was starting on their morning walks.

'Hey, lovely. I overslept. Why didn't you wake me?'

'Because you had a long day yesterday and I thought you were probably tired out.'

'You look pretty tired yourself.' He studied her face. 'Did you sleep OK? You were tossing and turning quite a bit.'

'Was I? Sorry. I hope I didn't wake you.'

'You didn't. I think I was a bit strung out on adrenaline still from the day.' He paused. 'So what's going on with you? Are you OK?'

'Grab a couple of dogs and come across to the dog-walking field and I'll tell you.'

'OK.'

A few minutes later, as they walked three greyhounds around the outer track of the field, Jade told him about the letter she'd sent to the address that she thought was her father's. Then she handed him the response she'd got back.

Finn listened, then read the pages in silence before finally turning to her and asking quietly, 'Why didn't you tell me?'

'I think for the same reason you didn't tell me when you started the search for Bridie. In case nothing came of it.'

'I meant about this one. When did it come?'

'Yesterday. But I didn't want to spoil your day.' She felt her eyes fill with tears and then Finn was taking the greyhounds' rope leads from her and dropping them onto the grass.

'Oh, my love, I'm so sorry. I would have been there for you. It must have been terrible seeing this.'

'It wasn't the best start...' She hated that her voice was thick with tears and her throat so tight with emotion. 'I was trying not to care,' she managed to get out, and in answer, Finn took her in his arms.

'Of course you would care. It's impossible not to care about this stuff.' He held her close while she sobbed on his shoulder. It took a minute or so before she could stop.

'The greyhounds,' she managed.

'They're fine. They can't get out of this field.'

'Milo can,' she contradicted. 'That's why I keep them on the lead. If he sees a rabbit he'll be through the fence. Where are they anyway?'

They caught up with Milo, who was sniffing around where the grass grew long and wild in the centre of the field. The fawn-coloured greyhound gave them a doe-eyed look that implied butter wouldn't melt in his mouth and that of course he had no intention of chasing any rabbits.

Finn grabbed the rope handles of the leads and they walked back to the five-bar gate.

'I'm sorry I didn't tell you,' Jade said again. 'Do I look like I've been crying?' Two volunteers were heading their way.

'Not too bad.' Finn was hopeless at lying and she glanced at him suspiciously. 'OK, just blame it on hay fever,' he amended.

'At the end of September.'

'I think you can get hay fever any time, these days.' He looked up at the white sky over their heads. 'We can talk more about this later, can't we?'

'There's not much else to say,' Jade said ruefully. 'I don't have any more leads at all as far as my biological father goes. Besides, I'm pretty sure it was him who sent that letter. Don't you think the red capitals were a giveaway? Surely if it was just a random person that lived there they'd have put in a note or something. They wouldn't have just scribbled that curt message in red pen.'

'Maybe they only had a red pen to hand?' he said, lifting an eyebrow, and she knew he was trying to make her feel better and she loved him for it.

They greeted the volunteers who'd come in early to walk dogs, which Jade was very grateful for, and then just before they reached the back door of Duck Pond Cottage, Finn pulled Jade close again. 'We have each other and we'll have our own family one day. And until then, you're very much part of my family. Ray and Dorrie love you. Ben adores you – that goes without saying – and I worship the ground you walk on. I can't wait to marry you.'

'Thanks.' Jade smiled at his passionate sincerity and tried to swallow the well of emotion still in her throat. It should have been enough; it was enough on so many levels, but there was still a fragile insecure part of her that yearned for someone who shared her blood to love her, too.

37

In October, Finn went out for lunch with Eleanor Smythe, who confirmed that all the paintings that had been reserved at the fair had now been paid for and that she'd be transferring the remittance to his bank account shortly. They included the ones the Stones had bought, as well as another that had also been reserved and one that Henry the art dealer had sold to one of his clients. Eleanor was in very high spirits about all of this. Finn couldn't bring himself to tell her that Bridie was his mother.

Then, a few days after the lunch, Bridie herself phoned to invite Finn round to the family house to meet his siblings.

'It won't be all of us because Molly's still in Spain, but you can meet Alice, and you can meet my husband, Christopher, and Declan will be there too, of course. And by all means bring your lovely partner along. Ben too, if you'd like to, and if his mother thinks it's appropriate.' She paused. 'Please come, even if you can't bring Ben and Jade. It would mean a lot to all of us. Alice and Christopher are both really longing to meet you.'

Finn bet Declan wasn't, but it would at least give him the

chance to apologise for thumping him and hopefully come to some sort of a truce with his brother.

'Bridie, I need to ask you something,' he said just before they closed the conversation. 'It's about some paintings you bought recently.'

He heard her sudden intake of breath. 'What about them?'

The edge of defensiveness in her voice told him all he needed to know. The fact that he'd painted them had been her main motivation for buying them.

She denied this as soon as he'd called her out on it. 'It's Christopher and Nick who are the art buffs. They wouldn't have bought them if they hadn't loved them.'

Finn had to be content with that. There was no way she was ever going to tell him the truth. That was for sure.

Finn, Jade, Ben and Sarah also went pumpkin picking in a local farm and bought two pumpkins to hollow out and make faces with for Halloween, one for Ben's house and one for Duck Pond Cottage. The Duck Pond Cottage pumpkin had to be moved out of reception after a day because Mickey barked his head off every time he saw it.

'He thinks it's a baddie,' Ben shouted in glee. 'It's OK, Mickey, it's a goodie pumpkin. No need to bark.'

But Mickey wouldn't be soothed so the pumpkin ended up outside the main gates on a wooden table out of the cockerpoo's sight.

In the end, Finn and Sarah decided it would be best if Ben didn't meet Bridie's side of the family at the same time as Finn did.

'Just in case it's a disaster and we decide not to keep in touch,' Finn told Sarah, only half-jokingly. 'It would just be too confusing for him, wouldn't it?'

'I agree.' Her blue eyes were cautious. 'It's not long ago he discovered he had a dad and a grandad he didn't know he had. Not to mention a Dorrie,' she added lightly.

Jade said she would go with him. 'If you can bear it,' Finn said. 'I could really use some moral support.'

'Of course I can bear it. It'll be fun.'

Finn raised his eyebrows.

'Like speed dating,' she continued, 'but with a family you didn't know you had. Hey, that would make a good TV programme, wouldn't it. You could swap places with a different brother, sister or cousin every three minutes. Well, you could in your case anyway, as there seem to be quite a few of them.'

Finn saw right through her bravado and hugged her.

Bridie had told them to arrive about 7 p.m. and on the appointed Friday, having misjudged how long it would take, they got there far too early.

'I think I'll just park up round the corner for a while,' Jade said as they cruised past an impressive set of electric gates that led up a long drive lined with tall yellowing poplar trees. 'That was the right address, wasn't it?'

'Yeah,' Finn said, craning his neck to look back. 'Definitely. Bridie said they had a long drive. She didn't say you couldn't see the house from the road though.'

'How the other half live,' Jade murmured as she parked the Land Rover around the corner.

'I know.' Finn blinked a few times. 'I didn't realise they'd live in a place like this. Although I guess I should have done from what Declan said to me at the art exhibition.'

'He's a bit of a bad egg, isn't he! Let's hope he's the only one.'

At just after seven, Jade drove them back to the posh address. Finn jumped out and pressed the button on an intercom and the black electric gates swung open silently to allow them entry.

A few minutes later, they were parking on the wide gravel

frontage of an impressive-looking black and white Tudor-style house which seemed to have lights blazing from most of its numerous paned windows. There were several cars there already. They included Declan's black Range Rover Sport and a couple of new electric black BMWs. Jade didn't usually feel as though her Land Rover was old and dowdy, but today it was definitely the poor cousin. Not to mention the only car that wasn't black! Sarah would have had a field day with that!

The front door swung open before they had a chance to ring the bell and Finn was relieved to see it was Bridie who'd come to greet them.

He was aware of Jade, standing a step behind him with a big bunch of flowers, as he held out the bottle of wine to Bridie that they'd bought en route. Thank God it was an expensive one he'd got especially. He'd very nearly brought one of the reds with a screw top from the cottage.

'Thank you so much. Come in, come in. Welcome.'

A smiling Bridie ushered them both through a big square hall into a huge oblong lounge, which was dominated by three coffee-coloured sofas grouped in a three-sided square shape around a geometric-design yellow and brown rug. The room, which was lit by several tall standard lamps, smelled sweetly of something vaguely coconutty and there were dozens of pictures on every wall. Finn found himself praying none of his would be amongst them. It was bad enough that he himself was here on display. He had never felt more vulnerable in his life as he and Jade stood facing what looked like an interview panel of people, who were lounging on the middle sofa.

Declan was in the middle, and on his right was the woman Finn had seen him talking to at the exhibition. Could that be Alice, his sister? On Declan's left was an older man with grey hair, who Finn thought was probably Bridie's husband, Christopher. On one of the other sofas was an even older man with very bright blue eyes who could have been who Eleanor had referred to as old man Stone.

'Meet the clan.' Bridie introduced everyone and Finn realised he'd been spot on about who they all were. The atmosphere felt pretty tense, but at least they were all smiling.

A few minutes later, when he and Jade were seated comfortably on the unoccupied sofa and they'd been given drinks – he'd opted to drive and was drinking orange juice – Finn began to relax. His family felt less like an interview panel now.

Christopher Stone was a charming host. Finn could see the engaging and interested persona – one of the qualities that made up a great salesperson – was very much in evidence. Nicholas Stone was sharper, shrewder, less polished. Alice was lovely, a real sweetie with a genuinely warm smile. Finn felt oddly protective of this younger sister he'd never met.

Even Declan was on his best behaviour. Chatty and charming, he was a young replica of his father. There hadn't been a chance for Finn to get him on his own and apologise yet, but he hoped there would be at some point in the evening.

They ate supper in a room everyone referred to as the snug, which turned out to be only slightly smaller than the lounge, but with a mahogany dining table and ten chairs. A coordinating but not matching mahogany bar with a rolled wood surround and optics behind took up the whole of one corner.

There were even tall stools by the bar, which Christopher told Finn proudly he'd had shipped back from Egypt when he'd taken a liking to it after a business trip there. The meal was served in several big-lidded bowls which contained rice and various fragrant delicious-looking casseroles, a couple of which were vegetarian, Finn was relieved to discover.

He'd somehow forgotten to mention Jade was vegetarian, but

Bridie had pre-empted this. She might have abandoned him as a child, but there was nothing callous about her actions this evening. She was thoughtful, kind, and hugely interested in both his and Jade's lives. It was impossible not to warm to her.

Finn finally managed to get Declan alone towards the end of the evening when Bridie, Alice and Jade were carrying the dirty plates through to the kitchen and Christopher and Nicholas had excused themselves briefly.

They were back in the big lounge again and the two brothers were sitting close to each other, albeit on different sofas.

'I'm sorry I hit you,' Finn said quietly to the younger man. 'It's not the kind of thing I usually do.'

'Mmm.' Declan's voice was noncommittal, and he leaned back slightly on his sofa.

'I hope we can be friends going forward.' Finn held out his hand.

Declan frowned, but didn't take it. And then he jumped and looked guilty and Finn realised Bridie had just come back into the room.

'I hope you two are playing nicely,' she said in a soft voice shot through with steel. 'Remember that Finn is our guest, Declan, and should be treated as such.'

Finn realised she was completely aware of Declan's hostility and wasn't going to stand for it. That was something at least.

'I'm sure we'll be best buddies,' Declan said cheerily, even if his eyes didn't quite match his words.

'Me too,' Finn agreed.

Bridie nodded approvingly. It was the best he was going to get for now, Finn thought, and it was definitely better than the bristling resentment he'd got from Declan at the exhibition.

They finally left just after ten thirty, having thanked their hosts profusely and promised a delighted Bridie they would bring Ben to meet her another time.

As they went back down the drive, Finn glanced in his rear-view mirror. The oblong of light shone out from the open door-way, silhouetting Bridie's slender frame and her waving hand. The door didn't close until the electric gates had shut behind them.

'What did you think?' Finn asked Jade as they headed for home.

'They all seemed very nice. More importantly, what did you think? How do you feel?'

'Like it's all still a bit surreal. Like I still might wake up and discover this is all some weird dream.'

'Yes, I bet.' She touched his knee. 'I'm really proud of you.'

'Proud? Why?'

'Because of the way you handle yourself. You never seem fazed. You're always the same wherever you are. You never seem to put on an act.'

'That's a really nice thing to say.' He caught hold of her hand. Then he told her about Declan. 'I think I've made an enemy there. I did try apologising but he's definitely not up for any brotherly bonding.'

'Maybe he will be in time. You've only just met, and it was unfortunate, that first meeting. You'll joke about it one day, I'm sure.'

Finn wasn't at all convinced of this and he could see by Jade's face, even in the darkened car, that she wasn't either. It was still early days, though. Only time would tell how his relationship with Declan would pan out.

38

Finn took Sarah and Ben to meet Bridie one Sunday lunchtime a few days after Halloween. Jade had offered to stay at home. 'It's Ben she wants to see, not me. He's her grandson. And won't it be best if we keep it all low key? For Ben's sake, I mean?'

'You're part of my family,' Finn had told her softly. 'As far as I'm concerned you always will be, and I want you there. So does Sarah.'

That was true. Sarah had told Jade the prospect of meeting Ben's posh grandmother scared the pants off her. 'I'm not good with posh people. I don't know what knife and fork to use. I don't even know what side the bread roll plate goes on.'

'The left,' Jade told her.

'It doesn't matter how many times someone tells me, I just forget again. I've got a complete mental block about it.'

'There probably won't be any side plates to worry about,' Finn said, overhearing this conversation. 'Bridie said something about having a barbecue outside if the weather was nice.'

'A barbecue in November is flaming optimistic,' Sarah said with a mock shiver.

'Early November can be lovely,' Jade said. 'We've been to lots of firework parties where we've eaten outside.'

'Yeah, but we had mugs of steaming hot soup to warm our hands on, and hot chestnuts roasted over a roaring fire.'

'Maybe the Stones have a firepit,' Jade mused. 'It's that kind of place. It wouldn't surprise me if they had those patio heaters either.'

'Not very climate friendly, those heaters. Anyway, what are they like – in general I mean? Did they strike you as fly-by-night builders or people of integrity?' Sarah's question wasn't directed at anyone in particular, but now they both looked at Finn.

His face was reflective. 'I think they're generally an honourable company. Old man Stone built the company up from zero. And I liked Christopher too when we met him. He seemed pretty authentic. I did some digging around on the internet too. If you'll excuse the pun.' He grinned. 'Rural Developments is a member of the FMB. That's the Federation of Master Builders for the uninitiated. I couldn't find too many people slating their houses. They have a decent reputation.'

'Blimey.' Jade looked at him in astonishment. 'You are a dark horse. You didn't tell me you'd done all that.'

'I just have, haven't I? It's probably daft but I wanted to know if the family I'm getting involved with is generally a good bunch. And I think they are. I think Bridie is great, now I've spoken to her a few times, and I think that Declan is spoilt. And I think she probably spoilt him because she felt so guilty that she'd abandoned me and Dad.'

'Wow,' Sarah said, shaking her head. 'You have been thinking about it. But yes, that would make total sense.'

'And it explains a lot,' Jade murmured. 'A spoilt little mummy's boy, who wants all the toys, no matter whether they're his or not.'

'That's enough amateur psychology for one day,' Finn said. 'But yes, my thoughts precisely. Let's hope the weather's good enough for a barbecue. It would be a lot less formal for Ben and let's hope Declan's got something else to do and doesn't decide to rock up and cause trouble.'

* * *

As it turned out, it was cloudy and overcast on the day they'd arranged, but it wasn't actually raining. Bridie messaged first thing and told them all to dress for outside so presumably the barbecue was still on, despite the nip in the air.

There was still evidence of Halloween as they drove towards the Stones' residence. There was still the odd pumpkin sitting on a table outside a house, and Ben pointed out a witch on a broomstick outlined in black on someone's window.

There was nothing like that at the end of the Stones' driveway. Maybe the locked ten-foot-high gates at the house end of the drive made 'trick or treat' expeditions difficult. Even though the gates swung silently open as they drew up without a person to be seen.

When they'd parked and had rung the bell, Bridie greeted them with her coat on. 'Hello, everyone,' she said as she opened the front door of her beautiful house. 'Who fancies a barbecue?'

Ben, who was already wide eyed because of the 'invisible man gates', took to Bridie immediately. The fact he adored barbecues, no matter what time of year it was, helped, but he'd have liked her anyway, Finn realised, because she was totally on his son's wavelength.

She chatted to Ben about school, instantly discovering that art was his favourite subject, and asking him if he'd like to see some drawings of animals they had in the garden.

'We've got a barbecue hut,' she explained to the adults, leading them across a wide lawn that looked like emerald felt it was so smooth, towards a paved patio section in one corner, where there was a circular wooden hut with a black bitumen roof, oblong windows all the way around it and a smoking black chimney protruding from the top.

Bridie opened a door on the front and beckoned them in. The inside of the hut smelled wonderfully of hot cedar wood and warmth. It was dominated by a circular central barbecue sprinkled with smouldering red-hot coals, covered by metal grills on which the food would be cooked.

A chimney led up from the centre of the barbecue, taking the smoke outside. Around the perimeter of the hut ran a low wooden bench, decorated with sheepskin rugs and a scattering of oversized blue and terracotta cushions, clearly meant for lounging. The inside of the hut was adorned with sparkling silver and gold fairy lights, lending the little space a touch of magic.

'Wow,' said Ben, and Finn knew his son spoke for them all. It was a breathtakingly cosy space.

Bridie smiled in delight at their reactions. 'It's one of my favourite places,' she said, spreading out her hands. 'Welcome.'

On the walls where there were no windows hung a selection of black and white framed sketches of badgers and deer and hares.

They'd been drawn by a talented artist, Finn observed, wondering if they were part of the Stones' collection and trying to see the names.

'Molly draws,' Bridie told them. 'My middle daughter,' she explained to Sarah and Ben. 'A talent for art definitely does seem to run in the family.'

She didn't elaborate too much. They had told Ben he was

going to meet Finn's mum who he hadn't grown up with but who had lived with Grandpa Ray a long time ago, and had left it at that.

Bridie had also agreed that for now the rest of the family wouldn't be present. The others could be introduced as and when Ben was ready.

Sarah and Finn had thought it was enough for now, to ease Ben into the idea of having yet another blood relative pop up out of the woodwork.

It was a magical afternoon. They gathered around the central barbecue, and coats definitely weren't needed in the hut. They ate sizzling brown sausages, a mixture of vegetarian and meat, and kebabs on sticks with glistening yellow and red peppers interspersed with chunks of fragrant monkfish and chicken. All this was washed down with fizzy drinks that Bridie had brought down from the house.

Ben was now telling Bridie about the puppies that had lost their mother, and how he'd been instrumental in saving their lives by helping to hand feed them until they were properly weaned.

'I did, Dad, didn't I?' He turned to Finn for reassurance.

'You did, son,' Finn confirmed.

The three pups were now ten weeks old and wriggling bundles of mischief, and Ben was totally besotted with the brown female, who he'd named Chocko, and who Finn, Sarah and Jade had agreed he could take home to keep. He was old enough for his first dog, and he'd have all of them on hand to help.

'I love them all, but Chocko is the cutest and she's coming to live with us next week.'

Bridie clapped her hands in excitement. There was something very childlike about his mother, Finn thought. No wonder she was on Ben's wavelength.

'How fantastic. Will Chocko be her forever name?'

Ben scratched his chin and looked serious. 'I think so. I thought it might just be her baby name. I was gonna call her Banksy, but it doesn't really match.'

'Because she's a girl?' Bridie asked.

'No, because I don't think she's a graffiti kind of pup. I called one of the other pups Banksy though,' he said happily, drawing his knees up to his chest on the bench seat. 'Grandpa Ray is taking Banksy home. And Dawn, who helps Auntie Jade, is having the other one. I called her Monet.'

'Artistic names,' Bridie said. 'Lovely. But Chocko is great as well. You two are going to have such fun together.'

'I know.' Ben sounded completely sure of himself and Finn blinked a few times.

He was thrilled Ben and Bridie were getting on so well, although it was bittersweet watching her with his son. Ben wasn't much older than he'd been when she had left him and his father, and it had taken him some soul searching before he'd agreed to bring Ben to meet her.

'I won't have him let down,' he'd said to Bridie with steel in his voice. 'So you'd better be pretty damn sure you want him in your life before I bring him anywhere near you.'

She had taken that. She'd bowed her head slightly and bitten her lip.

'I won't let him down. I can promise you that, Finn. And I won't let you down again either.'

'Can we come again to see Bridie, Mum?' Ben asked when they were finally ready to go home.

'We can if Bridie invites us,' Sarah told him. It was obvious that she too had been a bit blown away by how well her son and his new grandmother had clicked.

'You'd be very welcome anytime,' Bridie said. 'All of you. It's been a delight to have you here.' The truth of this shone out of her eyes and Finn, who'd been standing on Ben's other side, squeezed his son's hand.

'We'll arrange something soon, I'm sure,' he told Ben.

'Yay, yay, yay,' Ben shrieked, and Finn and Jade swapped glances.

So far so good, their look said.

With the possible exception of Declan, things had gone very well with the meeting of his family, Finn thought as they finally waved goodbye to Bridie and the barbecue hut.

He hoped Declan would come round too. They might never be best buddies, but some acceptance from Declan's side would be good.

'Rome wasn't built in a day,' Bridie said when he'd phoned her the day after the barbecue to say thank you. 'But I'm really hoping we can have a relationship going forward, Finn. If you want that. I also understand if you decide that it's all too much.'

'I do want it,' he told her. 'I want to get to know all of you properly.'

'That's fantastic. Tank you, tank you.'

He could hear the relief in her voice.

'Although I'm not so sure Declan's as keen,' he added.

'He'll come round. All this has been a shock for him.' She paused. 'And Finn, I'm partly to blame for the way Declan is. I've spoiled him terribly. I've let him have his own way far too much... But he has a good heart. Beneath the arrogant front. Baby steps, hey?'

Finn had agreed baby steps were definitely the way forward.

He wished things could be different for Jade and her father. But he was realistic enough to know that not all estranged families could have happy-ever-after endings. They'd both suffered enough heartbreak in their past to know that fairy-tale endings when it came to families were the exception, and not the rule.

39

Bonfire night came and went peacefully. Jade was always relieved when 5 November was over. Most animals were scared of fireworks but luckily Duck Pond Rescue was far enough away from the nearest organised display for it not to be too disturbing for her charges. They were also far enough away from most houses for bonfire parties in gardens not to be an issue.

That would change when they had a housing estate next door to them. Although news on the development had gone ultra-quiet lately.

Finn had spoken to Bridie about it and she'd confirmed that Rural Developments were currently looking at plans to clear and remove the invasive plant species, but that this was a long-term project. Jade felt slightly guilty about the damning survey that Ursula had produced, but not guilty enough to say anything. After all, it wasn't as though Ursula had lied. There *was* Japanese knotweed on the site and there *was* bamboo. Rural Developments would have to do something about both of these plants before they could proceed, no matter what the extent of the infestation.

Ursula was at the sanctuary a lot lately. She mostly helped out with dog walking and she'd bonded with Milo, big time.

'As soon as I'm retired, which will be at the end of December, I'd like to offer this one a home,' she said to Jade one morning as she stroked the greyhound's fawn coat, and he leant against her legs, lapping up the attention, clearly besotted with her.

'Why don't you take him home for weekends now?' Jade suggested. 'Have a trial period. He'd love that. And you can bring him back here when you're working.'

'Could I? Could I really do that?' Ursula's face lit up and she dropped a kiss on the greyhound's head, and he wagged his skinny tail in response, clearly equally happy with the plan. 'I'd need to get him a basket and some other bits and pieces first. But I'd love that.'

'He'd love it too. And there's no rush to take him home permanently. You can always bring him back with you when you come.'

It was a match made in heaven, Jade thought as she watched Ursula encourage Milo into her hatchback a few days later. The old greyhound looked pleased as punch, sitting proudly upright and looking out of the window as Ursula drove out of the main gates.

The only drawback was that Milo's mate, a sweet little bitch called Candy, pined for him when he wasn't there. But in the end this was resolved because Ursula, who wasn't unaware of the dogs' strong bond, said she would take Candy too.

Dawn and Jade both had tears in their eyes when Candy and Milo went home with Ursula in late November.

'That's perfect,' Dawn said. 'She's brilliant, isn't she, and those two dogs adore her as well as each other. She's got a log fire so they'll have their own hearth at Christmas. How fantastic is that. And talking of Christmas, what are your plans for the festive period? I'm happy to come in on Christmas Day and Boxing Day if you need me.'

'I wouldn't hear of it. You go and enjoy your grandchildren and that lovely new pup. I've got plenty of help.'

Dawn bent to stroke Monet, who was a shadow at her side when she was at the sanctuary. She and Jade often joked that the sanctuary hadn't as much rehomed Monet but gained another permanent resident because Dawn spent so much time there.

No doubt Milo and Candy would be the same because Ursula spent a lot of time there too. Jade loved the fact she got to see the animals she rehomed. Ben and Chocko were also frequent visitors of course, and when the pups saw each other they played and played.

It was true what Jade had told Dawn about Christmas. She would have plenty of help because as well as the surplus of volunteers who came in at Christmas because helping a charity was a nice altruistic thing to do, Ray and Dorrie were coming down from Nottingham to spend the holiday period with them. Dorrie was brilliant with the animals and Ray enjoyed helping with the dog walking. The pair of them were both besotted with Banksy too, and everyone was looking forward to the reunion of all three pups in the holiday period.

Ray and Dorrie were arriving on the 20th and staying till New Year. Sarah, Ben and Callum were coming for lunch on Christmas Day and they were providing much of the lunch too, a turkey for the meat eaters and a very posh nut roast, homemade by Callum, for Jade and anyone else who fancied a break from the meat-eating traditions.

Sarah, Ben and Callum were seeing her adoptive parents the day after Boxing Day and then heading to Dundee for New Year, which was a big celebration in Scotland. It would be all go.

But Christmas Day itself would be like any other time at

Duck Pond Rescue. At least it would be as far as the animals were concerned. They didn't care what time of year it was. They still needed feeding and watering and exercising.

The atmosphere was very festive. In the first week of December, Finn and Callum sprayed the reception windows with artificial snow, and Jade, Sarah and Ben made blue, green and red paper chains and pinned them up in reception, crisscrossing the ceiling, much to the delight of Mr Spock, who regularly pulled them down for entertainment and waited with glee for someone to put them back up so he could do it again.

Jade had done her research on what was toxic and what wasn't for parrots at yuletide and had bought a six-foot growing Christmas tree, which was in a tub outside the reception door, just in case Mr Spock decided to eat the decorations or got hurt on its sharp evergreen spikes.

The tree glittered with lights and wooden painted decorations of animals, many of them donated by volunteers. By mid-December, reception was jampacked with tubs of Christmas chocolates and biscuits.

Jade had bought loads and everyone who came by added to the pile. Several people brought in donations of animal food too – these ranged from the pensioner who'd bought two extra tins of Turkey Doggie Dinner to Reg Arnold, their food supplier, who'd delivered a duplicate of Jade's regular feed order and had refused to charge her for it. Jade had totally changed her opinion of Reg, who she'd once thought was tight fisted and mean minded.

Mr Spock had learned how to say 'Happy Christmas and a Merry New Year' and repeated it every time someone new came into reception. This could get wearing when it was busy.

Mickey loved Christmas because everyone gave him treats when they thought Jade wasn't looking. Even Diesel seemed to be catching fewer mice than usual. Or if he was catching them, he wasn't bringing bits of them into reception to frighten unsuspecting volunteers.

On the day before Christmas Eve, Aiden and Kate called by to drop off a bottle of wine and a big box of chocolates. In return, Jade and Finn gave them a bottle of port – Jade knew her vet was partial to a glass of port – and some red berry-scented candles, which Kate proclaimed were her favourites.

Thankfully Aiden was fully healed from his escapades in Venice and the couple stayed for mince pies and mulled wine, which Jade had been doing for the volunteers for the last week or so.

Jade didn't think she'd ever looked forward to a Christmas Day more. A proper Christmas Day when everything would happen at the right time. Christmas dinner, present opening, watching the King's speech, and best of all, feeling part of a loving family.

She hadn't forgotten the letter that had been returned to her, but with Finn's help she had managed to get some acceptance around it. She would always be a part of Finn and Ben's family. This time next year, she and Finn would be married. They would start their own family, and in the meantime she was surrounded by love. It didn't get much better than that.

40

Then Christmas Eve was upon them. Jade and Dorrie had gone to town on the vegetables – they'd prepared most of them already and had done eight different kinds – including buttered chestnut sprouts, roasted parsnips, creamed carrots and fennel, minted peas and two types of squash.

Dorrie had also made the Christmas pudding and Jade had bought a couple of lighter alternatives from the 'posh' section of the supermarket.

'We'll be too full to move for days,' Finn had said when he'd seen what they were up to.

'We don't need to eat it all at once,' Jade told him. 'Although we might need a second fridge to fit all the leftovers in.'

'In the meantime,' Finn said, at midday on Christmas Eve, 'is there actually anything we can eat now that isn't reserved for the main event tomorrow?' He peered closer into the fridge. 'Because all this lot looks like Christmas dinner stuff.'

'Um, good point.' Jade frowned as she joined him. 'I don't suppose you fancy cheese on toast?'

'There are some sausage rolls in the breadbin,' Dorrie said. 'Special offer from the Co-op.'

Finn flashed her a grateful smile. 'I think we might have to get you to move in permanently. I'm usually doing well to get cheese on toast.'

'Don't listen to him, Dorrie. He gets perfectly well fed.'

'I can see he does.' Dorrie laughed and added crisply, 'His father's the same, always complaining he's starving when outside appearances would suggest otherwise.'

'Are you saying I'm getting chunky?' Finn objected, patting his stomach.

Both women laughed. Everyone was in high spirits.

The magic of Christmas lay over everything and when that evening Ben phoned to tell them he and Sarah had just seen Carmelita in their garden, it was the icing on the cake.

'It was definitely her,' he said when Finn had put his phone on speaker so they could all listen. 'I recognised her instantly and... guess what...?'

'What?' chimed Finn, Jade, Ray and Dorrie, almost in unison.

'She brought her mate to see us too. She's got a boyfriend, Dad. I'm not making it up. A big dog fox, and Mum said that next year they're gonna have babies and they'll probably bring them to see us too. Didn't you, Mum?' His voice went up in volume so even though he moved away from the phone, they could still all hear him clearly.

'I said that might happen, Ben.' They could all hear Sarah's laughter in the background. 'What do you think, Jade?'

'I think you're very probably right,' Jade said, high with happiness. 'That'll be something to look forward to, won't it?'

'As well as a wee double wedding,' Callum said in the background. 'Although I'm guessing that can't compete with a fox visit for some of us.'

Everyone laughed again. It was a perfect moment.

* * *

Jade woke up on Christmas Day even earlier than usual.

'Where are you going?' Finn said sleepily as she extracted herself from the duvet.

'Downstairs. Why?'

'Because it's a tradition on Christmas Day to make love before daybreak.'

'No, it isn't.'

'Well, it's a tradition I think we should start,' Finn said, holding out his arms. 'Come back to bed.'

It was another twenty minutes, with the tradition well and truly established, before they both got up and went downstairs.

To their surprise, the fragrant smell of Danish pastries and coffee was coming from the kitchen and Dorrie turned from the cooker. 'Merry Christmas. I thought if I got up early enough, I'd beat you to it.'

A couple of hours later, the humans had feasted on a wonderful mix of Danish pastries and the animals had all been fed and they were busy getting the back room ready for later.

They'd pushed the sofa back to one wall so they could fit in an extra table to go with Jade's smaller table. A holly leaf-patterned tablecloth covered the join between them. The house Christmas tree had also been shifted as far as possible into the corner. It wasn't the tree that was technically the problem. It was the mountain of presents, most of which were for Ben, that were beneath it.

Jade had got Finn aftershave, plus some paint brushes and a new lightweight easel that was more transportable than the one he had. They'd bought Callum and Sarah a voucher for a slap-up meal at their favourite restaurant and they'd bought Ben loads of puppy things for Chocko as well as giving him a voucher for a puppy-training course that started in the New Year. They'd bought Dorrie and Ray a meal voucher too because the older couple insisted they had everything they needed already.

Then, of course, there were presents for the three dogs. It was always great fun watching dogs tearing the paper wrapping from their gifts. There were presents for the sanctuary animals too. No one would be left out.

Bridie had sent piles of presents for them all too – they were seeing Bridie and the rest of Finn's new family for a drink and midday nibbles on Boxing Day. Ray had said he would go for an hour or so. He bore Bridie no ill will and was fond of saying that if things hadn't turned out the way they had, he'd never have met Dorrie who was, without doubt, the love of his life.

Midway through Christmas Day morning, Finn had a phone discussion with Bridie. She'd left a message on the reception landline, asking him to call her when he had a second, and he sat in the office chair and dialled her number.

'Happy Christmas, Finn.' Her voice was soft. 'I'm so glad you're back in my life, so I am. Tank you for tracking me down.' Her Irish accent always sounded stronger on the phone and today was no exception.

'Me too,' he said. 'Happy Christmas, Mum.'

He heard her sharp intake of breath and knew the word Mum hadn't gone unnoticed.

There was a little pause and when she spoke again, her voice was husky.

'There's one more thing, Finn, before you go. Say you'll hear me out before you answer.'

'Of course I'll hear you out.'

'I know you and Jade were looking to expand the sanctuary into next door, but that Rural Developments acquired the land before you could purchase. We'd like to gift you some of that land.'

Finn began to object but Bridie stopped him. 'You said you'd hear me out.' She went on slowly. 'We can't give you as much as Jade originally wanted – because it's somewhere we'd still like to develop, once the invasive plants are sorted out, and there are access issues. But we'd like to give you some of it, Finn. It'll be in your name, but we'd assume that when you're married, you'd throw in your lot together, so to speak.'

For a few seconds, Finn was speechless. 'That's incredibly generous,' he said at last. 'Are you sure you can spare it?'

'Absolutely. Look at it this way, Finn. I've missed almost every Christmas and birthday you've had, and I can't make up for that. But I'm going to try in my own way to make some small amends.'

Again he was speechless and it was Bridie who broke the little silence.

'We can meet up in the New Year and talk about it properly. We can show you what Chris and I had in mind. I'll come over. We can walk around the plot.'

'Thank you,' he finally managed, and Bridie said, 'Think nothing of it. Enjoy Christmas, Finn. See you all tomorrow.'

Finn disconnected the landline and let out a deep breath. Wow, he hadn't been expecting that. Jade was going to be blown away by the news. Progress concerning the development had gone quiet lately but both of them had assumed it would be resurrected at some point in the future when the invasive plants had been dealt with. Now it seemed there might be a compromise. And one that didn't involve any more subterfuge.

Jade had told him about Ursula's survey and Finn had thought that sooner or later this would be exposed for what it was – an exaggeration of the facts that wouldn't permanently delay the building works. Sooner or later, money would win through. In Finn's experience, it always did.

But maybe he'd been wrong about that. Maybe love could occasionally trump money after all.

When he'd been on the phone, he'd seen Sarah's car pull into the yard, and she and Ben and Callum were in the process of lifting bags and packages out of the back.

He went out to help them.

'Happy Christmas, everyone.'

There was lots of hugging and back slapping and then they all went into the house where there were more hugs and back slaps and cries of 'Happy Christmas'.

Finn was bursting to tell Jade about Bridie's phone call and her oh so generous offer, but he decided it would be best to tell her later when they were alone. Another secret he was going to have to keep for later. At least it was a good secret.

Like the portrait he'd painted of Jade, which he'd been working on for weeks. Finn had painted it from a photo he'd taken of her and Mickey and Diesel. She'd been sitting at the picnic table outside one summer afternoon with Diesel curled on her lap and Mickey at her feet, looking at her adoringly.

Jade had looked up as Finn had approached and snapped the picture, and he'd captured her smile. She'd looked beautiful.

'It's because I'm in my natural environment,' she'd told him. 'Surrounded by animals.'

And Finn had agreed and immortalised it forever in paint. It was one of the best things he'd ever done, and he planned to give it to her after Christmas lunch. He couldn't wait.

* * *

Christmas lunch was almost perfect. Except that Dorrie completely forgot to cook the Christmas pudding.

'I'm so sorry,' she gasped, clapping her hand over her mouth. 'I'll do it now. It's just a matter of putting it in the steamer. But it will take a couple of hours. Can we have it later – after the presents?'

'I'll do it,' Callum said, standing up and grinning. 'I bet we're all far too full for pudding now anyway, aren't we?'

'Christmas pudding's yuck, anyway,' Ben shouted. 'We should have presents *now*.'

Sarah rolled her eyes and all the adults laughed.

'We should maybe take Chocko out for a quick wee first though,' Jade suggested, noticing the puppy was sniffing the carpet in the corner of the room.

Ben capitulated instantly and leapt to his feet.

'Can we take Mickey and Banksy out too?'

'I'll come as well,' Finn said.

'And me,' Sarah said. 'I need some fresh air.'

Outside, Sarah and Jade chattered, their breath rising up into the cool December sky while the three dogs sniffed about on the frosty ground, supervised by Finn and Ben.

'Are you having a good time?' Sarah asked Jade.

'Do you really need to ask? This is the best Christmas I've ever had.'

'Me too,' Sarah said. 'It's all about family, isn't it? I never knew it could feel like this.'

'Same,' Jade said. 'I'm so glad Finn's finally reconnected with his.'

'I didn't really mean that,' Sarah said quickly. 'Blood isn't always thicker than water, Jade, although I know that gets shoved down our throat at this time of year. There's so much hype around Christmas, isn't there? I meant the kind of family you choose, the kind you love, the kind that always has your back, no matter what. The friendship kind of family. And the fur and feathered kind.'

'I know what you mean.' Jade met Sarah's eyes, loving her for what she was saying.

They had paused just outside the back door, and Jade's attention was caught by the sight of a blue Astra parked up on the other side of the main gate. 'I wonder if that's someone who wants to drop off an animal. Maybe I should go and check.'

'If it was, I think they'd have come in before.' Finn arrived beside them, stamping his feet on the cold ground and blowing on his red hands. 'It's colder than it looks out here. That Astra was there earlier. Maybe it's someone having a stroll around the duck pond to walk off their Christmas dinner.'

'Yes, you're probably right.' Jade smiled at him. 'We were just talking about families. The friendship kind as well as the blood kind.'

'Both are equally important,' Finn said softly, and for a moment they all smiled at each other before Ben arrived, his face flushed with the cold air.

'Chocko's done her business. It wasn't just a wee so I've put it in a bag. But I might need to wash my hands now.'

'Kids sure keep you grounded,' Sarah said. 'Come on, love, let's get you sorted,' and they all laughed as they strolled back into the welcoming warmth of Duck Pond Cottage.

* * *

In the blue Astra outside the main gates, a man turned a piece of paper over and over in his hand. It was a photocopy of a letter he'd received three months ago. He'd regretted sending it back with the harsh 'RETURN TO SENDER' message scrawled on it as soon as he'd done it, but it had been such a shock to receive it. To know that his daughter was looking for him, that she might actually want to know him, despite the fact he'd left her and her mother. There were extenuating circumstances to that, but he'd never had the chance to give his side of the story. And he'd accepted, long ago, that he never would.

Then that letter had arrived and he'd panicked and sent it back. And he'd regretted it ever since. It had taken him all this time to pluck up the courage to come here. He was desperately hoping for a second chance. But he couldn't quite bring himself to finish the journey.

Hector Ajax Foster glanced through the main gates and saw two smiling women. Could one of them be his daughter? They were both about the right age. And this was the right address. He hesitated. Should he go in now? It was probably the wrong day. Or maybe it was absolutely the right day.

Who knew? Christmas was a funny time. He wiped his sweaty hands on his trouser legs, agonised with himself, opened the car door, then had second thoughts and closed it again. He put on the demister to clear the steamed-up windows. It was no good. He didn't have the nerve to go in there. Not today. He would do it though. He would do it one day soon.

* * *

MORE FROM DELLA GALTON

Another book from Della Galton, *Coming Home to Puddleduck Farm*, is available to order now here:

https://mybook.to/ComingHomeFarmBackAd

ACKNOWLEDGEMENTS

I started this series a long time ago (in my head) when I was a volunteer dog walker at the sanctuary that Duck Pond Rescue is based on, so it means a lot to me to see it brought to life as a series of novels. I loved my time there. Many of the dogs are based on real dogs I met and rehomed while I was there.

Thank you so much to Team Boldwood for giving me the opportunity to bring this series to my readers – you are amazing. Thank you to every single one of you who works so hard to bring my books to my readers in paperback, audio and digital.

As always, my special thanks go to my fabulous editor, Caroline Ridding, also to Cecily Blench, Jennifer Davies, and to Alice Moore for the gorgeous cover.

Thank you to Tony and Adam Millward, who were right there by my side, dog walking. Thank you to all the wonderful people who give rescued animals another chance.

Thank you also to the Dorset Wildlife Trust for helping with information on dormice and head shaving! Thank you to Elke Everton for suggesting apt names for babies. Thank you to Gordon Rawsthorne for being my first reader. Thank you, perhaps most of all, for the huge support of my many readers – without whom it would be pretty pointless writing novels. I love reading your emails, tweets and Facebook comments. Please keep them coming.

ABOUT THE AUTHOR

Della Galton writes short stories, teaches writing groups and is Agony Aunt for Writers Forum Magazine. Her stories feature strong female friendship, quirky characters and very often the animals she loves. When she is not writing she enjoys walking her dogs around the beautiful Dorset countryside.

Sign up to Della Galton's mailing list for news, competitions and updates on future books.

Visit Della's website: www.dellagalton.co.uk

Follow Della on social media:

facebook.com/DailyDella
x.com/DellaGalton
instagram.com/Dellagalton
bookbub.com/authors/della-galton

ALSO BY DELLA GALTON

The Bluebell Cliff Series

Sunshine Over Bluebell Cliff

Summer at Studland Bay

Shooting Stars Over Bluebell Cliff

Sunrise Over Pebble Bay

Confetti Over Bluebell Cliff

The Puddleduck Farm Series

Coming Home to Puddleduck Farm

Rainbows Over Puddleduck Farm

Love Blossoms at Puddleduck Farm

Living the Dream at Puddleduck Farm

Happy Ever After at Puddleduck Farm

The Duck Pond Cottage Series

A New Arrival at Duck Pond Cottage

Summer Secrets at Duck Pond Cottage

BECOME A MEMBER OF

THE SHELF CARE CLUB

The home of Boldwood's book club reads.

Find uplifting reads, sunny escapes, cosy romances, family dramas and more!

Sign up to the newsletter
https://bit.ly/theshelfcareclub

Boldw∞d

Boldwood Books is an award-winning fiction publishing company seeking out the best stories from around the world.

Find out more at www.boldwoodbooks.com

Join our reader community for brilliant books, competitions and offers!

Follow us
@BoldwoodBooks
@TheBoldBookClub

Sign up to our weekly deals newsletter

https://bit.ly/BoldwoodBNewsletter

Printed in Great Britain
by Amazon